THE
FIRST SON

Agents of Cosmic Intelligence | Episode 2
an alternate view of history

THE FIRST SON

Bill Harvey

The Human Effectiveness Institute
Gardiner, New York

Published in 2018 by
The Human Effectiveness Institute

ISBN: 978-0-918538-09-3 | 978-0-918538-10-9 [Hardcover]
978-0-918538-08-06 [eBook]

Library of Congress Control Number: 2018909983

For information write to:
The Human Effectiveness Institute
12 Amani Drive, Gardiner, NY 12525
HumanEffectivenessInstitute.org

Book design and typesetting by Yana Lambert
Cover art by Bruce Rolff

Maps throughout by Lynn Davis. www.lynnz.world.
Prologue – *The Universal Form*, painting by Pariksit Dasa, artwork courtesy of The Bhaktivedanta Book Trust International, Inc., www.Krishna.com. Used with permission.
Chapter 19 – *Moonrise Over Mytikas*, photo by Antonis Papagiannopoulos, www.olympusphotos.gr/. Used with permission.
Chapter 21 – Herod's Temple and The Sanhedrin, © Faithlife Corporation, makers of Logos Bible Software, www.logos.com. Used with permission.
Chapter 25 – *Waiting for Redemption*, painting by Baruch Nachshon. www.nachshonart.com/gallery/. Used with permission.
Chapter 34 – *Agony in the Garden*, painting by Andrea Mantegna, ca 1458-60. The National Gallery/UK collection. Used with permission.

for Robert A. Heinlein

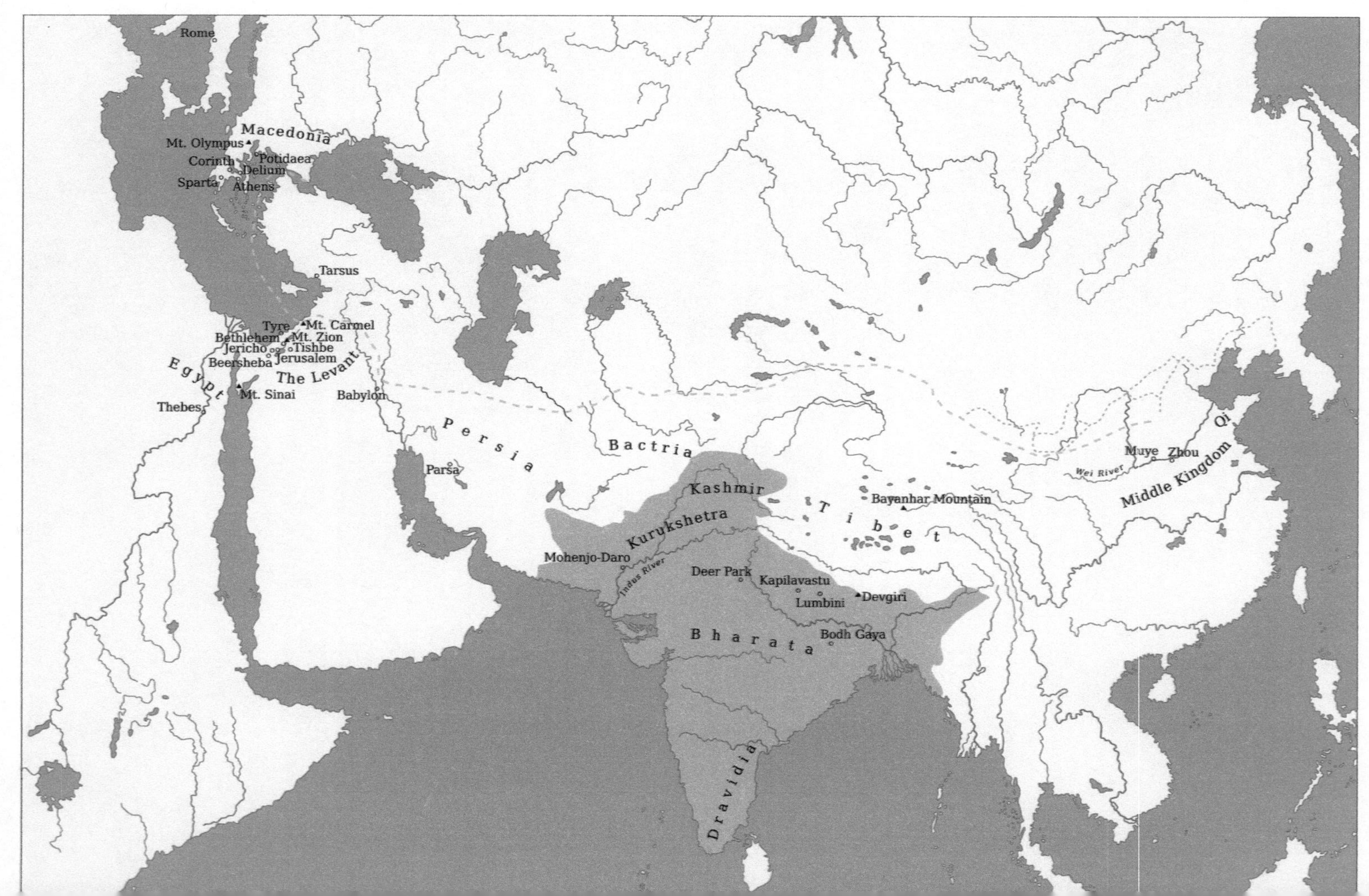

Rome
Macedonia
Mt. Olympus
Corinth
Potidaea
Delium
Sparta
Athens
Tarsus
Tyre
Mt. Carmel
Bethlehem
Mt. Zion
Jericho
Tishbe
Jerusalem
Beersheba
Egypt
The Levant
Mt. Sinai
Babylon
Thebes
Persia
Bactria
Parsa
Muye
Zhou
Qi
Wei River
Middle Kingdom
Kashmir
Bayanhar Mountain
Tibet
Kurukshetra
Mohenjo-Daro
Indus River
Deer Park
Kapilavastu
Lumbini
Devgiri
Bharata
Bodh Gaya
Dravidia

Preface

There is an invisible thread that runs through history. Not seeing this thread makes it seem as if events are disconnected, when they are actually highly connected.

In *The First Son*, the great turning points in history over a climactic 3100-year period are seen through the experiences of four young lovers caught up in a hidden war: formidable Templegard and his deeply intense Nastassia, playful Layla and the scholarly Melchizedek, her former teacher. And their mentor, Maitreya, one of the earliest avatars—a being of great powers and unsuspected secrets.

These five are all Agents of Cosmic Intelligence. They have been sent to a far distant outpost, Earth, where the Rebel leader is training a race of humans to become ruthless fighters to aid in the takeover of the multiverse.

It is the beginning of a new Age, one in which darkness could reach its apex, an era known to local seers as the Kali Yuga. The mission of these Agents is to push back the darkness and free the indigenous race from the Rebel forces that have taken complete control of the planet.

The Agents had been incarnating on the planet for nearly 200,000 years. They and other Agents had fought heroically against impossible odds. The Rebels continued to break the rules of the Lost Lamb Game by using obvious off-planet weapons.

Everything the Agents had done so far, playing by the rules, had come to naught. The Rebels controlled the planet, and the Agents were greatly outnumbered. But now, coming to their rescue was the second most powerful entity in the multiverse, second only to The One Self.

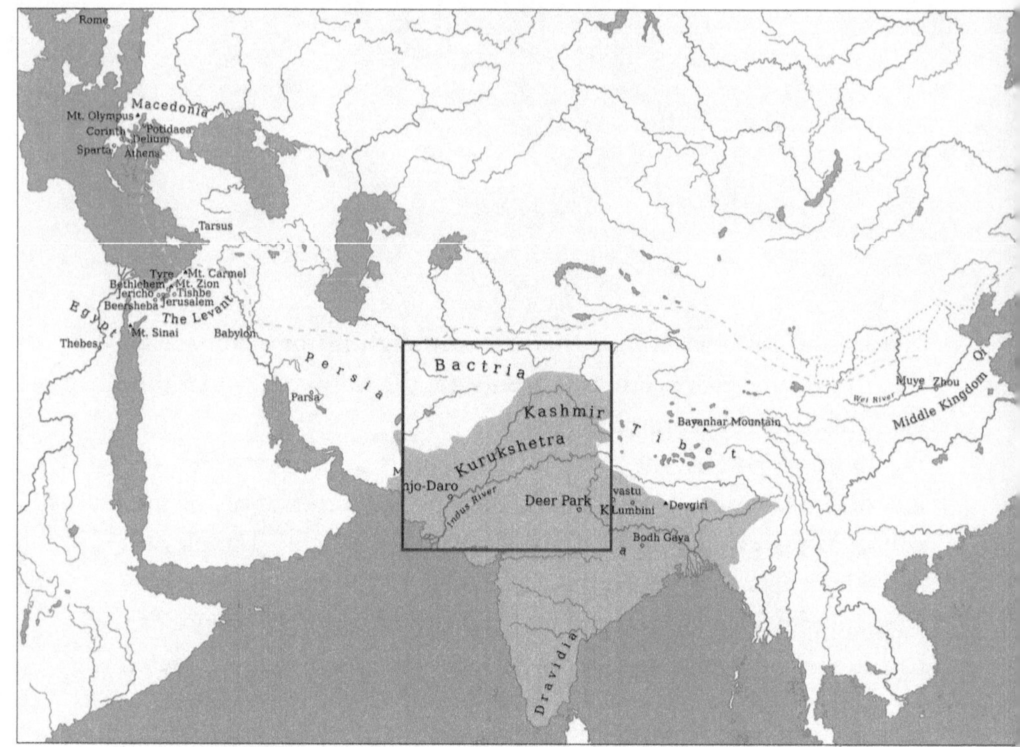

Prologue

Kurukshetra, A Sacred Place…
3067 BC

… a fertile bowl in the mountains with two parallel rivers to the north and south. Up in the foothills to the east and west, two great armies were amassing, with rainbow-ornamented elephants, horse-drawn chariots and infantry. The charioteer General would normally be up for this battle and couldn't understand his own hesitation. Sure, they were outnumbered eleven divisions to seven, sporting odds. He felt as if he had prepared all his life for just this moment, yet when the moment came he found himself thinking more like a priest than a warrior. What had come over him? It wasn't fear, nor did he have any premonition of doom. He held a realistic picture in his mind of what was about to happen and suddenly all that carnage seemed wrong. These were his relatives and teachers on both sides. Wasn't he in a position to stop the whole thing? Wasn't that his real duty?

His driver, handsome and blue-skinned, was reading his mind. This came easily to The First Son, appearing in one of his favorite forms. He laughed gently.

"The real conflict today is in the battlefield of your soul," he said.

"Surely our right action would be to forgive them, isn't that true?" Arjuna asked, looking truly confused. Arjuna was an incarnation of the Agent Templegard but he didn't remember that, as he was imprisoned in a human brain.

"We have forgiven them," Krishna answered, "a few times. Those actions led us here. Do you think it will really reduce suffering if you back off now?"

"How can one know?"

"Picture the situation. The Kauravas will interpret your actions as surrender, and that will easily become the judgment of the whole world. Half the Bharatas will enslave the other half, and this war will be kicked down the road to the next generation," Krishna said with certainty. The Kauravas and Pandavas were cousins with common ancestry as Bharatas, both living in the Northern India region known as Bharata. The Agents were on the side of the Pandavas, and the Rebels were on both sides, so the only hope of pushing back the Rebels in this strategic area was to have this fight. The Pandavas would probably win, which could reduce suffering on a cosmic scale by being the first turn in the tide of this war against the enslavement of the multiverse.

How does he know? Arjuna thought, transparently to The First Son. *Of course, they say he is really the god Krishna, an avatar of Vishnu, but they say so many unbelievable things, how does one really know?*

"Causing death is not what it seems," Krishna said. "It is like changing clothes." Arjuna seemed unconvinced.

"Tell me how to do righteously today," Arjuna asked humbly. The First Son sensed that deep down inside, Templegard was shattered by finding himself indecisive as if for the first time. His heart went out to his Agent.

"Do it as carrying out your training and your life's meaning as a warrior, without caring about winning or losing, or thinking about abstract moral principles. Follow your intuition and let your body do what it will do. By acting without desire, you free yourself from karma," Krishna answered.

Arjuna held his head. "So many words… I have heard so many words…"

The First Son ached with compassion for Arjuna, who of course saw himself as mortal, not knowing that on the inside he was The One Self, just as The First Son was, and all the Rebels were, and everything in creation is.

Don't pull your punches, dear! Nastassia urged him. Nastassia looked as she always did, long black hair, petite sensuous body, her queenly, small oval face and pillowy lips, now held in a sad pout. Arjuna felt a muse encouraging him to not hold back. Nastassia, Maitreya, Melchizedek, Layla and The First Son were all present in their causal/subtle/astral bodies, but the Agents were remaining invisible and The First Son was manifesting in human form, as Krishna. None of them had to contend with the human brain, and The First Son could feel their concern for Templegard. They too could read his loss of faith in himself owing to his sudden indecision, and it hurt them more than it did him.

Nastassia had a sudden flashback and sensed it was all taking place in a microsecond while time outside her vision seemed to stand still. She was scantily clad in rags, feathers and body paint, in a hot jungle, releasing an arrow carrying enough poison to kill an elephant. Templegard was there to receive the arrow in his body. She had killed him, this beautiful man, whoever he was. She suddenly returned to the present moment.

Be confident he's safe in our hands, The First Son advised. *Stay detached.*

I've lost him so many times, Nastassia thought to herself in a tearful voice, but the others could hear it.

The number of off-planet weapons here on both sides suggests mutual annihilation, Sir, Maitreya explained. The vibration of compassion in his psychic voice felt like bittersweet cellos and violins resonating in the heart of The First Son.

Will our shields hold over Templegard? Her voice trembling, Layla voiced another thought they all had.

Melchizedek finally said the thing that no one wanted to be the one to say. *What really concerns us is that you, Sir, will play by the rules, and Templegard doesn't want to hurt these people, but the Rebels will be waging all-out war.*

So will we, The First Son said. *If I must, I will cross the line to protect you all.*

By *cross the line* they understood him to mean he would break the rules of the Lost Lamb Game. This was The One Self's favorite game whereby, in part of the multiverse—also known as Mystery Planets—life was a mystery because no one remembered that they are The One Self, and they must wake up and remember, each for their self.

Crossing the line meant obvious miracles, obvious use of off-planet weaponry or technology, telling it like it is. The First Son remembered another situation like this, on a faraway planet. He started to tell a story to Arjuna/Templegard for the other Agents to also hear.

"These are the same words as I imparted them millions of years ago," Krishna said aloud, and The First Son remembered many scenes from many lives on many planets.

Arjuna blurted, "How can I accept this? It appears that you were born in this world only recently."

Krishna said, "Birth is as much an illusion as death," and revealed himself to Arjuna.

Arjuna saw many deities spring from Krishna, seeing that Krishna was every deity he knew and many more he did not know, and he strangely also saw that Krishna was himself, and his brothers, and his enemies, and everyone. He saw this not as in a dream but right in front of him in every way as real as anything he had ever seen before.

The Universal Form
painting by Pariksit Dasa

*Arjuna was filled with wonder as he looked upon the
Universal Form; and he began to pray to Krishna with folded hands.*

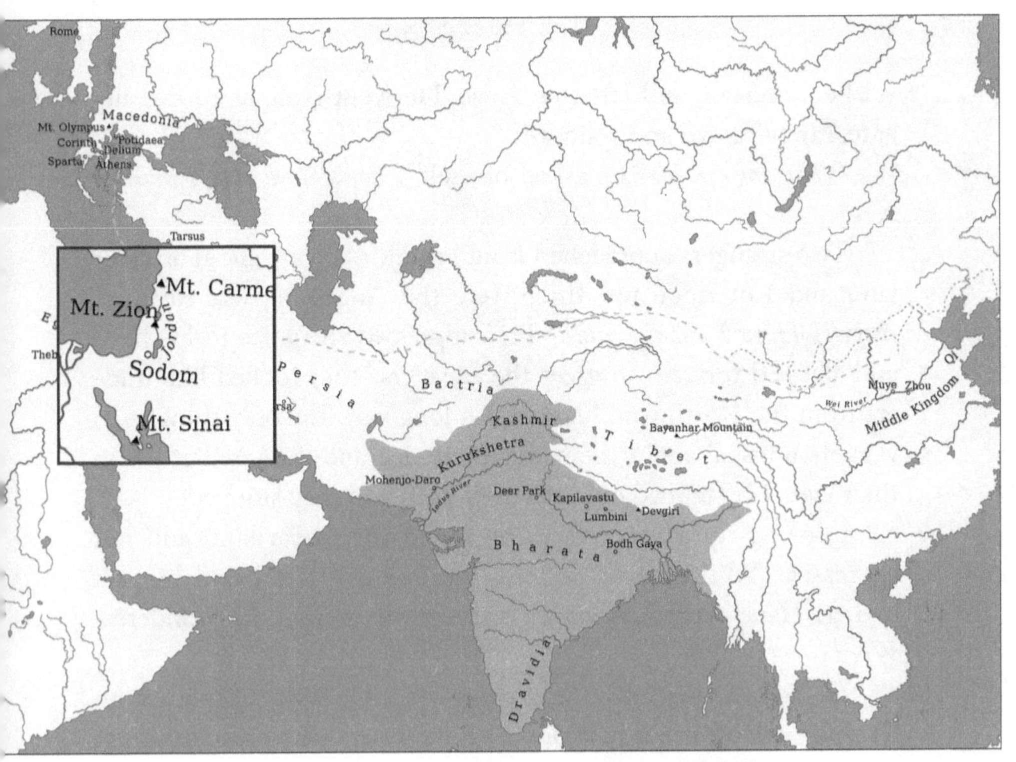

1

LOT, AN EARTH HUMAN

2068 BC

Something weird got into Lot as he was napping, and he woke up in a strange state, not at all himself. For some reason this did not frighten him, and he silently stole from his couch with a sense of resolve, something important to do. Without making noise that would roust his wife and daughters talking in the kitchen, he quietly washed, dressed, and left the house. He went straight to the city gate. He sat down and waited.

What am I doing? he asked himself. *I don't know, but I must be here.*

Two strangers approached from beyond the gate about an hour later and Lot stood up. These were the Angels he was to meet. *Angels? Have I lost my mind?* He suppressed the voice in his head and stepped forward to greet the travelers. They looked like traders from the North who had come a long way. The only thing even vaguely unusual about them was their size and the intelligence in their eyes. He stepped out into their path and they stopped.

Looking up at their faces he noted they were kind and not aggressive. "Welcome to Sodom, my friends," Lot heard himself saying. *How is my body acting without my control?* he wondered. *What is going on?*

He doesn't know why he is doing this, Maitreya telepathed to Templegard. Maitreya had blond-brown hair, a wiry muscular body, and a naturally friendly face.

Could he be under Rebel control? Templegard responded. Templegard looked to Lot like a young ladies' man, very handsome, with casually disheveled hair. Lot's "Angels" were Agents, in a different branch of the service than Angels. They were not actually in human bodies but assumed that form now and then.

"Have you made arrangements for where you'll be staying?" Lot asked.

"We'll sleep in the village square," Maitreya told him, and Lot became animated.

"Oh, no," Lot anguished, "you don't want to do that. This is a very rough town. You must stay with us, we have extra rooms and baths, and we'll serve you a fine meal, as our honored guests."

"We'll be fine in the square," Templegard assured him with a confident smile, "although you're a fine fellow to be so generous to us. We're just traders from up North and will only be in town one night. We've been sleeping under the sky for this entire journey."

"I know who you are," came out of Lot's mouth as if he were dream walking. "I've been told to help you and our lives will be spared." *Spared from what*, he thought, becoming apprehensive.

The Agents became situationally aware of the crowd moving around them in both directions and that some of those ears could be Rebels. Maitreya took Lot's arm and began walking through the gate into the city. "Yes, we're charmed by your offer, and cannot refuse. What did you say your name was?" Maitreya asked in a natural voice that could be heard by nosy pedestrians nearby. If the fellow was going to talk like that, they had best get him off the street. The Agents controlled the conversation and kept it to small talk.

This is Abram's nephew Lot, Maitreya informed Templegard, having had a moment to read Lot's mind.

Okay, so this is not only recon but an extraction then, Templegard said.

Right. In the chaos on Earth, Agents often got their orders in unusual ways, and always at the last minute, so nothing was surprising.

Lot's comely wife and daughters were happy that he had brought back such handsome strangers for dinner and an evening's conversation. The ladies loved learning about how people lived in other city-states, as it was always so different than the world they knew.

Maitreya noted with contentment that Lot's daughters were very beautiful. The younger one reminded him of Venus—the teasing eyes, high cheekbones, rosebud lips. He was suddenly in a flashback of his first incarnation where he fell in love with her at first sight. He was still carrying the torch.

Dinner and the talk afterward were sublimely pleasurable for Lot. He was starting to get used to whatever was happening to him, which he now realized was some form of intercession caused by God Almighty to save him and his family. He thanked God devoutly in his heart. But save them from what?

Suddenly there was the sound of a large crash against the front door and they all went to look. Lot opened the front door with mounting trepidation as he saw a large crowd of mean-looking armed toughs, and a large rock on the ground that must have been thrown hard against his front door, which was looking the worse for wear.

"What do you want?" Lot asked in a shaking voice.

"Send out your visitors," their leader, a large man with one closed eye, demanded. "They'll need to earn our approval to stay in our fair city."

"They're under my protection," Lot said, steadying his voice, "I'm their host." Throughout the region this was the code, the unwritten law. "I'd sooner give you my daughters," he said and realized he'd gone too far in his nervousness.

Templegard pulled him back inside and closed the door. "We're going to have to take you and your family out of this city, which will soon be destroyed and everyone in it. Good people should all leave the city now, with us."

"How will we get past—them! Outside!" Lot blurted, pointing.

"They're taken care of," Maitreya said. "Quickly pack what you must have and can carry a long way."

Lot's family was in shock and expected to be tortured and killed once they went outside, but they needed these strong men or Angels or whatever they were, else they would be totally helpless. So, they did what they were told.

When the Agents led them outside, they were almost hysterical with fear. The gang was still there but feeling around for where they were, as they had been rendered sightless by Maitreya. The Agents pushed through the crowd, leading and protecting Lot's family. They went out the gate and continued walking.

"Go as fast as you can, we have unfinished business, don't stop to look back or anything. Yes, right, keep going that way," Maitreya exhorted them.

Lot's family kept going, over one dune or hill after the next, through desert patches and groves of trees, over rock outcroppings. Lot was in the lead, heading down into the next valley. Not sure how far ahead he was, he stopped and turned. His daughters were only a few yards behind him, but his wife was atop the last ridge looking back at the city.

There was a deafening sound and the sky turned a bright red that forced Lot's eyes shut.

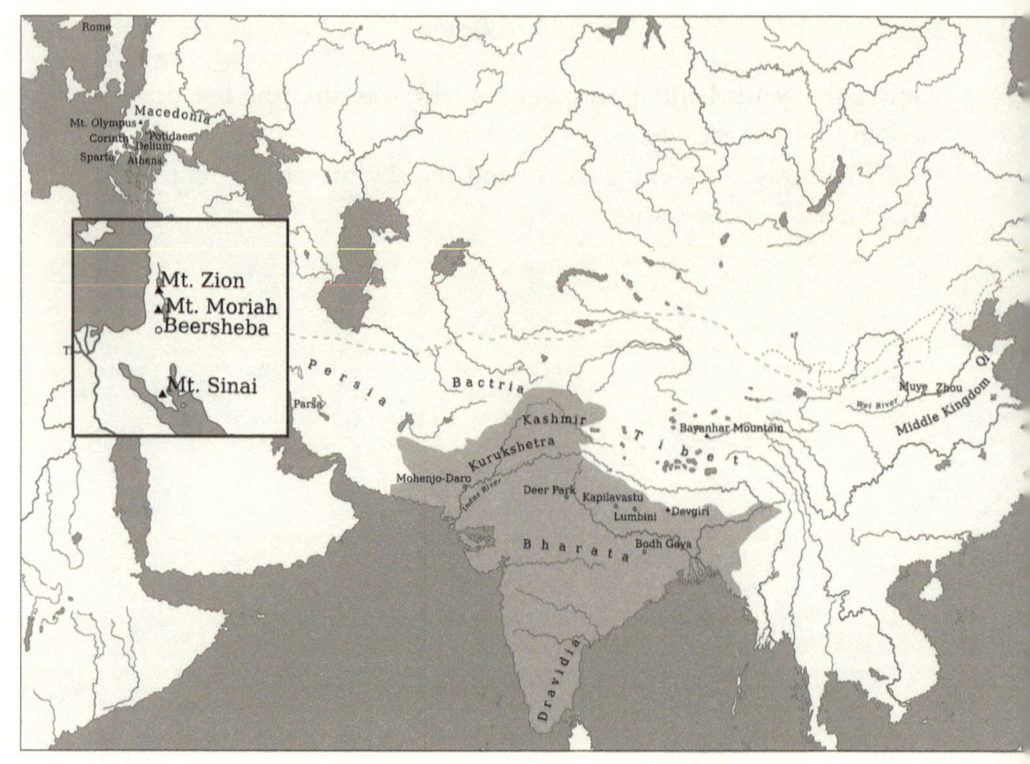

2

Beersheba, A Place

2055 BC

These smiles on the faces I see are surely the smiles one sees in heaven,
Abraham thought. The dream went back and forth, intermingling
their wedding day, and the day that Isaac was born, 80 years later.
That miracle was the high point of my life, he thought. *All those who
followed me had such trust that they stayed with me their whole lives
waiting the vindication of the promise from God, which had always*

been postponed every time it seemed imminent. Then Isaac had been born when Sarah was long past childbearing age. This was proof that God was not just in Abraham's imagination.

In his dream, Abraham was being lifted on a chair and danced around the room, not something he remembered from either real-life event, but it was happening now, and it was wonderful. The happiness he saw in the faces around him was inside him as well. He had never felt this happy before.

He loved his first son Ishmael and when God sent him away to establish his own nation, Abraham had been sick with sorrow. To have another son now, and with the woman he truly loved, born under such miraculous stars, *it's the fulfillment of my life,* he thought.

He was feeling lovingly toward God, and then he suddenly remembered something. It was a cold and dark something and he tried to turn away from it, back into the happiness, but it was too late. He was awake.

First light was just coming over the desert horizon. There were the donkey and two of his most able men, a father and son, loading the wood, sacrificial knife, flint, bitumen, rope, and other supplies for the journey, on her back.

Reality came back to him. God had required that Isaac be sacrificed. As was his first principle, Abraham accepted whatever God wanted. Inside, underneath this lifelong resolve that was the true meaning of his life, of who he was, some remaining seed of doubt—or disobedience, he imagined it was—anguished him to the brink of exploding.

He was unusually quiet and of few words as he said his good-byes to Sarah and the family and his other helpers who had risen early to see them off, Abraham and Isaac, the two bodyguards and the donkey. Others were pretending to be asleep to avoid seeing the horrible scene.

Sarah's eyes were red and swollen but she was of the same resolve as her husband. They were God's creations and he owned them; their proper way of being was to love and trust that whatever God ordained was the best course of action for whatever unfathomable reason. The lovers kissed ardently as if generations younger, and Abraham turned and led the departing few out from under the cooling shade of the tamarisk trees, into the slanting sun rays of early morning.

On the third day, during the day's march, they could see their destination rise high above the horizon. Isaac was having a wonderful time. Seeing sights he had wanted to see again for a long time, like the city of Hebron, where a bird in a cage picked out a leaf with his fortune written on it. It said, "You shall laugh," which pleased Isaac, as he knew his name means, "He laughs".

Being with his father so constantly, he took this *wanderjahr* to be some sort of a gift for himself, perhaps a rite of passage of which he had not been informed.

His father was as affectionate as always but not full of talk. This was unusual, but Isaac did not let it ruin his wondrous trip.

To Abraham, the weak and disloyal part of him that he hated, which is the way he thought of his doubt, was all but breaking out of the prison to which he had consigned it almost a hundred years ago. It had become fiendishly clever, offering him arguments that snuck into his thoughts as if they were his own thoughts—but they were things he would never think. Like *How could God be saying this?* And then giving him reason after reason why this did not sound like the same God he knew and loved—though as a child Abraham had firmly and permanently convinced himself with the soundest logic that there could only be one God.

Every time these rebellious thoughts stirred up in his mind he cut them off sharply by an act of will. But on this long walk they kept coming back and seemed to gain strength.

God is disgusted by human sacrifice. He has told you this more than once.

Shut up. Go away.

When you pushed back on God about Sodom, He agreed that even if He found only ten good people he would not destroy all life in the city. That is the way God behaves. This other voice in your head must be an imposter!

STOP IT!

Finally, they were at the base of the mountain, and Abraham bade his men to guard each other and the donkey for their return. Sharing the load with Isaac, the two began the long climb up Mount Moriah.

Isaac noticed what they were carrying and realized they were supplies for a burnt offering. "Father, but where is the lamb?" he asked.

Abraham fought back tears and tried to find his voice. Finally, he said, brushing his face, in a choked voice, "God will furnish a lamb."

Isaac noticed the tear and thought *Father is such a kind-hearted soul, he weeps for animals.*

They reached a saddle between two higher hills, which were the twin peaks of the mountain, to the East and West. Abraham suddenly remembered being here once before when he had come to Salem and first met King Melchizedek. *Melchizedek took me up here and showed me what the Temple would look like when it would be built here. He said I'd build another Temple—that must be the one at Kaaba that Ishmael and I refurbished. That was before we were married,* he realized. He thought again of Sarah—he still thought of her as Sarai, and of himself as Abram—the one being he loved almost as much as God. Here he was about to destroy the only fruit of their union.

Abraham bade Isaac to set up the wood and bitumen as he had been trained to do. Then he told him the truth about what God had required. Isaac looked very serious but not at all disturbed. Of course, if this was what God wanted, it was also what Isaac wanted. He was the son of two people who exemplified this attitude and so he was thoroughly steeped in it. Isaac felt suddenly honored at being this important to God to set up such a ceremony even though it would end his life. He felt sure that God would have something else for him to do after this life. Isaac's face began to shine, and Abraham saw it, and understood that this was Isaac's way of showing his love for God, to sanctify the ceremony himself.

Suddenly Abraham saw again the Temple crystallizing into existence around him, as Melchizedek had shown him so long ago. Unbeknownst to Abraham, Melchizedek was there with him right now.

Melchizedek was the Agent left behind to protect Abraham when his colleagues were ordered to head to the valley of the Indus River, the new front in the war with the Rebels. Melchizedek had been asked to be King of many city states and had chosen Salem over Ur or Babylon. He met Abraham when he was still called Abram and Melchizedek was King of Salem, later called Jerusalem. Now he had died and was not visible to Abraham. In normal times, Melchizedek was able to still telepathically communicate with Abraham, who thought of Melchizedek as an Angel, and could tell the difference between his voice and God's. Most humans in these recently-evolved brains could not distinguish the different voices in their heads.

But these were not normal times. Three days ago, some force had seized Melchizedek and paralyzed him. He could neither communicate nor telekinetically interfere with matter-energy. He was effectively neutralized, yet his consciousness seemed to automatically stay with Abraham.

He had only been able to pray. He prayed that Abraham would think logically about the consistency of messages and realize that someone else was impersonating God. Melchizedek did not even retain his ability to read minds and so he had no idea if his prayers were being neutralized too. He also prayed that The One Self—the Being that Abraham called God—would send someone stronger in time to avert a needless tragedy and defilement of the temple site.

At this point Melchizedek was energetically striving by act of will to regain control of his functions, but to no avail. It pained him to be helpless, watching events unfold that were exactly the things he was here to prevent. He knew that he had come up against some Rebel or group of Rebels whose combined power was overwhelming him and who were sadistically enjoying his distress. This had never happened before, and he had been at this line of work for millions of years. He was a top Agent, not of the caliber of his teacher Maitreya of course, but pretty sure of himself against Rebels—normally.

He experienced an unusual moment of homicidal rage against the Rebels. He had watched and felt the suffering of enormous numbers of individuals caused by the Rebels for a very long time and had never felt this sort of thing before. He wondered if that was a bad feeling to have, if he was being drawn into being as cruel as they were. All those feelings passed as strange curiosities.

He realized this might be the end for him, at least this time around. Or it might be a very long eternity of time before he was rescued. The hardest part of that would be not being with Layla. He again relinquished these distracting emotional thoughts and fought the bonds with everything he had.

Abraham bound Isaac and positioned him. Isaac was perfectly calm, watching as his father unwrapped the knife from its velvet cloth. Abraham stepped behind Isaac and gently held his chin, saying goodbye to him in his heart as tears leaked silently down his face.

Suddenly Abraham heard God intercede and stay his upraised hand. This, Melchizedek was able to hear too. In plain sight, The First Son had taken the form of a brilliantly white ram stuck in a hedge, freeing Melchizedek from his paralysis.

The First Son signaled to Melchizedek to go with Abraham after the sacrifice.

I will stay here and converse with the intruder, The First Son said.

3

Reunion

2055 BC

The sacrifice had followed all the proper forms, and once completed, Abraham and Isaac in joy had descended the mountain.

The First Son now stood casually by a great column of the Temple, which appeared to be fully material now, although no humans in the area would see it. It was there merely for the two of them, the long-lost brothers, now reunited after so much strife.

"You can come out now," he said. "It's just us!"

From the darkness of an inner corridor strode The Second Son. Both of them affected the garb and mien of men of the Negev. The First Son noted the highly polished and flawless hooves on his brother but said nothing of it. His brother observed that, and walked around The First Son, studying him.

"I guess I'd best use my long fork if we're to dine together," The First Son, who soon would be called Yeshua, quipped.

"Perhaps I'll grace you with my pitchfork," the other bantered back. At the same time, something in his movements suggested that he might bodily attack Yeshua.

Yeshua made a motion as if to hug his brother, but the other jumped back and struck a martial pose. Yeshua remembered that his younger brother had always been jealous of him because of his greater similarity with The One Self. Lucifer had been created specifically to experiment with someone seemingly very different from

The One Self, although, of course, both were occupied inside by The One Self.

He also remembered that although he was stronger, when Lucifer as a child had attacked him using the element of surprise, he could win. Lucifer was capable of whipping himself into frenzy with attached motivation about things, whereas The First Son tended more toward detachment, and The First Son knew that this too could work against him in the current situation. The stakes were much higher now. Unexpectedly this had escalated into a serious war. Although The First Son did not know if his personality could be exterminated, all creatures needed to be concerned about long-term hypnotic enslavement or unconsciousness, which were horrific situations to which all creatures were subject, now that this war was happening

"Lucifer," Yeshua began, but the other cut him off.

"Lucifer is dead," he declared. "I killed him. You see before you a new being I have created. I call him Perse."

"For that pretty blue color you always liked," Yeshua said, and Perse nodded.

"Why did you kill Lucifer?" Yeshua asked, assuming his brother was speaking metaphorically. Nothing in the universe could really be permanently killed, or at least so far none had ever been.

"He would have been too weak to win the war," Perse responded.

"The war—yes," Yeshua said, feeling sorry for his brother, "I imagine that you must tire of the war, and perhaps we should end it…"

Perse laughed roughly. "Sure, now that you and he are losing!"

Yeshua shook his head slowly in disbelief, perceiving that his brother indeed thought he was winning, that he even *could* win. This had started as play but along the way his brother had lost touch with reality. This was amazing. The One had never shared this with him, but of course knew everything, since on the inside of Perse was The One, having the experience of being Perse. Over the millennia Perse must have forgotten his real identity and was now fully merged with his game character!

Yeshua and Perse had begun to stroll, several feet apart, down a long well-lit hallway, each carefully observing the other. Perse wanted a fight but had just been paralyzed by his brother, as he himself had paralyzed Melchizedek, and he knew better than to attack when Yeshua clearly had the upper hand. He also wanted to lull The First Son into believing that he was invulnerable and that Perse was intimidated by him, because Perse had a plan.

Yeshua was still getting used to the idea that Lucifer had lost it and really believed that he was not an avatar of The One Self. If The One could go insane in one of his projected roles, did that mean there was any chance that the insanity could creep upstairs through the system of consciousness to infect The One Self, and would it then be shared with all the avatars, himself included? Intuitively he knew this was not possible, but then again, he had never experienced a being at his own level going insane. Yeshua had been the first experiment of The One Self inhabiting an avatar, and Lucifer had been the second.

"You do remember—don't you? Inside us is The One Self, masquerading as us, and as everyone else," Yeshua began, intending to unwind the knot in Lucifer's mind.

Perse laughed. "Yes, I remember the party line, propaganda with which to subjugate the entire universe. But I also remember that in the beginning there were many of us of equal powers, and the being you call The One Self tricked us and stole our birthright, and now claims to be the one true God—from whose despotism I will free us all."

Perse had gotten himself worked up while saying this and now gestured angrily and the Temple collapsed around them, burning furiously fast and becoming ashes in moments.

"Feeling better now?" Yeshua inquired gently. "These beings that live here in the Lost Lamb Game have an excuse as to why they don't know they are The One Self playing their roles. What's your excuse?"

The First Son saw now the whole picture clearly and did not see any point in continuing the conversation, and so he disappeared.

He sent a recording of the experience including his own after-thought tracks to the five Agents that were his general staff in the long wargame with Lucifer. They were of course flabbergasted. Even as a game it was hard on them to witness all the suffering and not be able to turn it all off at once. Especially they were heart-stricken for the humans, who did not know it was all a game and that they each were the One game player, playing a role. When they finally figure this out, the Agents' incredible happiness for the humans would be all the greater. But meanwhile it was hard for such compassionate beings as the Agents to bear.

Now with the new news that it wasn't really a game anymore—Lucifer had gone mad and forgotten who he really is, an avatar of The One—and the possibility that this was catching and could infect The One and therefore everything in Creation, ending the beautiful multiverse in all its awesome wonder and turning it into an endless nightmare—that was no game.

What are your orders, Sir? Maitreya finally asked The First Son.

The only thing we can do is to cautiously peel away ignorance among the humans and the Rebel invaders, The First Son replied.

Sir, if I may, why cautiously? Templegard asked. He felt that all of the Agents and Angels should exert themselves *en masse* as quickly as possible.

Because we are still operating under the rules The One Self has set forth for the Lost Lamb Game, and this is a mystery planet in that game, The First Son answered. *We can't just come out and tell the whole truth suddenly.*

The full significance struck them all: The One of course knew everything so HeShe had known of Lucifer's madness, and no change in game rules had been announced, so what The First Son was saying had to be right. They each set their minds to imagining what forms their work would be taking.

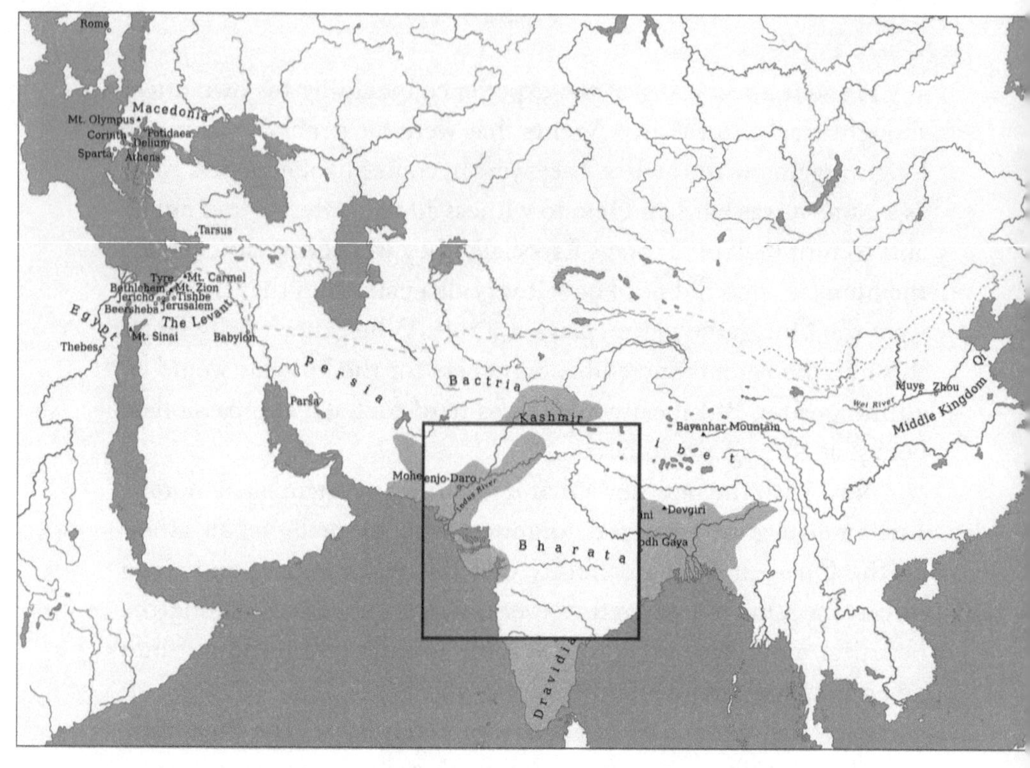

4

BHARATA, A PLACE
1717 BC

Melchizedek could have made the walk, but instead teleported. His work was temporarily done in the Levant, and the center of the action was now Bharata. He had never been there and was eager to rejoin his comrades.

As he entered the flowery grove surrounding the villa he immediately fell in love with the place. The villa was built on, around, and through the end of a lake. Water birds waded, and birds of many other kinds flitted about. They stared at Melchizedek, not recognizing him as one of the regulars here. Strongly built and with a winning smile, he wore a distinctive moustache and a large leather belt, as was his wont. His senses were in bliss. Flowers of all colors grew over the construction, which was partly of walls and partly of gaily colored tents with sides turned back mostly open to nature. Inside he could hear an ascending cheery realization of his arrival, and his friends were soon outside hugging him, with Layla poured on him and monopolizing his lips. She was wearing her hair redder than usual he noted.

"That was Perse himself you were grappling with," Templegard said, having engaged with Perse once himself.

"I thought so," Melchizedek said belatedly when he was able to come up for air, and would have continued, but Layla had caught her breath quickly. Nastassia laughed, as did Maitreya.

Later, on one open tent-covered deck of the villa looking out over the lake, the joys of reunion segued into the business at hand.

"Rebels have started using biological weapons," Melchizedek reported somberly, and everyone's smiles disappeared. "They manipulated a flea bacterium and brought a plague across Egypt. Now they are taking ancient parasite cells that can only live within other cells and manipulating them into even more deadly bioweps."

The genetically altered flea bacterium would thousands of years later be called bubonic plague. Rebel non-bacterial parasite weapons were also discovered by the human race, specifically the botanist Dmitri Ivanoski, in 1892 AD. He called them viruses.

This escalation was not a big surprise. Every planet that became a warfront eventually got to this point when the Rebels, fearing themselves stalemated, began to escalate.

"We've set up this place on the road into Bharata from the West, from where we are receiving what has gradually become what you might call a soft invasion from Perses," Maitreya briefed Melchizedek. When they first got to the region, it had been called Parsa, and now more explicitly was called Perses, as in "Perse's", since it was now his home state on the planet.

"Soft as in like tourists?" Melchizedek asked.

"Exactly," Maitreya replied. "They are well armed and armored for fight, but act like good guests when they stop here for rest and refreshment."

"They even act respectfully toward us," Layla said, indicating herself and Nastassia lounged on one couch. The others saw Melchizedek's eyes stay lovingly on Layla's curvaceous form, draped over the back and seat of the couch.

"Not just humans I take it?" Melchizedek intuited, and they all nodded.

"Some few asuras not in human bodies, lots of asuras in human bodies, only half-aware of who they really are," Nastassia said, and Melchizedek raised an eyebrow.

"You mean Rebels?" he asked, and she nodded. "Yes," she said, "the natives of Bharata are all seers, so they can see that they live among non-humans, even when the latter happen to be masquerading as humans (and even think they *are* humans)! So naturally they have made up names for them. They call us devas and they call the Rebels asuras."

The Bharatas are shamans, Melchizedek thought. *Their ancestors must have been Agents inside.*

Exactly, Maitreya pathed.

"Don't be surprised when you also see demons come into the place," Templegard warned with a grin. *The Rebels have totally broken the Mystery Planet rule, bringing in many types of extraterrestrials in plain sight of everyone,* he pathed, along with a feeling that it was all somehow suddenly ridiculous.

"Oh yes, the Bharatas call those rakshasas," Layla put in with a smile, "kind of like a cross between a ghoul and a vampire, some Rebel race that loves human flesh and blood and was easy to recruit for Earth duty."

"Also capable of flying, invisibility and shapeshifting," Templegard added, as if this was all fun.

They suddenly all found this extremely mirthful and couldn't stop themselves from laughing. They were really just so happy to be together again, all five of them. They wanted to laugh.

"And don't confuse rakshasas with gandharvas," Nastassia said, breaking herself up and falling over. Layla shriek-laughed and their male comrades wiped tears.

"Wait," Maitreya said, and then they all got it too. Someone was coming. They all studied the approaching beings coming from the West, still a few miles off, thirteen beings not counting animals. Melchizedek realized with a start that whenever someone was coming, the first thing all of them thought was "Uh-oh, this is the day that Perse finds us." Since Perse had taken over Melchizedek, all five of them wondered whether he could overpower all of them put together, and force them all to work for him, the way he did with Templegard millennia earlier.

"Three Aryans," Layla reported, her remote sensing being almost equal to Maitreya's.

"Are they Persians?" Melchizedek asked, since he had first heard that word in the Levant referring to people from Perses.

"No," Layla said, "They're part of a seer's club. They call themselves Aryans, which means lions in Aramaic. And it's more than a club, it's like a guild or lodge."

"Started in the Levant?" Melchizedek asked, since the lodge was named in Aramaic. Layla nodded and added, "But many Aryans who stop by here are from Perses. Some are fine folk, and some are Rebels."

None of them picked up anything close to the power of Perse and so the tension abated somewhat.

Melchizedek turned to Maitreya and asked, "What's our brief here? What's our cover?"

"We're spies, as usual, and currently focused on understanding this migration from Perses, whether it's simply a buildup to attack, or something more. Our cover is that we happen to like it in this beautiful spot and being very conversational and cosmopolitan ourselves, we enjoy meeting other wealthy tourists, so we're staying here for a while until we feel like moving somewhere else." Maitreya then downloaded many petabytes of detail into Melchizedek's consciousness all at once, and Melchizedek went into meditative contemplation in order to most quickly assimilate it.

5

ANGIRAS, A COVER IDENTITY
1717 BC

Melchizedek was still assimilating his cover when the visitors arrived from the West. He knew now that his name was Brhaspati, and that he was married to Layla, whose name was Tara. Maitreya was his father, Angiras, whose wife was Nastassia, named Angirasas. He and Layla—Tara that is—had a child, who was Templegard, named Bharadvaja Barhaspatya. *That would be easy to remember,* he thought wryly.

They welcomed their tired and hungry guests the way good hosts everywhere did. (If later they were to be offered payment, the Agents would accept it to preserve their cover as normally greedy wealthy people living the high life. Or if no payment was offered they would act exactly the same in bidding fond farewell. They were aware that this non-attachment to money potentially undermined their cover but had not figured out a better plan. As good spies, they were method actors and preferred not to take actions contrary to their inner real personalities. It was easier to keep track of a cover with no lies—or as few as possible.)

During the arrival of the guests, their cover was suddenly penetrated.

Rati, the Bharatan princess, was indeed a seer for she saw the five of them and knew immediately that they were devas, and threw herself down, worshipping their unshod feet.

27

Upon seeing her, her two bodyguards did the same. The rest of the travelers stared, and the looks of the three probably-asleep-Rebel Persian mercenaries showed nascent hostility.

The three Aryans thought of themselves as seers, but they were unable to see what the princess saw. The Agents to them looked like humans. The three traders looked on, politely trying to hide their lecherous tendencies as princess Rati was an overt sex goddess and proud of it.

The Bharatan guide, Maargadarshak, who knew his hosts from many previous stopovers to be merely the usual idle rich, wondered now if he had offended these now apparent celestials by not having recognized them himself. But he was afraid of becoming a fool by imitating a young girl who probably was already acting the fool, so he just stood there vacillating.

Cover probably compromised, Maitreya pathed to somebody far away. They would probably be moved soon to another theater. How quickly would it go up the Rebel chain of command? How soon would Perse be here?

This girl is an asleep Agent, Melchizedek pronounced, and they all checked it out and then projected agreement.

She's the same Rati we worked with here centuries ago, who became a famous goddess across this region, Nastassia identified, and there was a telepathic murmur of confirmation.

"Rise, beautiful one," Templegard-now-Bharadvaja adlibbed, and nodded to the bodyguards to do the same. The Agents then got down and worshipped Rati's bare feet, much to her surprise. The other Agents noticed Maitreya spending a little more time kissing each toe individually and took this for devoutness. Maitreya had a secret, however, which he had never shared with anyone. This exotic asleep Agent now worshipped as a sex goddess was once his mate. She was called Venus then. Maitreya applied his iron discipline so as not to be staring at her. He was such a good actor no one noticed his arousal. He was wide awake and fully attentive, and his heart was soaring just to be in her presence for a little while. He sent waves of gratitude to The One.

"You're just like us," Layla whispered to her, kissing her cheek to cover the whisper, as the Agents stood up again. "Taking incarnation in this human brain usually shuts down awareness of who we really are." Almost 200,000 years ago, when Melchizedek and Layla introduced the current human brain with its large frontal cortex, the Rebels had gotten wind in advance, and sabotaged the brain to be overly powerful, so as to eclipse and narcotize the true consciousness residing within. But that had backfired by causing Rebels incarnated as humans to also lose awareness of their real identities.

"Devas?" one of the mercs asked menacingly, his hand resting on the hilt of his scimitar, still in its scabbard.

"Asuras," Maitreya-now-Angiras said with a smile, and everyone palpably relaxed. If the mercs weren't asleep Rebels or didn't even know about the existence of Rebels, they instinctively felt safer with asuras than with the mysterious devas. Rebels had indoctrinated their more talkative human pawns to disseminate the Rebel party line and controlled most conversations that way. Rati on the other hand, now having been told that she was a deva, quickly adapted to maintaining that fact under cover. If asked why the hosts kissed her feet she would say she is an asura too.

Layla saw the understanding in Princess Rati's eyes. No one had ever told her she was a deva, but she believed it easily, and knew that asuras and devas were deadly enemies.

"We'll talk later," Nastassia-now-Angirasas said to Rati, holding both her hands and tapping her wrist in Agent code so no one could see, but Rati would get the message that we should say no more in front of this company. Somehow Rati remembered that three taps meant "don't speak". She was amazed but showed nothing.

"Let's show the guests their quarters and where the towels are. They are sure to want to bathe before dinner," she went on in the manner of the matron character she was playing.

After the guests were sorted out the mental conversation debriefed on what had been learned about the travelers so far.

Rati's bodyguards are actually her boyfriends, Layla disclosed. *They pretend to be eunuchs and get away with it because their testicles are undescended. Rati practices sodomy and oral sex with them to maintain her hymen. And there's also her deep bosom—*

Too much information, Nastassia interrupted, and projected a pretend blush.

This spy stuff can cause nosy habits, Layla apologized.

The bodyguards were Kshatriyas, warrior caste, the ones who became kings, and were humans who had become steeped in the ways of the Rebels. Guarding and serving the princess on holiday in the West, they were seeing things none of them had ever seen before, and enjoying the time spent away from the prying eyes of the court.

The guide Maargadarshak was well known to them from many previous stays at their oasis on the long journey. He was also human, and he was family, despite the fact that he hung out with Rebels. He had no idea of the Agents' true identities. He was a middle-aged adventurer with no real family and of low caste, and so had taken to the road and discovered the profits to be made by leading wealthy Westerners over the difficult roads to Bharata for holiday, trade, or whatever occasion brought them to the region. He was not nosy.

The three Aryans were Persians and appeared to be Rebels, although it was hard to tell as they were able to maintain their mental shields.

The three Persian freebooters were all obviously Rebels asleep in human brains, and warriors.

The other three people were traders, one from the Levant, one from Perses, and a Gaul from the far West. They brought valuables from their own cultures as samples to establish trade.

The guests came down for dinner at different times and so a revolving party began, floating around the house as new hungry people were drawn to the food area where wines were also ready to pour for oneself. Sunset was visible through the thrown-back tent walls, reflecting in the lake. A few bold birds hopped around looking for table scraps. They robbed from the plates Maargadarshak had piled around him on the floor, where he was playing the flute.

"Oh, are you too going to see Mohenjo-Daro while you are in the area?" Angiras overheard one man ask another. The nearby city, now in ruins, was a popular tourist attraction.

"Oh, you must!" Layla-now-Tara interjected gaily. "It could be the oldest city on Earth!"

At the first sitting, Angiras led with a hymn to Agni, the god of fire, who despite being a deva was well-liked among Rebels and so the guests that leaned the Rebel way were not offended and everyone chanted along. Although a hymn to anyone other than Perse was somewhat of a slap in the face, they could let it pass under the circumstances of hunger and the smell of the cooking.

Over dinner, Rati recounted one of the stories her parents had told her about Agni, passed down over the ages.

"As we were chanting, I remembered when I was a little girl I had a dream in which Agni and Ushas got high on Soma and sported on the rim of the hill where the dawn rises," Rati said. "And that which we see as the dawn is the gentle fire of their passion." Maitreya/Angiras noticed that she was flirting with him and a part of him swelled up and wanted to show recognition, but he did not. The other Agents noticed that Maitreya's mind had been shielded for a few seconds but communicated nothing of it.

Then Ganesh, the darker of the bodyguard swains, said, "I have heard that Mitra and Ushas fight over which shall sit on Agni's lap." Many of the human male guests leered.

"In your usual taste, Ganesh," said Punji, nicknamed after a booby-trap weapon and the lighter-skinned aspirant to Rati's affections. "It's true, though, your highness, that the gods do sport just as we do, sometimes even involving rape—if you ladies will excuse my speaking of such things, even spiritually."

Maargadarshak then added, "It is okay, Mister Punji. These our hosts are the most open-minded people I know—their salons always allow for the freest conversations. And you're right about our traditions. Even Krishna once advised Arjuna to steal a young woman by force."

At this point, thinking of The First Son whom he knew well as the number two in the entire multiverse, the commander in chief of the Agents who appeared in this region as Krishna, Angiras said, "Oh, I'm sure Krishna would not do that."

The initial reaction of the Bharatas was mild shock. Angiras hastened to continue. "Oh, please let me explain. I'm not denying our traditions. Our greatest teaching story, sung by minstrels for thousands of years, the Mahabharata, contains a number of falsehoods. Although the main exhortation is Nivritti—attach to nothing—in other places profit is placed over everything else, including Nivritti. How can one great song contain opposing ideas? Because many devas and asuras added to it over the ages. Also, some advice pertains to beginners and other advice to those already well-advanced." The faces of the mercs darkened as this sunk in, because they saw it as counter to their own benefactors' propaganda, which it was.

The Bharatas listened with respect but confusion as the conversation spread out to cover a number of falsities—according to Angiras—embedded in the teaching stories of the culture, which went back at least 15,000 years. The Rebels had injected their own propaganda into these otherwise true and valuable morality plays transmitted orally across a thousand generations. He couldn't speak openly about Rebels, so he simplified by saying, "Celestials who became confused added in these twisted ideas, and since they made colorful story material, they stayed in over the ages."

"Esteemed and divine Angiras," Rati began with ultimate respect, and a lingering tinge of flirtation in her eyes, "if abducting a woman by force is not proper, what else have we been mis-taught?"

Angiras showed no reaction to the flirtation and went through a litany of inconsistent ideas in the tradition of the country. A hierarchical system of castes, women as secondary citizens, the warrior caste being the only ones eligible to rule—all were standard Rebel ideas. To virtue and salvation, ideas spread through the Agents' emissaries, the Rebels had contaminated the oral teachings with profit and pleasure and non-egalitarian ideas. Of course, their basic disbelief in the multiverse as one consciousness would lead them to this selfish might-makes-right attitude.

Esmaeel, the largest of the soldiers of fortune, challenged his host, "You seem quite certain, Angiras, but how can you know which way it really is? How can any of us know?"

Angiras laughed. "Good question, my young friend. What we learn and experience from yogic meditation and contemplation is, to us, very compelling proof; but to a non-meditator we have no means of validly transmitting that proof. I can only urge everyone to meditate, as the practice over time leads to one's own certainty of what the world is, and how to best serve the dharma." The Aryans nodded at this.

The salon continued well into the night, with the Agents playing a propaganda game with the Rebel-leaning guests but keeping it friendly. The Bharatas' heads went back and forth between the debaters. An idea gradually formed in Maitreya's consciousness, a way of cleansing Rebel poisons out of the stories parents told their children.

Later, when all the guests and the other Agents were asleep, Maitreya quietly went to a table overlooking the moon on the lake. Part of him was fantasizing about a conjugal visit with his wife. He was not in a human body; she was. He could invisibly get past the two bodyguards and other peeping eyes and make love to her in her dreams. She was the goddess of sex and since they were eternal soulmates it would seem to be consensual. Was this what The One had intended?

He felt even more strongly that what The One wanted him to do right now was to take dictation. The One probably gave him the idea he had been having all night. He sighed and gave up the idea of slipping into Venus's dreams, which seemed somehow inappropriate. He was the senior officer in a situation that could be threatening everyone in the multiverse with endless suffering for eternity. How could he take any time off, for anything, let alone surreptitious sex with a sleeping being, even if she was his wife? Instead he took up ink and quill and began to write on an Egyptian papyrus, notes for a book:

Rig

Om—I praise Agni, the god of fire, the family priest, the divine priest of the ritual of worship...

THOU, mighty Agni, gatherest up all that is precious for thy friend. Bring us all treasures as thou art enkindled in libation's place.

Assemble, speak together: let your minds be all of one accord,
As ancient Gods unanimous sit down to their appointed share.

The place is common, common the assembly, common the mind, so be their thought united.

A common purpose do I lay before you, and worship with your general oblation.

One and the same be your resolve and be your minds of one accord.

United be the thoughts of all that all may happily agree.

Much later, Maitreya's notes would come to be known as the Rig Veda, the first of the great books of wisdom that the Agents would plant on Earth. Each book had the same purpose: lead the reader inward to self-discover the One True Identity.

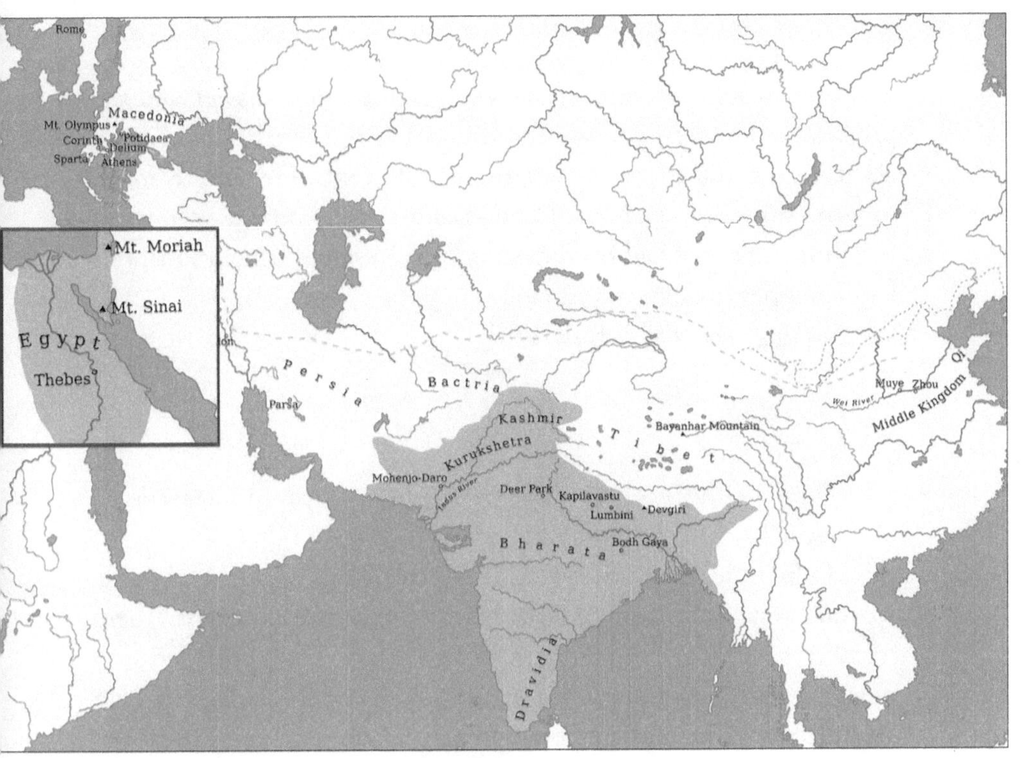

6

THEBES, A PLACE

1380 BC

As a prince he was given a lot of latitude, of which he took advantage, he thought now. But he himself still did not know why he did these things, like what he was doing now. If he was caught he would be questioned and that thought was agonizing. He did not like speaking. It took him too long to decide among the many warring voices that rose up within him seeking to be spoken out of his mouth. It would be better if one was given time to answer, and the privilege of answering by writing things down. There he could reach clarity and certainty before sharing his thoughts. He secretly loved to write things down. Most Hibirus didn't even know how to write yet, though people had been writing for a hundred generations. His endless inner dialogue continued.

Nothing's going to happen here.

Who says?

I'm going home.

No, I'm not!

Why am I always arguing with myself? Who else is in here with me, in my head?

He had picked a brilliant hiding place from which to observe. No one was likely to find him here if he remained silent. There seemed to be many hidden passages like this one that provided spy-holes through which to watch into other chambers undetected. He loved to slip away and explore and watch and listen and learn the secrets of the priests. His little boy's body could easily fit into these tight places where most adults would probably not dare to go.

If I'm caught, I'll have to answer questions.

You hate that.

Yes, I hate it because I don't really know why I do what I do. When I am challenged with a question I have too many answers to choose from. I somehow want to put them all together and by that time the questioner has moved on to something else. I hate that!

Like the warring voices in Moshe's mind—as if factions existed inside him, or outside factions sought to control his mind by some kind of magic—the priests had been at war for some time. He was drawn in to understanding which of their two chief gods, Amun and Aten, was the real number one god of this country, and which the imposter. The country itself was still trying to decide. Were they really one and the same? This was his secret hunch. He was excited at the possibility of becoming the one to discover the truth. He shared this with no one, not even his brother, with whom he shared almost everything.

Looking out into the large stone chamber, he breathed silently, squeezing himself below to control his feeling of needing to urinate, which he often felt while hiding and spying.

In the chamber he had been watching, an older prince, an actual Egyptian dressed in one of their most elaborate costumes, had been led in by priests and placed into a beautifully carved and painted box. When the cover of the box was being closed, Moshe had seen the terror flash over the older boy's face before he covered it up and again looked regally brave.

Can he even breathe in there? Moshe pondered. He was glad it wasn't him.

Now it had been quite some time since the prince had been in that box. The priests had been softly chanting and walking around the box carrying their candles, while other candles flickered in the wall sconces, sending dancing shadows around the chamber.

Are they killing him? Moshe wondered. The kid would have suffocated by now. What if he was dead? Should Moshe tell anybody? Was this part of their war between the Amunites and the Atenites? Was this a political or religious assassination? He could be in much worse trouble than he thought if he were to be caught spying on this scene.

The chanting came to a stop. Moshe was almost shaking with excitement or fear, and he strove to breathe more deeply to calm himself, yet without making even the smallest sound.

The priests ceremoniously lifted off the top of the box and looked down inside. The chief priest among them, an old man, gave an order and the others reached down and lifted the seemingly lifeless corpse up while others closed the box again. Then they all placed the body on top of the closed lid and arranged it decorously.

The chief priest then bent down and kissed the boy on the mouth for a long time. A moment came when Moshe realized that the priest was trying to breathe life back into the boy. *Wow,* Moshe thought. If the dead could be brought back to life this way, what pay dirt he had struck. This could be invaluable knowledge for the Hibiru people.

Suddenly the boy coughed and the priest pulled away, allowing the corpse to revive itself. The boy looked up and saw the priests, and Moshe could see the recognition and remembering on his face, but it was a different face, the boy had somehow changed. His face was no longer boyish, for it had an air of great knowing. The young prince with some difficulty sat himself up, and the priests aided him.

With a degree of challenge in his voice, the chief priest asked, "What was your experience, sire?"

"I could not breathe," the boy said. "Darkness closed in on me. I wanted to scream or to pound on the lid in order to get out but I knew that was unacceptable. I wondered who wanted me dead and how they had gotten to you. I felt my breathing stop. I felt my heart stop. Then I must have died because there was nothing."

"And then you experienced waking up and looking up at us just now," the chief priest suggested.

"Oh no," the young prince objected. "There was nothing, and then everything changed. I still existed. Some force bore me upward and I emerged into a great light. God spoke to me, telling me there is no final end, that spirit is eternal, everyone's spirit, not just the Pharaoh's—and that death is an illusion—"

"That is a secret, sire," the chief priest warned, but Moshe realized the priest's attitude had changed. The prince had passed a test of some kind. Perhaps it was not true that everyone persisted after death, and the prince would have failed the test if he had not reported having experienced life within death. What would have become of him had he not passed the test?

Moshe had an instant fantasy of being in the boy's position and upon reawakening into this life, clamming up and not telling the priests what he had experienced. Would they kill him? Or would he be simply left out of the line of succession? Moshe had no illusion that he, the son of slaves, would ever rule Egypt, although he fantasized about it all the time and daydreamed about righting all the wrongs and making everyone happy.

After the procession filed out again and no one was in the adjacent chamber for some time, Moshe dared to slip back out of his hiding place and cautiously repair to his room, by way of the bathroom. Once his body was at ease again and he was back in his room, he felt the urge to write. Something inside him felt strongly that something significant was going to come through him onto the papyrus. He was in the rare state he got into sometimes where he knew that the voice already thinking the words to write was what he called his Master, the one voice he knew he could always trust and allow out of his mouth or onto papyrus. Then the words began to flow out of him into hieroglyphics:

The Book of Emerging into the Light

O nobly born, you who are about to embark upon a
great journey
I am the egg of the world
What a journey I have made, the things I have seen
I am but one of you.

Those notes would grow into a book that he would hide where the chief priest would find it. Later generations would also find a copy and rename it *The Egyptian Book of the Dead.*

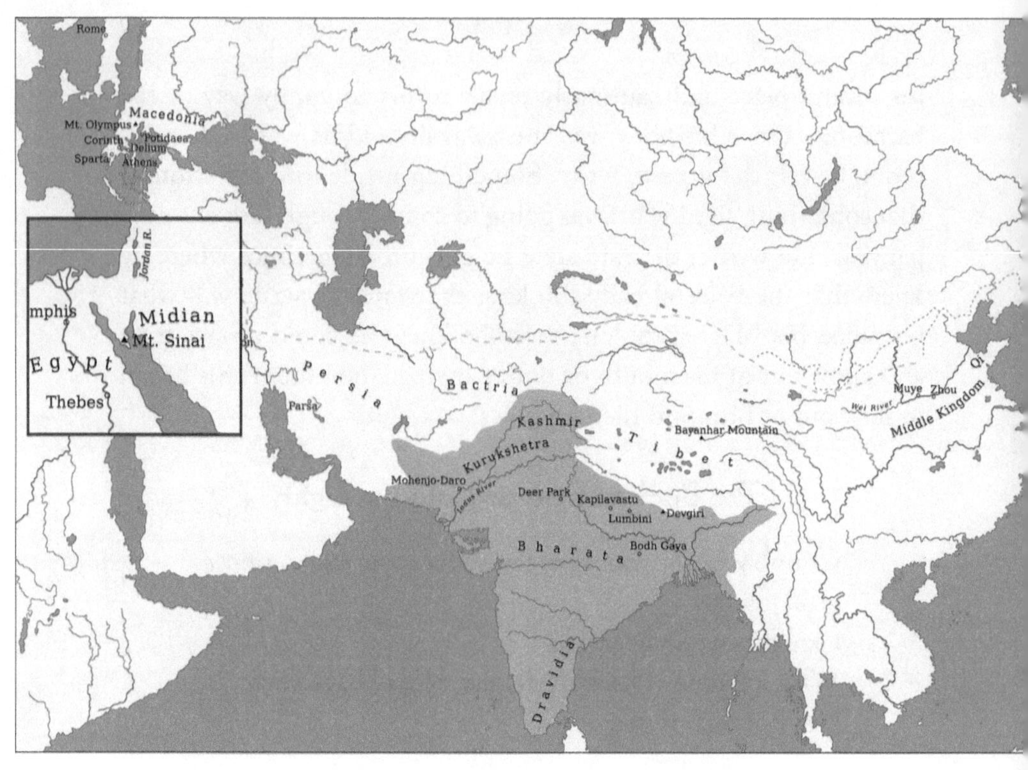

7

MIDIAN, A PLACE

1313 BC

This has something to do with all my fighting, Moshe somehow realized, although he did not know how he knew. Before his eyes a bush was burning in a way that was impossible—it was not being consumed, blackened, or crackling, it wasn't withering and breaking off and falling. It appeared to not mind at all. *Why is the god of fire dancing on the goddess of nature?* he wondered. You'd think the gods

40

would know enough not to fight. He himself should know better. *You were just defending other people.*

The strange sight in front of him triggered self-examination and he noted that he had become obsessive about fighting injustice. *Why was that?* Something deep inside was compelling him. *If it is me, then why can't I see it?*

Now the bush spoke to him in his mind, claiming to be an Angel, a messenger of the Most High, the chief of the gods.

Moshe, they will remember you as Moses, which means, "To pull out", because you are here to draw the Hibirus out of Egypt, and to help draw out the best in each person.

He was being asked to go back to Egypt to convince the Pharaoh to let the Hibirus go. He had killed an Egyptian some years back, so going back there seemed like a really bad idea.

Strange voices were no stranger to his mind. He had been wrestling with himself internally all of his life, as if there were more than one of him. Sometimes he was almost sure that a voice in his mind was not his own but was implanted by somebody far away or close by and invisible. Now with the bush identifying itself as the speaker in his mind, finally here was verification of what he had guessed long ago: some of what we hear in our mind as coming from our own self is not.

From that moment on his world changed forever. The One Self, whom Moshe and everyone else on Earth thought of as God, El Elyon, the Most High, the highest chief among the gods, began speaking to Moshe directly, once he began to accept the assignment. These audiences with God uplifted him to a rapturous state of bliss and near omniscience, which Moshe prized. The mental clarity would fade away when God was not speaking to him. That's when his normal warring voices, wherever they came from, took *over* again.

The One gave Moshe a telekinetic/telepathic augmenter in the form of a stout walking staff, although The One could change its appearance. The staff was an instrument to give more power to the Agents supporting Moshe.

Through the device the Agents could carry out The One's wishes, which was the way The One liked to operate. HeSheWe preferred not doing everything alone, and that's why the Awake Creatures game and then the Lost Lambs game started in the first place. However, certain miracles God just upped and did directly.

The deck was stacked against Moshe although he didn't know it. He was only human, and strategic to both the Agents and the Rebels; hence his lifelong inner war, as he was constantly being communicated to by both sides.

Add in that his followers were not just normal humans. A good number were Rebels in human bodies, some awake and some half-asleep, but all disposed to rabblerousing and inciting riots. Moshe identified some as causing trouble on purpose, finding grievances that others took up as well. He actually called them rebels without knowing how right he was.

Whenever he turned his back, he totally lost power over the community and it sank back into something much like Sodom. Thus, was the power of the Rebels over the human mind, trapped within the interfering brain the Rebels had genetically sabotaged to be overly helpful and overactive.

The One regretted having to decide that it was for the greater Good that some of these people be kept from entering the Promised Land. The Rebels constituted most of the warrior class and so Moshe was given orders to *not* let in, the military-census-registered males over 20 who had grumbled against God. This was effectively the Rebels. Moshe and his brother Aaron would have to make judgment calls to keep out the rest, and to let through all non-Rebels.

This of course was wise. The One is the wisest of all. He knew how far he could rely upon Moshe, since Perse could successfully trick Moshe, such as when he imitated The One's mental voice and gave Moshe instructions to slay every man, woman, and child resisting the Hibiru presence except virgin girls who were to become slaves. The Agents would have to take it the rest of the way, and Moshe and Aaron left to control who made it across.

When the time came, it was a hurtful thing that Moshe would not be allowed to enter the land of milk and honey. Moshe sensed it was because God did not trust him. Or was it that God was offended when Moshe said, "Then blot me out too," when God had spoken of blotting out the Hibirus. He had taken the side of the Hibirus rather than God's side. He chastised himself. *Who am I to think I have the right to do that, to put my judgment over God's?*

The One looked on with compassion as Moshe tortured himself. Moshe would be with him soon and he would explain it all to him, revealing that Perse was the one who spoke angrily of blotting out the Hibirus. The One Self did not blame Moshe for not being able to distinguish HimHer from Perse. The new Rebel-sabotaged human brains were not Moshe's fault. The One Self was totally pleased with Moshe.

In his remaining time on Earth, Moshe was transcribing something that would teach humanity how to make the right decisions, and how not to be swayed by tempting delusions.

Moshe sat in his tent and wrote in Hibiru.

Torah

In the beginning God created the heaven and the earth. And the earth was without form, and void; and darkness was upon the face of the deep.

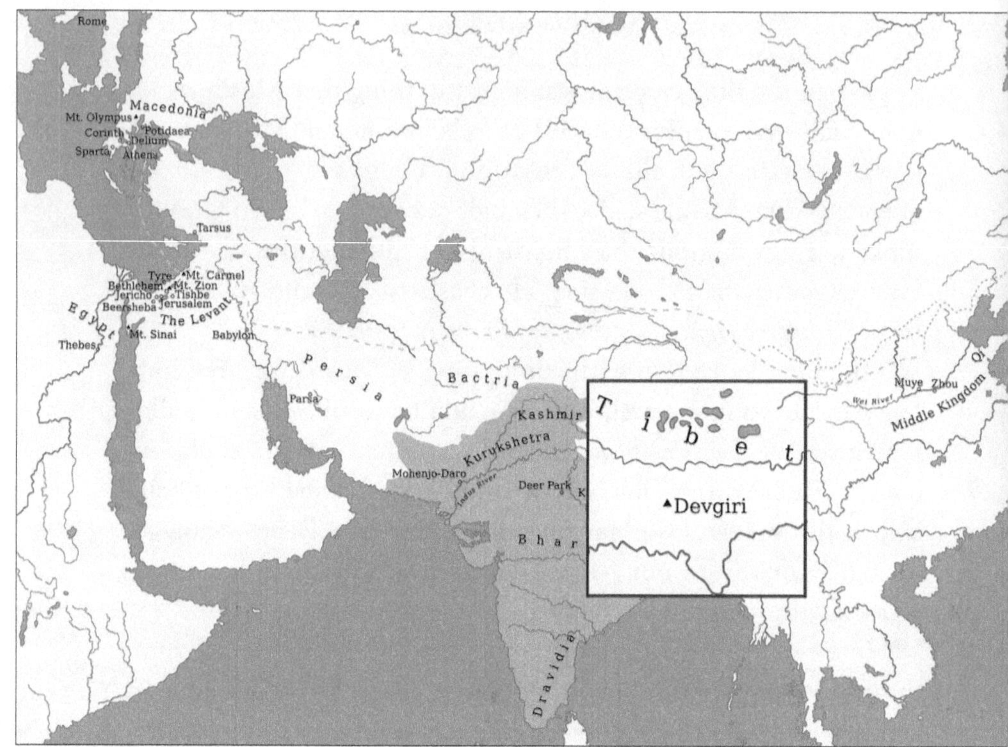

8

CHANGE IN TACTICS

1312 BC

The Agents had been operating for some time in their invisible
bodies, able to appear in any form and safe from takeover by the
booby-trapped human brains. At the same time, they were not succeeding in slowing the enslavement of the planet by Rebel forces. In
order to consider their options, they met for a retreat atop Devgiri,

which would come to be called Mount Everest, where humans and Rebels had never been detected.

They took on human form, just in case there were surprise visitors of any kind, and they appeared dressed in heavy garb for warmth, gathering around an actual fire to keep their cover plausible. Each pair of lovers was intertwined, looking like a two-headed being encased in furs. They were wearing their preferred human appearances. Templegard found Nastassia's dark regal small oval face seductive and intimidatingly beautiful. She made her face even more seductive for him without moving at all. He was wearing his tall swimmer's body and young handsome face. Layla, who was often blond or red haired, was a bit of both now and she bit Melchizedek on his ear. Maitreya smiled indulgently at the lovers' antics and called the meeting to order.

"We need to consider some creative solutions," Maitreya said. "We're not winning." The other Agents made subtle sounds and gestures of agreement with Maitreya.

"Is it too soon to second-guess ourselves?" Melchizedek wondered. "We've just begun planting the Truth in books. It could take centuries or millennia for the books to do their job at any kind of scale, even with our help."

Maitreya smiled. "I think the books may be there to keep reminding *us* and to wake *us* up whenever *we* go native." Though written through them and Moshe and others, they knew the books weren't their own idea, they were inspired from above. They always started with little snatches of sentences they heard in their heads, and from their training they knew to start taking dictation at those times.

"I *thought* these books were a little advanced for humans, at least the humans on this planet, with the brains they've got now," Templegard said.

Layla murmured assent. "Yes, judging from how quickly Moshe's words and miracles were forgotten by his followers and even his brother, time after time."

A fierce wind blew up and sent particles of hard snow in a sideways storm, having no effect on their bubble bodies, despite their human appearance. Looking into the wind, there was just a wall of glittering white blowing past and through them. Looking the other way, the panorama was beautiful, the sky blue and pink, the mountains and ravines twisting down into verdant valleys and lakes far below and far away.

"I don't know," Maitreya began, "it's just a hunch…" They all looked at him, knowing he had an idea. "We've been staying out of human bodies to avoid getting taken over by the spiked brains… the downside is that we are not seeing things the way humans see them, we're not experiencing what they experience. Maybe we'd be able to sharpen our tactics if we could see the world through their eyes, which might make us able to communicate more effectively with them. Maybe we have to risk it and go back to Plan A, being born as humans and learning how to stay awake in those brains. Maybe we can evolve techniques that work for us, to stay awake, and teach those techniques to other humans."

This seemed frightening to all of them. They had each experienced being taken over and made to suffer by the Rebel-altered human brains, rendering them quite unlike themselves and instead as pathetically weak creatures without psychic defenses or powers— a nightmare. Exactly the outcome they were striving to prevent from overtaking the whole multiverse, at which point they could never come back again to the heavenly paradise it all was at the beginning. It seemed like a really bad idea. But it was true that what they had been doing was not working. They *had* to do something different.

And that was when the Agents made either their biggest mistake or their smartest move, shifting back into being born as humans. It was a huge decision, seeing as it affected not only the five of them, but also another half million Agents under Maitreya's command currently on the ground.

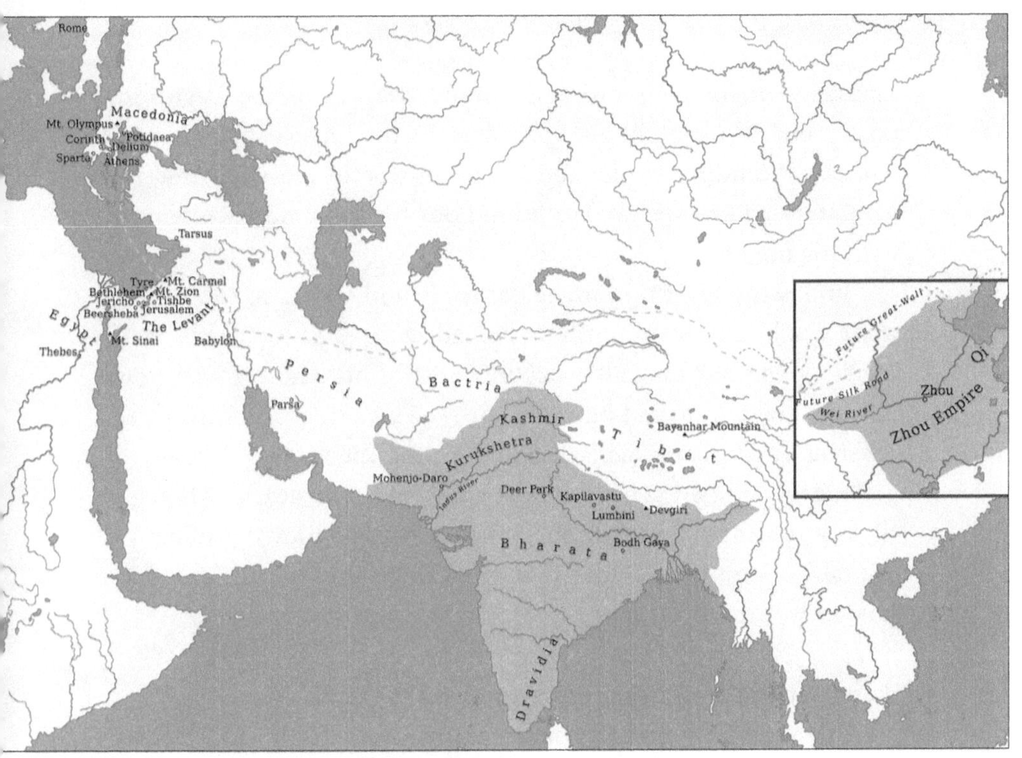

9

Permanent Connection

1046–1006 BC

Today you will meet the woman of your life, Jiang heard a voice in his dream say. Although used to psychic experiences, this was a new one. His wife Ma-shi was supposed to have been the woman of his life but she had left him long ago.

He opened his eyes and saw the dawn out his window, illuminating the windowsill flowers, as well as the golden and cream tapestries of his bedroom and around the top of the large four-poster bed. Pink highlights reflected in his impeccable silver silk pajamas. Standing, he looked in the mirror to see what this new woman would be seeing. He fluffed out his short neat white beard with his fingers.

Following his intuition, he got ready and set out to the West on what would a millennium later be called the Silk Road. His walking stick was not his only weapon. Most of his Zhou troops would not recognize him, and he would be seen as a target by the bandits, deserters, and Shang diehards still fighting the war.

He was guided to a roadhouse catering to the nearby Zhou garrison and went inside. Although the sun was not down yet, many of the tables were filled with off-duty soldiers already drinking. Jiang saw no women.

Oh, there's one. No one was at the bar but the barmaid was busy doing something. Jiang went up and sat at the bar.

"What will it be?" the perky barmaid asked him in a friendly open manner as if ignoring his age. He was 92. She looked about 15. There was something familiar about her. How could she be the woman of his life? He smiled at the joke someone was playing on him.

"Baijiu, please," he answered.

She served him the 120-proof vodka. "I'm Nu Wa," she introduced herself. He took a sip. "Ah!" he said, offering his hand, "I'm Jiang Ziya, it's my pleasure to meet you." He smiled at her name. Fu Xi and Nu Wa were the Adam and Eve of this culture, whose folklore said they were descended from a dragon identified with the creative principle.

He looked at her smiling face and as they shook hands he got the strong feeling that this was not a joke, but that he had a strong future connection with this little girl. She was indeed little, but so beautiful, especially her eyes and mouth. Her face was small and oval, her lips pouty, her smile dazzling. Her skin was pale mulatto rather than yellow. He had seen or imagined this face before but he had no clear memory of it.

"Jiang Ziya, I've heard of you—weren't you King Wu's strategist at the battle of Muye?"

"Still am," Jiang admitted, speaking more softly, just to her. "The strategy is just beginning," he joked seriously.

"Wow," Nu Wa said, keeping her voice down, following his lead to be discreet. She gulped. "How... does one become the King's strategist?" She believed he was who he said he was, partly because he was so old. She had not seen that many people of his age, though he looked to be in pretty good condition. He looked handsome to her beneath the short white beard, which was meticulous.

"You have to be patient," Jiang said, "and trust your inner guide." She nodded enthusiastically, feeling like she had so much in common with this old man, as he continued. "I used to work for King Zhou and grew to loathe him, and only escaped him by pretending to go insane. For many years something told me to wait, and one day someone would come for me, and make me his strategist, and together we would bring down King Zhou's Shang dynasty and replace it with a new one. So, I sat by the banks of a stream with a string in the water. After a few years my wife left me."

"Did you catch many fish? Is that the way you survived?"

"I never used a hook. I only wanted the fish that were sent to give up their lives for me. So, I was almost always hungry. But some fish always came and I lived. One day a man came to me. He said that he was King Wen, the head of the Zhou state, and that his viziers had foretold that while hunting on the north bank of the Wei River he would find a duke whom Heaven had sent to be his teacher."

"And that's where he found you?"

"Yes. He sat down and we talked military and political strategy for a while. We still talk about it for hours every day."

"I was wondering... what brings you out this way?" She was thinking how such a man found time to hang out in bars, especially so early in the evening. She was slightly suspicious that maybe he was merely impersonating Jiang, but the man had such a presence this seemed unlikely.

He was about to tell her of his dream but something changed his course. "I was actually myself curious as to why an intelligent woman like you would be working in a dangerous place like this."

She laughed. "I need the money, and nobody knows me in this area. I came from far to the South, so it wasn't easy to get a job."

"I'll give you a better job, with more pay and no danger."

"Why would you do that?" she asked and then repented. "Oh, I'm sorry. I didn't mean to imply that you might have bad motives. I'm very grateful actually! Forget I asked that. What kind of job?"

"I need another assistant who is willing to learn and who understands the reality of inner sensing as you do."

"Wow that is so great! Listen, my next shift replacement is about to come in. I'm staying in a little room upstairs, and I have almost nothing so it will take just a minute to pack." Jiang nodded agreement.

It was getting dark and as they set off back to King Wen's palace, they had a bit of a dustup with three men. Jiang recognized them as three off-duty soldiers he'd seen at one of the tables. He'd seen them looking at Nu Wa in the roadhouse and wasn't surprised to see them planning to rape her and easily kill him.

Jiang seized the left forearm of the man to his right and hung off that arm while whirling 360 degrees in an aikido move that produced a spiral fracture and loud scream. Coming out of that whirl, he kicked the teeth down the throat of the man to his left, noting that Nu Wa had stomped on the foot of the third man and painfully broken the small bones there. In shock and pain, the men backed away.

"You *are* Jiang Ziya!" Nu Wa said.

Jiang gave Nu Wa more than a job and training. He took her on as his personal protégé and sought her counsel, verifying as he expected that she picked up on subtle messages, which added to the ones he received. She was accepted at court as Jiang's adopted granddaughter. Jiang was Duke of a territory within the Zhou Empire called Qi, as well as being King Wen's main adviser, and so she was treated with utmost respect.

This was the very first year of the Zhou Empire. Ironically, King Zhou was the name of the head of the Shang Dynasty, which the Zhou Dynasty had replaced after the battle of Muye, just months before the voice spoke to Jiang. King Zhou had burned himself to death after losing that battle. He had been an asleep Rebel. Most every state in China had an asleep or awake Rebel in charge, except for the Zhou state, where King Wen was an asleep Agent.

The Rebels had destabilized the entire region, whose nation-states had lived in relative peace for thousands of years. Earlier border disputes had been settled through aristocratic chariot battles with relatively few casualties. The Rebels had changed that, introducing mass infantry warfare, iron weapons, and assembly line production of crossbows and pikes. Now millions of massed peasants killed each other annually. In place of chariot warriors running each of the nation-states, now there was a Rebel-infused bureaucracy everywhere in the Middle Kingdom except here in Qi.

Nu Wa lived in adjoining quarters to Jiang and they spent a lot of time together. They told each other the story of their lives and noted many parallels in terms of hidden guidance systems, the reading of messages in dreams and other odd experiences. They discovered that they both felt they had lived before, and both had a sense of being on some kind of mission.

She taught Jiang a method she had learned as a child from shamans in her own tribe far to the South. One needed to put the shell of a dead turtle over a fire, and cracks would appear on the turtle shell, which could then be read. She had memorized the 64 patterns that could each be read as a message, and the 6 changing lines, which could provide still more messages. At Jiang's strong feeling, the two wrote down the messages for all of the hexagrams and then hid the papyrus manuscript. Jiang was amazed to notice that one of the pieces of advice given by the method was to feign insanity—just as he had done to escape King Zhou.

One night, Nu Wa complained of a stiff neck and Jiang offered to massage her neck. She happily agreed but said she wanted to take a bath first.

While she bathed Jiang laid towels on her bed so that she wouldn't get the silks wet when she came out. Then he sat down to wait for what turned out to be a long while. Eventually she called out to him.

"Jiang, can you help please?" He went into the bathroom and without looking her way asked, "How can I help?"

"Because of my neck, it hurts to try to get up and out of the bath in the usual way. Could you please give me a hand?"

Jiang stepped into the bathroom, averting his eyes and stepping slowly until his leg intercepted the tub, then he reached down under her back and lifted her carefully out of the tub, getting soaking wet. She giggled. He felt himself getting an erection. He carried her to the bed and gently deposited her there, still without looking at her.

"Okay," she said, and he turned and cautiously opened his eyes. She was face down on the bed, a towel over her. He sat down on the bed and began working gently on her neck and trapezius. She made soft pleasure sounds.

Sometime later he asked, "How's that?" He felt her neck and trapezius were no longer exhibiting stiff resistance to his fingers. *Is she awake?*

"My feet, please," she said in a muffled voice. "Thank you. You did a great job. My feet need it next," she explained.

A little later she said, "Let me turn over," and immediately did so, exposing her body fully and then putting the towel over herself again, as if not giving it a thought.

He went back to work on her feet from the new angle, where he was able to work each toe separately. He watched her face, which showed she was in ecstasy and his erection came back.

"The calves too," she said, and so he started working on her calves.

A minute or two later she said, "Higher," and so he started working her knees.

"Higher," she said again a minute later, and he began cautiously working her thighs.

"Do you have any oil?" she asked, and he went to the bathroom and found the oil and brought it. For completeness, he put it first on her neck and shoulders, then on her feet and legs. He was up to the thighs again when she said, "Higher." And so, he started working on her hips and sides, and she reached down and placed his right hand on her *mons veneris*.

At this, he kissed her. She kissed back. In the hours that followed, some of Templegard's and Nastassia's memories started to come back.

Before they culminated their first lovemaking, Jiang held Nu Wa still for a moment and she looked curiously and playfully in his eyes, wondering what he was going to do or say.

"That night I came to the roadhouse, I was sent by a voice who said I would meet the woman of my life there." Then he kissed her.

From that night, the other courtiers sensed that the relationship had changed, and adapted smoothly to it, exhibiting their understanding. The court of Zhou was mostly asleep Agents.

They successfully counseled the king for tens of years, keeping the province independent, despite endless attacks from all directions. Meanwhile their health deteriorated as fallout from the genetically altered diseases ravaging mankind—bioweaponry loosed by the Rebels who then could not control it. Life spans became dramatically shorter than oral histories remembered them to be for their revered ancestors, and old age had become hell on Earth, and it was their turn to suffer it. Now they were very old, and Jiang was on his deathbed. He was 132. No one lived that long nowadays but he did. Those 40 more years had laid a very strong keel to the Agents longterm plan in China. Nu Wa would not live much longer without him, she would want to go to him wherever he was going next. She was 55. They looked the same age.

"What shall we do without you?!" King Wu, son of King Wen, implored them, hoping for a magical solution. Jiang just coughed. His voice no longer obeyed his commands. He knew he was at the end as he barely had the strength to breathe, let alone talk. He depended on his partner to complete the mission. He steeled himself to stay alive just a little while longer, to back her up if need be. The king put his head in his hands.

"Noble king, although we leave you soon," Nu Wa said in a slow and feeble voice, "you and your children and their children will be able to have our advice forever. No, it is better than that, you will have the advice of our own teachers." Jiang and Nu Wa knew intuitively that they were the channels for sage advice and not the originators of it.

She sat at Jiang's bedside, her body conserving its energy by hardly moving. The king looked up hopefully. "You mean your spirits will stay with us?" he asked.

She shook her head. "No," she said in a weak voice, "I don't know where our spirits will go. But we have taught you the eight trigrams and their sixty-four combinations, which are at the root of all situations in the world…" she had a coughing fit. The king helpfully offered, "Yes, yes, this understanding we shall never lose, and we shall pass it down to posterity forever, but without you and Jiang we shall become confused, and not know which part of what you have taught us to apply in any given moment." He realized that there was nothing this dying woman could do about it. He should let her feel good in her last days, thank her for her great work, and let her die in peace thinking it would be all right after she was gone, rather than tormenting her with the awful truth that doom was upon them all.

Her coughing eventually stopped. "Yes, we know that, wise king. We have prepared for that. Over on the table you will find we have created a book for you, and a *method* that will show you which part of the book to read and apply at any given time."

The king got up and crossed the room. On the eucalyptus table sat a leather-bound book of papyrus pages, sitting next to a small pile of yarrow stalks. The couple had found a method of replacing the turtle shells with the stalks. His shaking hand reached out and gently opened the book to the first page. There in the calligraphy he read, "The Book of Changes". In the regional dialect, he read it as "I Ching".

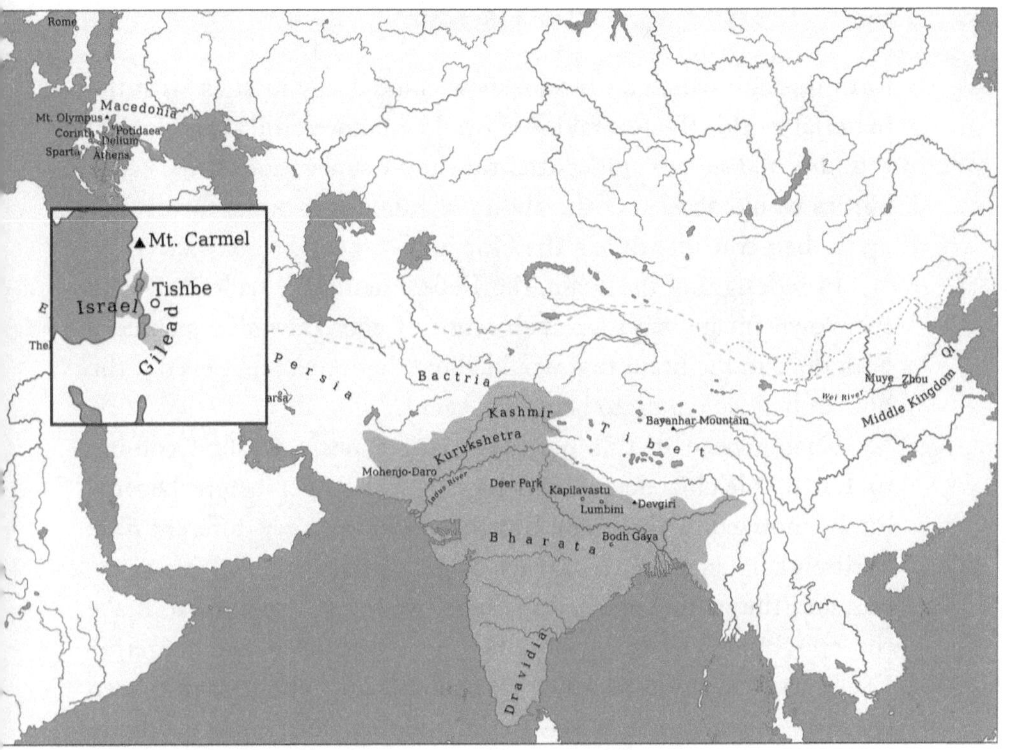

10

ELIJAH, AN EARTH HUMAN WITH AN AGENT SOUL

872–855 BC

Melchizedek took human birth at Tishbe in Gilead, northeast of the Dead Sea, and almost immediately capitulated to the brain. The One Self had originally designed this highly evolved new human brain, introduced almost 200,000 years earlier, to be a useful platform through which a consciousness could easily interact with the material world. The frontal lobes would enhance ethical and logical thinking and support inner attention and visualization. Those capabilities would accelerate the ability of humans to wake themselves up to their true identity as The One Self.

In redesigning the brain, the Rebels naturally made it over in their own image, with a selfish sense of ego. They also planted a back door in the brain that would allow them to hack it even if the human had woken up to being an Agent.

Having been in this position many times since first coming to Earth, Melchizedek should have lasted longer before becoming hypnotized by the brain. But the world was very different now. Written language, the resurgence of polytheism in Israel, bioweapons, and the culture steeped in Rebel ways, all combined to make the enlightened consciousness far more distracted and forgetful. Every year the world became more complicated and harder to keep up with—always more things to think about, never enough time to absorb it all fully and reach clarity. In between incarnations, when they were all awake again, the Agents called this "Acceleritis". The combination of the sabotaged brains and Acceleritis made things more challenging all the time.

Maitreya had seen the future where Acceleritis reached incredible heights and the average person on the planet could not keep up with the input stream. Even the relatively slight increase in complications was already making life more difficult in 872 BC.

Although Melchizedek, now called Elijah, had succumbed and had no memory of his true identity, he began to meditate from a very early age, for it was ingrained in his spirit. Seeing the boy sitting in meditation so much earned him the family nickname, Elijah the sitter, in Hebrew slang, Elijah the Tishbite. This nickname stuck and everyone called him that. People who didn't know him assumed it meant that he came from Tishbe.

The Rebels were aware of him as an Agent but were prevented from harming him by the other Agents who were always around him, invisibly warding off the almost constant attempts on his life and mind. On a few occasions the Rebels managed to bring Elijah down from a higher state of consciousness, but never for long.

In meditation Elijah learned that one true God existed, just as the Hibiru tribes believed. That God, of course, was and is The One Self in all of us and in everything.

Elijah discovered that only in the quietude of his stilled mind could God communicate with him, as a whispering voice that would be drowned out by the overactive thinking brain except in a deep state of meditation. He became a servant of God, a priest, seer and prophet, establishing and training a guild of prophets of God.

The One Self took over giving Elijah assignments directly. This impressed the other Agents and made them aware of the strategic importance of Elijah's mission. At the times when The One had taken him over, he could do whatever miracles he wanted. In view of the Lost Lamb Game rules, he was very sparing with these, not to give away the Big Secret.

Once Perse had managed to demoralize Elijah so that for a moment he forgot that God existed and protected everything so there was nothing to worry about. Everything around him changed. It was the same landscape but now it looked menacing, the trees seemed to be reaching out their zigzag tentacles for him. Deep inside, a memory stirred within the sleeping Melchizedek in him. He remembered this was some sort of trick he had been taught long ago but he didn't understand what that could have meant. He remembered God and the beauty returned to the landscape. He sensed his own breath deepening and slowing again, and his shoulders relaxed and broadened.

What had happened is that he had dropped into the shadow reality called Hell. This is what a being could put himself or herself through by having a runaway mind. Humans on Earth were already falling into accepting life as a nightmare—for which they had good reason. Agents are trained to use method acting to practice the trick of putting themselves into Hell by dark hopeless imaginings. The original purpose of this trick was to be able to perform recon missions to observe the Rebels, because this is the domain they dominate. When an Agent projects being in Hell, he or she makes visual and other contact with others in that state at great distances—including Rebels and their victims. That was the trick Melchizedek/Elijah was remembering, but he couldn't place the memory.

The trick had special significance on Earth because of the tendency of the sabotaged brains to put themselves into Hell often. There the trick was used by Agents not in bodies to get on the same wavelength as humans. And by Agents in bodies to use the trick backwards, to get out of Hell.

The Rebels had managed to frustrate and reverse virtually all of the good that had been done by Agent activity on Earth for the last 200,000 years. The One confided in Elijah that of the hundreds of thousands who had been taught the truth, only about 7000 remained awake to that truth, while the rest were hypocrites who were mostly unaware of their hypocrisy.

As Elijah came of age and was ready, The One ordered him to go to the king and queen of Israel, Ahab and Jezebel, human pawns of the Rebels, and tell them of God's displeasure with their work, warning of a long drought that would be visited upon them. The royals laughed though secretly were frightened. They wanted to have him killed but found that their mouths could not give those orders, which frightened them even more.

Now, Perse was coming after him and The One sent Elijah into hiding, cloaking the location from Perse. The prophesied drought became a reality, lasting three and a half years. As directed by God, Elijah hid out to the East in the Kerith Valley and was fed by ravens. Finally, The One sent Elijah back to the king and queen to announce the end of the drought, which then soon ended.

Although the royals and their Rebel puppeteers were happy to see the drought end, word of these displays of the prophet's power over them had leaked to the populace, threatening their rule. So, King Ahab had no choice but to agree when challenged by Elijah to a duel on Mount Carmel against hundreds of the king's magicians, all of whom had strong Rebel backing.

The duel was focused on the burnt offering of two bulls. The question was whether Baal, the "god" of the Rebels (secretly Perse) would be able to set *his* bull on fire, or whether Yahweh, the God of Israel and Judah (The One Self) would be able to set *his* bull on fire. Thousands of Ahab's subjects and other onlookers massed to watch the event. By direct intervention of The One, Perse with all of his weaponry found that nothing worked, while The One easily sent down a fireball to cook the other bull. The crowd set upon the royal magicians and slaughtered them. "Don't let any of them get away! Kill them to the last man!" Elijah yelled.

That is a very bad sign, Maitreya observed with great sadness. *The One surely did not inspire him to say that. He* cannot *discern the difference between the voices in his head any more.*

How did that one get through? Usually we can block Rebel attempts to put words in his mouth, Templegard agreed with concern. He wondered with guilt if it was he who had let his guard down.

It must be Perse, Nastassia surmised. Who else could get past them without their even sensing it?

In fact, her guess was right. Perse was having a fit of frustration and needed to kill somebody, even if it was his own people. He saw them as letting him down rather than the reverse, which protected his ego and justified the slaughter in his demented mind.

That's not my Melchi saying that, Layla pathed in a quavering voice. *We've got to get him out of there. He's gone native!*

It's very hard, Maitreya consoled her. They could all sense Layla's pain. *I'll ask for approval to extract him,* Maitreya promised.

This would take a while. Maitreya could sense the wheels of cosmic consciousness reordering the battle plan to accommodate the request. Always the guiding principles were to minimize suffering but to play out the game fairly, without resorting to any *deus ex machina* moves.

Elijah sometime later was sitting on a hill in meditation when accosted by a captain in King Ehaziah's army with fifty of his troops. Ehaziah was the son and successor to King Ahab. Elijah casually called down fire and wiped out all fifty-one soldiers. Another captain came with another fifty soldiers and suffered the same fate. The hellish stench of incinerated human flesh hung heavy in the air.

How can he think he is getting orders like that from The One? Layla agonized.

Melchizedek does not have any of his own memories, Maitreya pathed. *He knows to serve The One but imagines The One to be a jealous God who rules from a volcano and is interested only in war. These people have never known peace.*

We've got to get him out of there now, Layla pleaded. *When he realizes the way he acted, he will never forgive himself. He's being used as Perse's pawn, Perse has turned him!*

But Maitreya restrained their shared impulse to intercede and sent up another more urgent request for orders and permission to extract.

Soon the orders came down, with an elaborate plan the Agents could only partially understand.

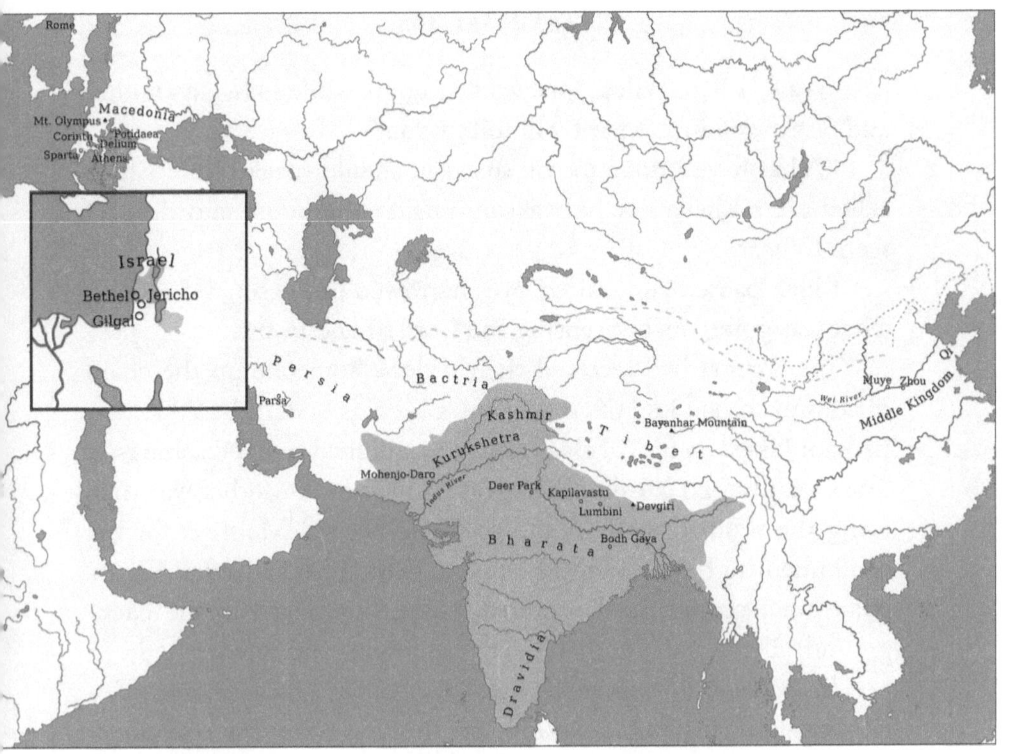

11

ELISHA, AN EARTH HUMAN
TEMPORARILY INDWELT BY AN AGENT
853 BC

Elijah saw a young man plowing a field, driving twelve oxen before him. A spirit moved within Elijah that caused him to walk up to the man and throw his own cloak over the lad's shoulders. Then Elijah, wondering what made him do that, started to walk off.

"Wait!" Elisha yelled. "Just wait a minute while I kiss my mother and father goodbye, then I will follow you!"

"What have I done to you that you should speak thus?" Elijah called after Elisha but he was running to the house and did not seem to hear.

Elijah paused and waited, eyes narrowed in the sun, wondering what was going on, but sensing the Lord's hand in this.

The Agents had received their orders. Someone up the chain of command had identified this boy Elisha as one of the 7000 that had not kissed an idol of Baal, and who still held to the teachings of The One through Moshe. There was no time for any other way than using the walk-in method and so Layla begged Maitreya for the assignment to be the one to go in and extract Melchizedek-Elijah. Maitreya assented. Layla entered Elisha but stayed in the background, allowing the human to stay conscious and rule his body.

He looks just like my Melchizedek, just hairier, Layla observed Elijah through Elisha's human eyes for the first time. The consciousness had projected its favorite self-image upon the flesh, a rugged noble face with caring eyes. Human eyes saw just the surface of things, filtering out the greater details also seen from bubble bodies. Looking at his leather belt-girdle she felt a sentimental twinge. *Melchi always loved leather.*

Still the time had not yet come, and there was work for Elijah and Elisha to do. Elijah trained Elisha and introduced him to the prophets loyal to God.

Finally, the time had come. Elijah was told by God where to go, and he went to these places, as a way of calling attention to four concepts The One Self was assigning the Levites and all other beings to study. They were all historically significant places where the prophet's guild had built up large contingents, Gilgal, Bethel, Jericho, and the Jordan. The prophets were mostly asleep Agents, and many came awake at times.

Gilgal was the first camp of the Israelites after they crossed into the Holy Land in April, 1451 BC. The word *gilgal* means the transmigration of souls.

Bethel was where Abram built the first altar to The One Self, and where Jacob saw his vision of a stairway to heaven, the beginning of teaching Earth humans the truth of their Oneness with Angels and The One Self in all of them, and of the method for climbing that stairway. *Bethel* means house of God. It was the first point of communication with The One Self, before the shift to Jerusalem.

Jericho was where the lesson was first taught that anything could be accomplished without direct human action, by trusting the source of all things to accomplish it, whereby a fortress beyond the Israelites' power to conquer was brought down by following instructions from above to simply walk around it seven times. This symbolizes the ease by which one can conquer any obstacle, even inner ones, once focused on subtle feedback clues from The One Self.

The Jordan River was the obstacle the Israelites had to pass through in order to get in to the Holy Land. They had to entrust their lives to the belief that the waters would be parted for them. It was a lot harder this time than when the Egyptian army was at their back. They all could see themselves drowning and the option was simply to stay where they were. By accepting death, they underwent transformation, and the waters parted for them.

Great essential lessons were enshrined forever in those four places, just as in the celestially inspired books being left behind as records.

The prophets all knew that Elijah would be going away, and understood that they should now follow Elisha, although the two would not speak about it and instructed the others to not speak about it either.

Elisha was surprised that Elijah kept trying to get rid of him before each stage of this journey. Layla understood this to be a test to make sure that Elisha was the right person to entrust with the mission after Elijah's extraction.

Each time, without any help from Layla, Elisha indicated, "Nothing will ever stop me from following you."

Fifty prophets followed them as they approached the Jordan, watching as Elijah struck the water with his cloak. The waters parted to allow the two to cross, and then closed behind them, leaving the other prophets to watch from a distance.

"Before I'm taken from you, please ask for what I can give you before I go." Elijah said to Elisha as they walked along. This was the first time Elijah had spoken openly about being taken away.

Elisha thought a moment and answered, "I am half the man you are, and therefore I will need twice as much of God's help when you are gone."

"Watch very carefully what is about to happen, and if you have the spiritual sight to see, it will be a sign that your wish is granted," Elijah said.

Elisha became very alert and used the powers of concentration he had been taught. Layla helped focus his consciousness and then departed from him to help guard Melchizedek's ascent.

Suddenly Elisha saw pass between himself and Elijah a flaming chariot drawn by flaming horses. This was the closest representation his seer's mind could make of the Agents guarding a shuttle craft as it made a dangerous power dive through Earth's atmosphere, which greatly raised its skin temperature so that it was on fire, then beaming aboard Melchizedek's consciousness body, cremating his human body at the same time, and returning to the skies in a flash. If he had not been concentrating he would have seen very little, just a flash of something going by.

Elisha ripped his garments apart in sorrow, exclaiming the first words that shot into his mind, "My father! My father! The chariots and horses of Israel!"

12

COMING UP WITH SOMETHING ELSE
853 BC

The first thing Melchizedek sensed was the overpowering smell of flowers. Then he woke up completely.

He grinned with delight seeing the imaginary paradise Layla and he had created for their vacations, and there she was, holding him in her arms, while behind her were Maitreya, Nastassia and Templegard, all wearing concerned expressions. Layla's expression now registered upon him most deeply. She was in shock. He hugged her tight and eventually felt her relax a little. He smiled at his other companions and noticed that their smiles in response seemed rather cheerless. Something was amiss, but what?

Nothing could dampen Melchizedek's vast contentment at being home again with his loved ones, taking a break from the intense game The One had been playing with Maitreya and him for fourteen billion years so far, even though Layla, Templegard and Nastassia, as newer souls, were newfound friends in the game. The mountains in the distance, including some coming up out of the huge ocean, the surreal clouds drifting and unfolding overhead, the calls of many types of sea and land birds cavorting in the sky under two suns and a ringed moon, the turtles, crabs, dogs, cats and other animals having fun together on the beach, his loved ones in their bubble bodies in their favorite naked pseudohuman forms and ornamentation, himself in his bubble body once again without the constant aches of the old beat-up Elijah body, and that maddening mindspace vying for control with the robotic brain—all of this deliverance was heavenly bliss.

"Thanks for getting me out of there," Melchizedek said and the others merely nodded. The extreme extraction method had been used, he realized. They needed to get him out of there fast. The Elijah body had been stored as information in the Akashic Records, where everything was stored, ceasing to make its illusion in matter. More typically, the extraction would be handled by arranging for bodily death, since Earth was a Mystery Planet where the inhabitants would have to figure out for themselves what was really going on. An even more rare extraction method that also could have been used was the walk-out, where the body and its brain (which always wanted to take over anyway), would finally be left without an actual inhabiting consciousness to occasionally take back over. But walk-outs were very difficult on Earth due to the overthinking of the Rebel-sabotaged brains.

"Why the rush?" Melchizedek asked, speaking aloud for fun.

Normally Layla would wait for Maitreya to speak first, as he was the senior Agent in this out-of-the-way theater of war that had just become the spotlight as now The First Son was here. Layla was the most junior, having been launched out of The One Self for the first time less than a million years ago. Nevertheless, she spoke first.

"Sweetheart, do you remember what you were doing in there?" she blurted and then looked apologetically at the others, especially Maitreya, who smiled back softly.

Melchizedek read their minds in a flash and knew exactly what they were talking about. He had become bloodthirsty and casual about exterminating the Rebels and their pawns, which was a huge fallback for the height of his consciousness. For the first time in a billion years, he experienced a quickly-passing twinge of horrible shame and humiliation and even fear for what would become of him now. He was then as awestruck by the tendency to attachment as he was by having gone native and sunk to the level of the Rebels. Agents weren't here to exterminate Rebels but rather to save them and their victims from creating their own hell. They were teachers, not murderers like the Rebels.

The next thing that flashed through his mind was the image of him smiling and laughing off what his fellow Agents must be thinking, and then telling them that it was an act, all part of his new plan to make Perse think Melchizedek was capable of being turned, so as to lay a trap for Perse. This idea of lying also passed immediately.

Melchizedek made no effort to conceal any of his internal process. His eyes widened as the full extent of his fall became apparent.

Look, it's still trying to take me over, even though it's not here anymore, Melchizedek pathed, speaking about the booby-trapped human brain.

It's worse than I thought, then, Maitreya responded. *The egotistical "I must always be right" program natural to the punjied human brain* **can** *infect the way consciousness works even after that consciousness leaves the human body.* Maitreya of course knew that The First Son, when becoming acquainted with the current state of Perse, wondered if this insanity could creep up into the One Consciousness. Now Melchizedek's experience was the first piece of hard evidence that the concern was valid. They were all in shock and Maitreya reported the incident upstairs.

"I have a feeling that Perse got to Melchi toward the end there," Templegard submitted, speaking aloud because of his preference for action.

"Ed should know," Nastassia said, keeping her lover company in the out-loud domain. She had started calling him Ed for some reason, perhaps because it was simply shorter. "Ed's earliest memory was being mindblasted right after saying 'Hail to the Second Son'. That's when he became Perse's Rebel marionette, Stari-ki."

"It's possible," Melchizedek said, going along with speaking out loud to be polite, "Maitreya said that it was Perse that had paralyzed me when I was guarding Abram. If he got me once he could probably get me again."

"Sure sounded a lot like that stuff Perse snuck over on Moshe right after a conversation with God, slipping in his command to take no prisoners, kill every man woman and child, except take virgins as slaves…" Nastassia mused.

This was a lot of food for thought. Melchizedek stood up and with body language taking his leave of each of them, he ran into the ocean. They all played for a while in and out of the water, though Melchizedek swam off by himself and they let him alone as they knew he had a lot to process.

God, he thought, addressing The One, *I apologize for thinking I knew better than you.* He now remembered the moment in which he had decided that the world would work better if all of the king's magicians were killed. He had hesitated at the thought, wondering if that was a decision he had a right to make without checking. But then he had plunged along impulsively in the moment. In effect, he had taken the matter into his own hands, which smacked of thinking he could make the decision better than The One could. So he now accused himself of that.

Melchi, you were simply taken over, it wasn't you doing it, don't blame yourself at all. Melchizedek felt as if he were being swathed in love. His heart lit up.

Later, drying off under the suns, and petting a blackish-red cat that had approached them, they resumed battle plans.

"They have devised a very clever strategy for countering our teachings," Maitreya said, continuing to play at human speech, thinking *Perhaps we need the practice* to explain why they were inspired to speak aloud today, even though far from the Earth with no need to keep up appearances. "Instead of pushing back and saying we're wrong, they embellish what we write, bringing back beloved characters from ancient local superstitions and myths, and weaving it all together, thus gaining control of the agenda and putting their twisted ideas into our mouths." He was speaking of the several important books they had left behind to be found, copied, and distributed by humans over the past few thousand years. But he was also speaking of the oral tradition ideas they had promulgated starting tens of thousands of years before that, and the role models they had given Earth humans by a combination of inhabitation and inspiration.

"So far, we've been using two things in an attempt to free humans from Rebel enslavement," Melchizedek said, "spiritual advice and force."

"Force unfortunately didn't work," Templegard observed, remembering how the ship Atlantis had to drop shields to prevent Perse from splitting the Earth like an apple. *Since then we've counted solely on spiritual advice,* Templegard pathed. *And you can't say it's been working great.*

"Is there something else we can try?" Layla asked in all innocence. This was now worth considering, so they all went into meditation.

The next morning Maitreya had an idea. They were lying on the beach again as the first sun rose, and the morning birds were shaking themselves awake.

"It's easy for the Rebels to contaminate our spiritual teaching, since it can be highly abstract and subtle—nonattachment to outcome, unconditional omnidirectional love for all parts of your own Self, everything that needs to be taught to realign a being who is so delusionally certain of its own separateness. Once into such subtle matters, one resorts to metaphors for familiar things, so by choice of words a clever Rebel can make anything mean anything," he explained to much head-nodding as they all on some level had already realized all this.

"That's why Layla asked if there was something else we should be doing." Melchizedek was playing Captain Obvious in order to coax Maitreya to share his new solution.

"Science," Maitreya said. They all thought about this. What did he mean?

It's non-ambiguous, Maitreya pathed, *since twisting the words to mean something else doesn't work. Everything in science is explicitly defined.*

What do you mean by science? Templegard asked. *Controlled experiments?* It wasn't yet registering for him.

Demonstrable empirical proof, Maitreya explained as the way he was using the word. *Controlled experiments are one of its methods, along with inductive and deductive logic, mathematics, prediction, inspiration, and open-mindedness…*

Science is the objective search for truth by whatever methods might work, Melchizedek added.

Love does not question, and so love of all, or love of God, tends to not question, hence the idea of science does not crop up wherever love is the prime mover, Nastassia commented. *Science is questioning with the intention of getting the answer.* Her colleagues struggled to exhume her seemingly contradictory meanings about love and science.

Can you give an example? Templegard asked Maitreya. *What new actions will we take?*

Start with the creation myths, Maitreya answered. *They are anthropomorphic and counter-intuitive to any human except the most unquestioning. Tying the truth of Oneness to that kind of content is like tying the truth to a heavy anchor.*

Ah-ha! Now I see it, Templegard pathed. *Of course, we need to remove the trappings and leave only the pure truth—but wait! Won't that cross the line in terms of Earth being a Mystery Planet?*

Good, Maitreya said, pleased with Templegard's progress. *You've seen the key constraint—excellent, Ed. We can't cross that line, they have to cross it themselves, and they will cross it by a combination of spiritual, telepathic, and scientific development, stimulated by us.*

Someday, Melchizedek said softly. It sounded like a prayer, because it was.

Wait! He added an instant later. *You slipped in a second new factor—not just science, but also teaching them telepathy?*

Isn't that what we have been doing by teaching them to meditate? Maitreya instantly countered. *Once they can read their own mind—and separate their true self from the robotic brain—they become more sensitive to the self outside the brain—and to messages from The One Self. Telepathy comes along with that sensitivity. In time some of them could come to be able to discriminate The One from Perse in their own minds.*

You said something else, Layla said, as if to herself trying to remember. *Ah, yes, you said demonstrable empirical proof. How do we do that without crossing the line?*

We did it in Atlantis, Nastassia put in. *The One spoke directly and unveiled the truth in its complicated totality by direct perception, so they couldn't question what they saw, heard, smelled, touched, felt inside, and tasted…* She trailed off as she saw the objection that this would raise.

That didn't work too well on everyone, Templegard pathed gently to his beloved.

But it worked perfectly on some, Melchizedek noted.

If we can get 50% conversion I will be a very happy Agent, Maitreya said.

Where do we start, Templegard asked.

We have to go back to first principles. Strip away all assumptions and then slowly rebuild from scratch, only accepting an axiom after most rigorously pounding the heck out of it, Maitreya answered.

Thinking of the various theaters back on Earth, Rebel dominance everywhere, their own converts being just a tiny fraction of the population, the frustrations of the last 200,000 years, and momentarily succumbing to skepticism, Templegard asked, inclining his head to signify he was pointing to Earth, *who down there is going to initiate this?*

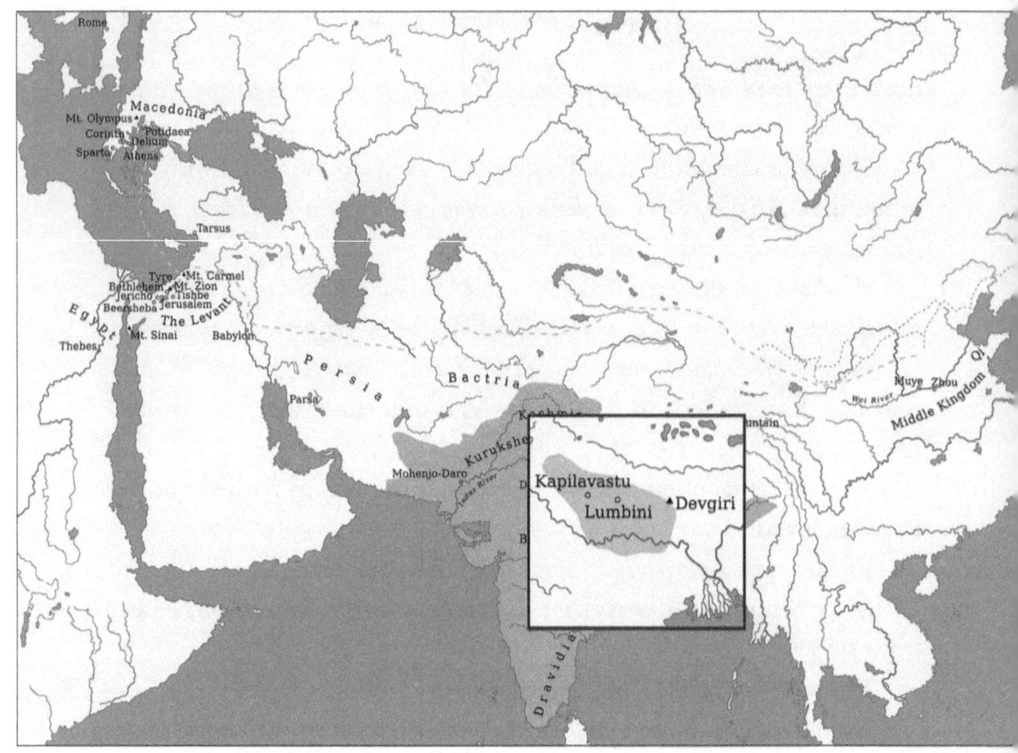

13

SIDDHARTHA, A HUMAN INCARNATION OF THE FIRST SON

563 BC

The First Son, twenty years earlier, had taken up residence on Everest in his bubble body and observed the goings-on on Earth, awaiting the right time and letting his thoughts be guided by what he was learning. From this vantage point, he could experience everything happening on the planet as if he were inches away from each event.

The idea of using Everest as his main base seemed apropos once he saw his Agents doing the same between physical incarnations. He paid very close attention to what his Agents were doing because this was the most curative activity on the planet. Nevertheless, their progress had been slow in reducing suffering, let alone freeing Earth humans from Rebel enslavement. He lived in a constant state of meditation and contemplation, awaiting the inspiration of the acts he would himself take to make a positive difference, learning what he could from their small successes and their huge shortfalls.

He very much appreciated the Agents' notion of adding science to what they taught Earth humans. He could see looking backward into their past and forward into their future, that every step they took teaching in the spiritual domain was countered by the Rebels contaminating the selfsame teachings. Logically, teaching science should be less subject to contamination. But what kind of science to teach that would most reduce suffering and undermine the program of the Rebels to continue to rule Earth?

Ever present was the constraint that he could not simply tell the whole truth straight out, that each person was the same One Self living through all, because this was a Mystery Planet and rules were rules.

The First Son and The One Self had frequent conversations about the "game".

You like it up there on Devgiri. For twenty years that's where I find you.

Well, you know it's really you that likes it so much in this projection of yours called me.

Yes. Well, how do you like the way the game is going? Is it fun yet? The One Self asked ironically.

I'm proud watching the Agents. They've now realized that contamination can work its way up into the soul, and that even You have skin in the game.

Makes it extra exciting doesn't it?

One could almost get attached to not being taken over by Perse's psychic viruses.

So long as it stays "almost" we'll win.

The First Son could see what the Rebels were already doing to counter Thales, the first scientist, who predicted an eclipse. It would take about a century for the Rebels to fully get their act together, but then they would have similar spokespeople that Earth humans would see as equally credible, who would be saying things that sounded the same to the natives and yet whose action implications would be exactly the opposite.

After Thales who was played by Maitreya, Anaximander who was Templegard, Parmenides whom Maitreya walked into when Thales died, Pythagoras, Heraclitus and Anaxagoras, there would be a Protagoras, who would sound the same but who would justify ethical relativism, the quest for money and power, or anything one wanted to rationalize. There would be an Aristippus, and an Epicurus, who would persuasively explain the logic of why unrestrained hedonism was the optimal response to the givens of life on Earth, a message that Rebel-trained ears wanted to hear. There would be a Pyrrho, who would compellingly teach that nothing could be known for certain, so everyone should give up thinking beyond the mundane basics, the perfect philosophy for enslavement. The First Son could foresee all of this happening within another three centuries and could almost hear the actual names of these Rebel-channeling Greek philosophers to come.

Why not? Just next door in Bactria, Zarathustra, to whom The First Son had appeared, had now been himself perverted by the Rebels. The truth was being put forth baked into a message that both came close to revealing the Rebellion, while twisting the story so that both the good and evil Gods had been present from the beginning, more along the lines of the Rebel explanation. They took every opportunity to emphasize that the good God was also the smarter and stronger one, so that the arrogant and clever Rebel personalities inhabiting some humans and influencing practically all the others would be identified as aligned with the good God.

The First Son knew he would not be able to stop these things from happening, and that he had to play a longer game. What science to teach? These cosmologies were easily turned around, so what kind of science would be harder for the Rebels to pervert?

It was not yet time for a major breakthrough. His Agents were already foretelling of the coming of The First Son, through prophets they inhabited like Elijah and Elisha, or inspired like Moshe, the two Isaiahs and Ezekiel. Much more of this preparation would be needed before there could be hope of creating a major turning point event. Even now, Perse and his Rebels regularly impersonated The One Self in the minds of the prophets and often fooled them.

He had an idea. He decided to test it. So, he conceived of a pilot test, and then set his mind to deciding where to carry it out. After three years of further planning, he took birth on April 8, 563 BC, as the son Siddhartha of King Suddhodana and Queen Maya, in Lumbini, Nepal.

The First Son, having infinite sensitivity and having never before been born into the sabotaged human brain, immediately forgot his true identity. He knew nothing of The One Self or the Rebels led by his insane brother Perse. However, he was immediately fully cognizant of everything going on within him and in range of his senses. Looking up, he saw his mother and her handmaidens who had assisted his birth. He could tell his mother was seriously ill and he was sure somehow that it had something to do with his birth. He sent her healing love, but he could tell that the strength of his love was not going to save her, which surprised him. He wondered why it surprised him and made a mental note of it. There were things he did not understand that he needed to figure out, but he didn't know what they were.

The Agents had all but lost touch with him. He did not perceive their presence. They had expected otherwise and thus became extremely concerned and prayed for cosmic fire support. They stayed close to him both to protect him and also for their own safety from Perse, although if he couldn't see or hear them, how much could he help them against Perse?

In fact, he *could* hear them but not the exact words, and so the flow of their ideas seemed to be his own, most of which he could only slightly understand.

He saw that their horse-drawn vehicles were pulled up on the side of a road. He was on a yellow silk blanket, being washed by a pretty handmaiden wearing a galaxy of colors and gold ornaments. Above them was an evergreen Sal tree providing lovely shade. Through the silk blanket he could sense the wetness of the earth. He heard polite bird conversations and could almost make out the meanings. He felt suddenly tired as if from a long journey and allowed himself to fall asleep.

He awoke once or twice on his mother's breast, rocking with the motion of the horse-drawn vehicles, and heard the music of the wheels over the rocky road, and had a feeling of great delight as he dropped back off to sleep. In his dream he saw himself inspecting his body parts and wondering what they were for. He guessed that his fingers were for pulling things closer so he could inspect them. In his dream he could see his actual body clearly.

He came fully awake as the horses rounded the circle in front of his father's main palace in Kapilavastu. This was an astonishing sight. The very size and complexity of it, the beauty of it, flowed into him and he was in bliss. He continued to marvel at it and study it for as long as he could.

"Siddhartha," his mother was saying, right after kissing a man, "this is your father King Suddhodana," and he saw that the man was a beautiful tough guy who obviously adored him, and at first staring in awe he was transfixed by the glory of his father's face.

"But you can call him Suddy," his mother added conspiratorially, "he lets me get away with it in private." This suddenly made Dad much more approachable and even cuddly, so he reached out for this father and Suddy grabbed him and hugged and kissed him, even as Siddhartha quickly learned to do the same. This amazed his parents and the many soldiers and courtiers standing about.

"Father," Siddhartha said distinctly as the King held him out to look at him again. If it were not for the trained Kshatriya reflexes he would have dropped the baby. The stunned crowd whispered amongst themselves. This was a deity or a demon, which is the way they thought of Agents and Rebels, as devas or asuras. Asuras were not all demonic but they palpably differed from devas in not being particularly interested in virtue. The crowd was obviously voting for a deva, or at least wanted the royal couple to think so.

Siddhartha began to be visited by all types of holy men, and they would all make predictions, usually "He will either be a great Kshatriya or a great Brahmin." Sidd thought they were covering their bets, not going out on a limb, and he was truly interested in what he was going to be. It remained his number one and two questions: "Why am I here? Who or what am 'I'?"

He immediately quite liked one such visitor, despite the fact that he was dirty and had long unkempt hair. He appreciated the way everyone else dressed and presented themselves but did not look down upon Kaundinya. In fact, he looked so young, Sidd wanted to play with him. So, when the man stooped down, Sidd put his feet in Kaundinya's long wavy black hair and twiddled his toes, grabbing the hair. The hermit monk just out of his teens laughed. Grabbing the feet gently, he made eye contact with Sidd and mentally asked for permission, and Sidd said, "Go ahead," and giggled, producing a gasp from the crowd. The monk seemed unsurprised and studied the birthmarks on the baby's feet. He began to nod in certainty and looked up at the royal couple.

"He will become the next Buddha," Kaundinya announced, "and I will be his first disciple."

Sidd would need to find out what a Buddha was, because he felt in strong agreement with Kaundinya, and he didn't know why.

The King soon privately offered Kaundinya the post of Royal Court Scholar, wherein he changed his appearance radically but was the same student of virtue on the inside. He was a human with an Agent advisor operating only at subconscious levels. Kaundinya was not sure if the Agent was another being, or part of himself, or a god. He was too humble and grateful to pry into the source of the good advice. The voice in his mind was always the same to him, as he didn't have an ear for discerning one mental voice from another.

But before Kaundinya came into the court, Queen Maya died. Sidd was about a week old. He had been in love with both his parents from the first moment. Visiting his mother's bedside many times a day, and spending hours with her at least once a day, the rest of his waking hours were spent with his father, reviewing troops performing fighting drills with various weapons, fast chariot maneuvers, and other exciting sights to be seen. To Sidd this was ballet, since he did not see anyone get hurt.

In the evenings the three of them were always together with Prajapati, the King's second wife and Maya's sister, and her son and daughter both named Nanda. To Sidd's evolving mental framework, this week was like a year in terms of how quickly and how much he learned. By carefully overhearing conversations, he had learned that a Buddha was a being that had become as enlightened as it gets and comes along once in a very long time. That sounded right to him.

He was not prepared to be kissing his mother goodnight and hearing her say "Goodbye." Suddy put a hand on Sidd's shoulder. Sidd totally got it that she was about to die. He didn't want her to die. He wanted to keep her with them—they were such a fabulous threesome, six with Prajapati and her children. He again tried his love healing and again found it didn't seem to be working.

Why did you think it would work, he asked himself.

Then seeing the look in her eyes, he forgot about himself. She was the priority. He saw that she was suffering, taking it very badly, not accepting that it was happening, and therefore she was in a very confused and tortured state, which he found he could not stand. He wanted to take her grief out of her, into him if necessary. But this didn't happen. Suddy got on the bed and kissed and consoled her. "I will love you forever," he heard his father whisper.

"Get him a full-time mother who loves him as we do, darling," Maya said, "I won't be jealous, please do it right away." The King nodded somberly. They all knew she was talking about her sister Prajapati, who would breast-feed Siddhartha now, he realized.

Looking into her eyes and holding her hands, Siddhartha said, "We will all be together again someday. Speak to me and I will hear you," he promised, wondering why he thought he could do *anything*.

In her eyes he saw that she believed him. She nodded, and then her spirit left the body.

Siddhartha cried himself to sleep beside her, with Suddy on the other side.

14

The Prince

547 BC

His father wanted him to become King, and Sidd wanted to make his father happy. He studied hard to learn what Kings had to know to care for the welfare of all the people. This involved training to be adept with many weapons, and in horsemanship, chariot driving, hand to hand combat. In the military arts he studied as hard as he studied anything, and rose to be expert, while managing not to hurt anyone. In a number of situations this caused him to get hurt himself, which he readily chose as the preferred outcome.

The King knew that Sidd could one day walk off and leave him to become the Buddha, and he did whatever he could to stave off that eventuality. Unseen and unnoticed Rebel advisors ensured that he would take this to extremes. Perse knew where The First Son was and what he was doing. He was determined to do everything he could to stop it.

Carefully sanitized routes were prepared whenever the Prince would leave the palace grounds, so that Sidd would have no inkling that suffering existed in the world. But it was impossible to hide reality from Siddhartha, who was so highly attuned to everything. He had personally experienced the death of his mother, a very strong first clue in the first week of his life. It was very hard to hide sickness and old age even on the palace grounds. But suffering takes place daily due to mere vanity and jealousy, and those things go everywhere, as Siddhartha observed every day. He studied each case in microscopic detail and off-handedly gave people veiled suggestions that in some cases reduced their personal suffering and the suffering of others. He was constantly developing solutions for common problems and sorting them out in his head into categories.

A high being that had been his beloved in many incarnations was now his cousin Yasodhara, daughter of his father's younger brother King Suppabuddha and Queen Pamita. Sidd didn't know why he liked her immediately because he was not able to remember past lives until much later. She had been born on the same day he was born. That, and how much he liked playing with her as they grew up together, were his reasons for supposing they might be meant for each other.

When they were both sixteen his parents decided it was time for him to be married. This started as a Perse idea. Distract The First Son even further with raging hormones and strong attachments to wife and children. Following the traditions, princesses from far and wide were invited to a gala event, at which the Prince would choose his bride. At the event, Sidd was attentive and courteous to every princess and gave out valuable gifts to them all but chose none. Yasodhara, who had been kept from the event by Rebel meddling, managed to get past the obstacles and make a tardy appearance. Every eye in the house was on her as she entered, unexplainably in disarray, yet strikingly beautiful with golden skin and blue-black hair down to her feet. Playing comedienne, she ad-libbed, "Are all the gifts given away?"

Siddhartha rose and came up to her and put the pearl necklace he had been wearing on Yasodhara and announced that he was choosing her to be his wife. Siddhartha experienced an erection as she kissed him, his first romantic kiss in this lifetime.

Her father was not happy about this, believing Siddhartha to be too unwarlike to be King, and figuring for sure he would go for Buddhahood instead. He insisted that Siddhartha be tested against other Princes in archery, riding, and swordsmanship. Everyone was surprised that Siddhartha bested all rivals in this competition.

For thirteen years, Siddhartha and Yasodhara lived happily at the palace, guided carefully whenever they left the grounds so as to never see suffering. Sidd caught onto this game and found it amusing but was never fooled. Each day he kept all of his obligations and inched closer toward a complete understanding of how we let our minds trick us into needless suffering.

Perhaps it was Perse's insanity creeping up into other parts of The One Consciousness, but the Agents were now also putting themselves through needless suffering, as they had become attached to saving the human race from the Rebels. Not being able to communicate with The First Son probably triggered it. They seemed to be acting more like they would if they were trapped in the sabotaged human brains. They noticed this themselves and brought each other out of it.

Early in the thirteenth year of marriage, Yasodhara informed Sidd that she was pregnant. In a flash he saw that someone behind the scenes was pulling strings and that from their point of view, he was falling into their trap: with a child and a wife how could he achieve Buddhahood, which he had been taught to associate with renunciations and asceticism and begging. She was looking expectantly at him and so he kissed her and expressed the joy she was expecting and which he was feeling too, while also feeling that nothing must stop the mission. A single word of explanation for his hesitation came out of his mouth, as if she would understand, and she did.

"Rahu," he said, meaning obstacle, and she smiled and nodded, understanding it all before he said a word. His father also understood and would name the child Rahula.

"Whatever you must do," she said in a choking voice, squeezing his hands, and looking bravely into his eyes.

No! No! This must not happen! Layla broke down momentarily and then, remembering, got herself back under control, with the others comforting her.

That night he left the palace and went out into the world with a single helper, with whom he sent back his possessions. He became an ascetic. Encouraged by his father who was concerned for his safety, five men followed Siddhartha on his quest, becoming his disciples. The first disciple was Kaundinya.

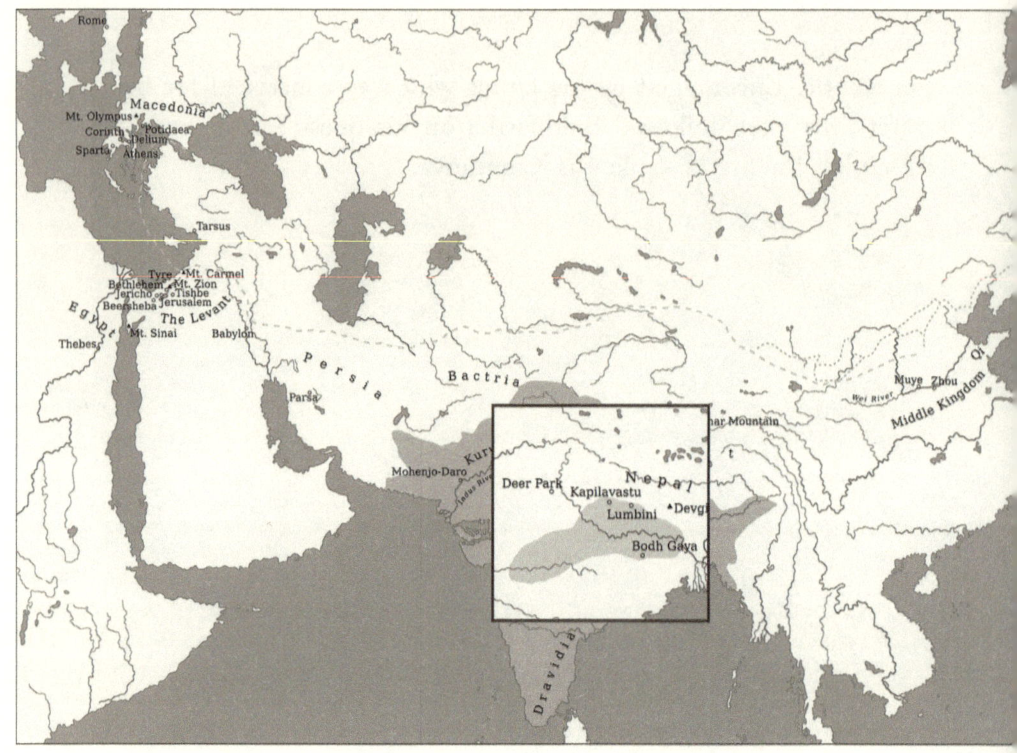

15

BUDDHA, A COSMIC STATE OF BEING

521 BC

Begging for food, then living on one mustard seed a day was what one did if setting out to become Buddha. Any other course of action would have been unthinkable, and probably ineffective. Being a realist and a very practical person, Sidd knew the limits of what he could get away with in regard to his audience.

On this part of the journey, he had a lot of time to think and to condense his teaching to something practical. He'd automatically believed that renunciation would have to be part of the program because it was so ingrained in the culture over millennia, not because it followed logically from his teachings.

His body of teachings consisted of lessons learned in the palace about how people make themselves suffer, and what they could say or do to get themselves out of it. He had discovered the fact of the self-fooling brain fashioned by the Rebels in their genetic intrusion, though he didn't think of it that way. He realized that his mind was capable of making decisions without explaining them to him or getting his agreement. He understood there was a part of consciousness of which one is unaware, yet which takes actions that cause suffering. And how those machinations could be brought to light and supervened by a mind on its way to complete realization of everything, Enlightenment.

Now he had just fainted and his disciples had revived him. He was unable to do much good in this state. Asceticism was not having the desired effect. He came to the conclusion that a middle path must be optimal for most people, somewhere between asceticism and the compound of greed, gluttony and hedonism that was its opposite. He decided to stick to his own teachings, to things that he found objectively worked in the real world for him and others taking his advice. His disciples left him, seeing his recoil from asceticism as giving up the path.

While gradually recovering by moving toward a minimum diet, but left alone, the Rebels tried to kill him. As they always do, first they started by trying to break his courage. They planted guilt feelings about leaving his family, failing as a householder, failing as a King/warrior, and now failing as a spiritual mendicant. Who would now believe a word he said? Why should they? He had given away all the power that he had in the world, with which he could have done a lot of good. Instead he was hurting people and causing suffering. How much suffering had he already added to the world, and did it not greatly outweigh the good he felt he had done?

Sidd laughed at these thoughts in his head. This was his field: he had discovered how we program ourselves with inner dialogues that trap us in lower ego states and degrade our noble true selves. Now his mind was trying to fool him—*good luck*, he bid it, knowing how not to get brought down by attachment to success or to how one is perceived by others.

He came to rest in Bodh Gaya under a Pipal tree now also known as a Bodhi tree. Finding his comfort there, he was determined to solve everything once and for all, to attain Enlightenment, to stay in that one spot for as long as it would take.

It took 49 days. Each day brought a new revelation, as if veil after veil were being removed. On the 49th day, he woke up to being The First Son. He was back in communication with The One Self, his Agents, the Angel network, and celestial beings of all kinds. He was 35 years old.

The Agents were beside themselves with joy to be back in touch with The First Son. Their human-like frailties became less frequent. Still, their daily mood was not as up as it had been for most of their memories— they were in a real war with real consequences.

Sidd realized that in his family were people he had been with before in many incarnations, and that part of his work would be to wake them up to being able to see that for their selves. These were some of the Agents who had originally come into Bharata millennia ago, whose telepathic genes were in most of the population by now. His work would restore great Agents back to the great work.

He remembered his current mission—reconnaissance through a human birth to test the introduction of a new science. He had subjected himself to the poisoned brain and experienced the worst it can offer, which included forgetting his true identity and mission. However, his nature prevailed anyway and led him back to the self-same mission. In fact, his new practical science for everyone was the remedy for the poisoned brain.

He set up shop in Deer Park near Varanasi in Northern India with four other monks, growing quickly to over a thousand. In a short period of time, simply by explaining his methods to the students, they gained degrees of freedom from conditioned behavior. This was so startling and obvious to other people that a following was continually attracted by the tangible results.

Rebels and many humans didn't like him. He accepted students of all castes, which particularly disturbed the warrior Kings. He stayed away from traditional subjects and so implied that they were not important, at which some Brahmins took offense. All he seemed to want to teach was a science of mind by which people would act more virtuously in their own enlightened self-interest, simply by a clearer understanding of their own mental processes. This did not seem spiritual at all. It seemed the opposite, more scientific.

Buddha did not opine about cosmology, which was taken as a form of non-support. The few times he did say something about that subject, what he said was spun by the Rebels to be something else, and so it seemed that he was against the idea of a creator. All he said was that there was no beginning or end to the universe, that it does this for eternity. He could have gone on to say that there are cycles, as if the universe is breathing when it expands into much diversity and then comes back together again like a Rubik's Cube and sleeps for a while, and when it starts again it still has all its memories… but that was far afield from his main intention, to reduce the most suffering the fastest, so he stayed focused on the main point, that we are the cause of everything we experience, and once we know that, here's how to control it.

Another Rebel distortion claimed Buddha denied the unity of all. The truth of the matter is that The First Son had to avoid spelling it out because Earth is a Mystery Planet and the plan is to keep it that way, for the fun of each being discovering the truth for his or herself. In one conversation, he quipped that one God would be lonely and that having so many gods is more fun, but that was totally taken out of context.

The Rebels also jumped on his idea that there was no separate self, always seeking to undermine the oneness of all things. Buddha never actually said that. He said that the current selfish human race did not experience the sort of soulful self they talked about. And that it would not end their suffering to get lost in metaphysical discussions about the self. In fact, the best way to end their suffering would be to act as if there were no self, to not dwell upon that lens but rather to let it go entirely. He knew that the contaminated brain had formed a puppet self, known as the ego, which masqueraded as the true self, making the inhabiting consciousness merely an unwitting observer, and therefore a sufferer. Dissolving the assumption of a self both denied power to the ego and caused perceptions and intuitions to be registered without bias.

His second mother, Prajapati, became a disciple and remembered their previous lives together. But that didn't happen easily. Buddha knew that some people felt threatened by him and some were even trying to kill him. Letting women into a school of higher learning was going to be the spark on the tinderbox, so he stalled, but eventually gave in to what he knew was right.

"Cause and effect are the things to stay focused on. By its desire for specific sensory experiences, the attached part of the mind is too distracted to keep such a focus, yet without that focus you will never escape being trapped in an out-of-control mind," he said to a new group. "You are the cause of all you experience, but you blame it on others because without this focus you actually can't see who is really doing it."

Miles away, Perse was questioning some of the Rebels he had sent to kill Buddha.

He's unkillable, Hassan said. *First my weapons wouldn't fire. Then they did fire but seemed to have no effect.*

He can't have changed the laws of physics! Perse ranted, next realizing that of course The First Son could do that, and so could he...

Perse excused the Rebels and sped away to where the Buddha was now sitting in meditation.

Good day to you my brother, The First Son said.

Any good reason why I shouldn't fry you right now? Perse asked.

I'm not done here yet. I'm going to see my son for the first time, and there are millions of people out there who will be willing to give my method a try. You should try it sometime... Buddha said.

Perse loosed his mightiest mindblast, which should have carbonized all the matter in the area, leaving Buddha without a human body, or at least inconveniencing him. But nothing happened. Perse felt that slightly logy feeling one feels after delivering such a mindblast, so he knew he had done it. It was simply neutralized. He found that very demoralizing, so disappeared.

The First Son concealed it but had come very close to succumbing.

Days later Buddha arrived in Kapilavastu to see his family after seven years, and to see his son Rahula for the first time. The Rebels sought to rain on the parade as much as they could and talked most of the senior royalty into not going out to greet Buddha. Remembering traditions of earlier Buddhas, he and his people took to the streets begging for alms. His father sent for him and acted insulted.

"Why didn't you come here?" the King demanded.

"You didn't invite me," Buddha said. A moment later they were laughing and hugging.

His family staged a wonderful ceremony during which he met Rahula. Yasodhara sang a song she had written, to Rahula, dedicated to the Buddha, called "The Lion of Men".

> Intent on the welfare of the world;
> That, indeed, is your father, lion of men.
> Like the full moon is His face;
> He is dear to gods and men;
> His gait is as graceful as that of an elephant of noble breed;
> That, indeed, is your father, lion of men.
> He is of noble lineage, sprung from the warrior caste;
> His feet have been honored by gods and men;
> His mind is well established in morality and concentration;
> That, indeed, is your father, lion of men.

After the ceremony, Rahula came up to Buddha. His first words to his father were, "Lord, even your shadow is pleasing to me."

Oooohh how sweet, Layla said, bursting into tears. She and Nastassia both crying with happiness hugged each other, and the other three Agents formed a hug-anism around them.

The family came together in a three-way hug. They stayed that way a long time. A sumptuous feast was enjoyed by all, and the threesome were physically inseparable.

As the party wound down, an invisible Rebel planted the thought in Yasodhara to cue up Rahula to ask for his inheritance, and she broke up with how funny that was, and said it to the boy in jest.

Rahula looked at her funny and wondered if it would make Daddy laugh too, so he ran up to Buddha and, laughing, muffed the line "Mommy says to ask Daddy for his inheritance." Buddha laughed and hugged the boy. He turned and started to walk, inviting the boy to walk with him. As they walked, Buddha considered the request and saw it would lead to the boy getting sucked deeper into Rebel enslavement and decided instead to reveal a little bit of his teachings, which would inspire the boy to become a disciple.

They were seated together in one of Buddha's rooms at the Nigrodharama monastery. Buddha explained to his son why honesty was the most important virtue. "A person who would tell lies would also be inclined to fake the other precepts. Above all, say nothing except the truth."

"There are actions which bring good to the people and actions which bring harm," Buddha said, holding up a mirror so Rahula could look at himself. "Before you say anything or do anything, reflect on what good it can do and what harm it could do. If there is any harm, do not say it, do not do it. Do this reflecting continuously. Only take actions that are purely for the good."

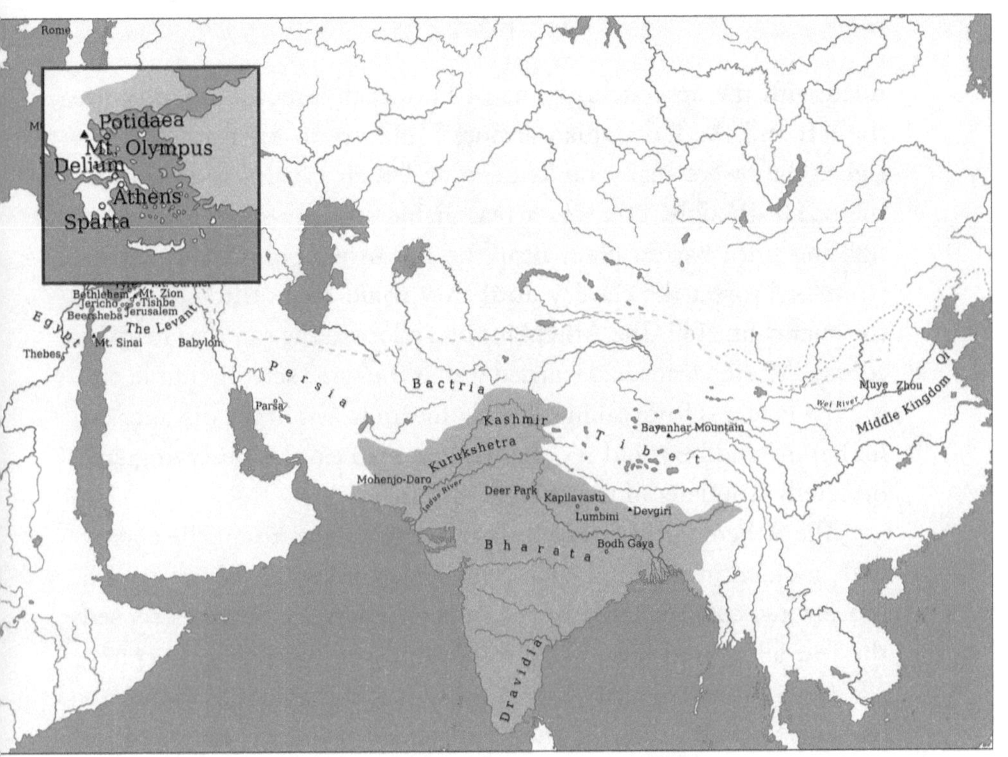

16

Potidaea, A Place

480 BC

Socrates and his four fighting partners moved forward, shoulder to
shoulder, shields high and spears forward. His mind was simply an
unattached observer now, and the beauty of the day suddenly pervaded his consciousness as if he were out on holiday. His peripheral
vision through the long slit of the face armor saw the seas at both
the right and left edge, while forward from far left to far right was

filled with the approaching line of Potidaean armored infantry on the left and the Corinthian armored infantry to his front and far right. They were many ranks deep and their cavalry rode behind them. He thought this was a reasonable strategy since they were fighting on a barren plain near the narrowest point of a narrow isthmus. Protect the cavalry until they could break through where the enemy line fell. The Athenians had adopted the same strategy of course. All Achaeans had learned war at the same school, thus keeping the Persians from taking their homelands. Far in the distance on higher ground he could see the Macedonian cavalry observing and he briefly wondered if they would join in.

The Athenians began to walk faster to be able to hit the enemy with momentum behind them, but not running as they were still too far away and needed to retain their energies. Socrates sensed the fear all around him. Deep inside him yet invisible to Socrates, Maitreya, his real identity, instinctively sent energy out to the whole division to center them in their bodies and take their minds off of outcomes. The opposing line had also sped up.

Now they were running and so too were the Corinthians coming toward them. He could no longer afford the luxury of peripheral vision and was focused on the phalanx in front of him that he and his comrades would be engaging in a second. The face armor masks made it impossible to see the faces or expressions of his foes but he could read the body language, and the man that was coming at him was much taller and seemed very eager to be the one that first broke the Athenian line. Their shields collided with great force but Socrates did not move backward, surprising his attacker during which moment Socrates' spear penetrated his leg, and as the man reacted to that, Socrates brought the spear up under the shield and quickly retracted the weapon. Using the dying man as a shield, he then found an unprotected piece of chest in the second Corinthian rank and sent a second soul back to the real world. Socrates was not aware of the whole truth or of his soul's identity or background, but he intuitively understood the nature of reality, that there was a world where the forms were ideal and not trapped in matter, where souls came from and returned to, and God dwelt.

The battle raged and gradually the Corinthians somehow managed to be breaking through to his right, not far away. He turned his attention to the priority of mending the line without becoming derelict to the responsibilities right in front of him. He began to fight to the right and as ranks had long since become more of a melee, he had liberty to do this. The Corinthian infantry made room for their cavalry to rush forward into the soft spot. Suddenly there was a counterattack from the Athenian Cavalry, and Socrates spotted Alcibiades, in the same hoplite armor as himself, racing to the center of the breach to square off with the lead cavalrymen trying to pour through. Alcibiades took down the first one but two others engaged him and Socrates saw him take an arm wound and flip his sword from his right to his left hand, in the same motion jumping and delivering a neck wound to a cavalryman, who went down. Socrates bolted through several pairs of men fighting hand to hand and a horse getting up and running away, to spear the cavalryman about to deal a deathblow to Alcibiades, who was then falling. Socrates grabbed him up and carried him quickly away from the battlefront.

Ω

The day was won on the other side of the field. The Athenians turned the enemy's right flank and their army retreated, pursued and harried by the Athenians. The Macedonians just watched. Perse also watched, with interest, seeing this battle as something like a football game that was a small part of watching the fruition of his fondest dreams coming true on Earth. Hellas had withstood the invasion from Persia, Perse's capital on Earth, and now he was experimenting with amusing ways to undermine Hellas from within. He didn't really care which city-states or countries dominated the world. It was all in their minds anyway, when they were all being manipulated by him. He was just having them fight each other to make them better fighters.

The Athenians pitched camp, intending to stay and take over, which they knew was not already accomplished and that there was a lot more fighting to be done first. Socrates was summoned and went to the tent of an officer who turned out to be Alcibiades. Knowing Alcibiades' penchant for male lovers, Socrates put two and two together, and realized he had been summoned by the aide and consort of Alcibiades. The two looked a bit alike, both incredibly handsome. Socrates himself was gnomish but didn't feel the least bit of envy. To him, all that mattered was the eternal soul.

Alcibiades hugged him and Socrates hugged back as a father would. Socrates had been a teacher to Alcibiades from his early childhood. He was twenty years older than Alcibiades, and had been born into poverty, while Alcibiades had been born into the top family in Athens.

"You saved my life!" Alcibiades said.

"Will you use it for Goodness, then?" Socrates asked, and Alcibiades laughed affectionately.

"Of course! Of course! I always promised you that," Alcibiades said, leading Socrates outside to a picnic on a blanket the aide had set up. The day was still lush and Socrates sat down with pleasure. Then he noticed the food and realized it was a lot better than what the other soldiers were getting and so he politely refused to eat it. Alcibiades knew better than to argue with him. Socrates drank water and ate a bit of bread as this was the general meal that day.

"What is Goodness, then?" Socrates got back to it.

While chewing thoughtfully and remembering the only time he had given a half decent answer to this, he couldn't quite remember what he'd said, so he improvised. "That which is pleasing to God."

"And what is God, then?"

This was a stumper. He didn't remember Socrates ever having asked him this, although it had been a long time since they'd seen each other so he should expect his idol to have come up with many new thoughts. It was ironic that he idolized Socrates, who was really

Maitreya, an Agent, because Alcibiades was an unconscious Rebel whose mission was to stir up trouble in Hellas, which he was managing to do on a small scale and would one day do on a grand scale, switching sides from Athens to Persia to Sparta. He didn't need to remain conscious of himself in order to carry out his mission. Being a megalomaniac, a trait common among Rebels, he had been unruly as a child, and Socrates couldn't seem to get him to see how his might makes right attitude differed from virtue or Goodness.

"Well, there are the gods, as we all know," he said, as a stall, knowing that he would be chivvied into a better answer by the next question. He had a well-developed strategy for coping with Socrates' polite inquisitions into truth, some of which he remembered.

"So, what's the difference we mean when we say 'God', singular, and 'gods', plural?"

"The head of all the gods must be the one called God," Alcibiades ventured.

"Who would that be?"

"Zeus, I gather."

"What makes you think that?"

"Well, I know that Zeus is chief among the gods."

"Have you heard Zeus referred to as God, or as one of the gods?"

"No, I have never heard Zeus referred to as God."

"What about Goodness? Have you been taught that the gods always act with Goodness, or do they sometimes, even Zeus, do things that hurt others, or are unjust?"

"No, of course, the gods have passions as we do, lust and other cravings. They fear for their image being tarnished, they are envious, they rape. You got me to see that a long time ago."

"So, when you say that Goodness means anything pleasing to God, what God are you talking about?"

"You know, I don't really know," Alcibiades admitted. Unlike most people he was not ready to change the subject or fly off the handle after being pummeled with Socrates' questioning, since he was used to it and he was grateful that this form of training had made him a great persuader.

"But you say that there is a God, and this God stands for Goodness, so we should only act having judged carefully that the intended action is one of which this God would approve?"

"Yes, that's it!" Alcibiades heartily agreed.

It was a sign of the Agents' success that the idea of a formless original God of Goodness had pervaded all Rebel-held territories. Greeks, as they were also beginning to call themselves, were unable to explain to themselves from whence had come this idea. That this One God was also the One Self was something the Agents could not teach on a Mystery Planet in the Lost Lambs region of the multiverse. Beings there needed to come to that realization on their own, through going inside. Socrates called it "Knowing Thyself", though not fully comprehending it due to the loss of contact with Maitreya's memory. Socrates intuited and said that we come from a higher reality and lose memory of it at the shock of birth, which is a close approximation of the truth resulting from the altered brains.

17

PLATO'S ACADEMY

367 BC

Seventeen-year-old Aristotle, destined to shape the mind of the human race, was humble as he strode into the Academy for the first time, awed by the huge marble fluted columns and his own attunement to numinosity. That was what had attracted him of course, the sense of something unearthly and better that one could feel but not name or justify.

Once inside the great hall, he was amazed to see a couple necking, a drunk and other common campus phenomena. He had every right to be amazed, as no one had ever seen a college before Plato invented them. In his terms, he manifested a copy of an ideal form that existed in a realer world.

Aristotle's expectations were more along the lines of a monastery, where people would be slightly stooped over as they walked mostly in silence. A moment later he was glad of the reality versus the expectation. He relaxed and felt at home as he strode through the great hall, getting oriented.

This would be his home for the next twenty years.

On that same day he met The Great Man for the first time. The founder of this place, Plato, came out into the garden as Aristotle was exploring there. Bluebirds were singing in the dappled sunlight. The two made instant eye contact with some strange kind of mutual recognition neither could explain. Plato was not surprised at anything, as he had no doubt that all he could experience was illusion anyway. This was going to be his prize pupil, he realized. Aristotle, having no prior psychic experience in his life, gulped as he expanded his notion of what nature is. Plato was the first person with whom he could not deny experiencing a psychic connection and he could tell it was mutually realized. This was the largest mind shift he had experienced up to that point. Being very mentally-oriented, he stood still and put it all together in his head, looking inward, as Plato and his retinue of students approached.

Broad-shouldered wrestler Plato held out his hand. Aristotle saw an aura around Plato, the second weirdest thing that ever happened in Aristotle's life. They shook hands sincerely.

"They call me Plato," Plato said simply, as if Aristotle would not otherwise know who he was.

"I'm Aristotle, teacher."

"Oh yes, from Stagira," Plato said. "The scientist."

"You've read my paper, sir?"

"Loved it. Good work. That's how you got in here." They shared a laugh.

18

Plato's Academy

348 BC

"What you're really telling me is that metaphysics is not worthy of anyone's time, given the priorities," Plato said with a smile.

"I apologize if I gave that impression, Sir," Aristotle said. "I myself have become very focused on the natural world, and the attitudes and ways we must continue to devise in order to gain direct knowledge of all we wish to know."

"And if I said that the world above deserves an even higher share of our attention—?" Plato asked gently.

"How could that be, Sir?"

"Some of the things we wish to know are of the world above," Plato said.

"Such as—?" Aristotle asked. He fell into ego—too much enjoying his apparent sudden equality with the teacher—and looked around at the class of fifty or so students, looking for their reaction. He came back from ego without noticing what had happened within himself.

"Death. Life. God. Love. Beauty. Truth. Righteousness. Purpose. To name a few," Plato said.

"I agree, Sir, those are subjects that continue to interest me greatly," Aristotle allowed. "I cannot see the method for investigating those things. Whereas I'm just naturally passionate about seeing things with my own eyes before ascribing 'knowledge'."

"The method for investigating the higher world is meditation, paying attention inwardly," Plato said.

Aristotle quickly agreed. "I spend most of my life now in a similar state you taught us, contemplation," he said.

"I don't want to change your focus, dear Aristotle," Plato said. "Just please don't forget about the clues coming at you from inside."

19

MOUNT OLYMPUS
322 BC

After the death of Plato and then Aristotle, the Agents—back in their bubble bodies—assumed human form and compared notes atop the Mytikas peak on Mount Olympus.

"Congratulations, Templegard!" Maitreya said. Everyone pounded Templegard, like patting him on the back, given his tank-like body. He had been Aristotle.

photo by Antonis Papagiannopoulos

"Thanks. Sorry about Alexander, though!" Helping yet another Rebel—Cyrus had been the first—to become a conqueror, from Iraq to the Indus River, was going to look bad on his resume, Templegard figured.

"Rebels are going to kill Rebels no matter what we do," Nastassia reminded him. "Your pupil was far less vicious than the norm down there."

"You must have taught him something," Melchizedek, who had been Plato, agreed.

"Cyrus picked up more," Templegard apologized.

"Alexander wasn't as bad as the Spartans," Layla put in. The others knew she meant the killing of slaves as a form of military training, as she'd made it known that to her this was one of the lowest forms of Rebel behaviors she had observed. It was an annual event, declaring war on their own slaves. When thousands of slaves proposed to become warriors and help the Spartans win the war against Athens in order to subsequently be made free men, they were summarily slaughtered. Maitreya never said it, but he had seen much worse on Earth and elsewhere.

"Congratulations to all of us," Templegard countered graciously. "Maitreya's Socrates might not have induced mass virtue, but the idea of doing what is right and not hurting others is now at least being taught by parents to their children, everywhere."

"And they still don't behave, but there has been a vast upswing in guilt," Maitreya quipped self-deprecatingly. They broke up at this. He was good at making them laugh.

"Apologies, my friend," Templegard said to Melchizedek. "I needn't have been so outspoken to Plato at the Academy."

"Not at all," Melchizedek said, and pathed an arm around Templegard's shoulder, which everyone could see and the active parties could feel. "I needed to be reminded that spiritual channeling *alone* was not the way to provide demonstrable proof. Your empirical emphasis was very much needed."

"But they had to know that the biggest revelations would come from inside," Templegard rejoined.

"Science needs both intuition and sensory verification," Layla said.

"Your cave metaphor was a very imaginative way to depict the real world of consciousness," Nastassia said to Melchizedek.

"If not to depict it," Maitreya differed, "at least to help the mind grasp that there could be a world more real than the one they know."

"What lasting effect have we accomplished in Hellas?" Maitreya asked.

Melchizedek looked at him. "You sound just like Socrates," and they all laughed.

"My guess," Layla said humbly, "is that what you guys just did is going to have a massive influence for the rest of time on Earth. You got them to—*think really clearly* for the first time."

"Couldn't have done it without you," Maitreya, Melchizedek and Templegard said in unison, bowing, having had a split microsecond to telepathically coordinate. Nastassia and Layla were the inner muses, cautioning and inspiring the three philosophers and showing them glimpses of probable futures they needed to see. Layla and Nastassia blushed modestly.

"Can an old man join your party?" asked The First Son, appearing among them in human form, wearing white, and speaking out loud as they had been, instead of pathing. They were delighted. Even though they were in constant touch with The One Self, they hadn't seen The First Son since he was Buddha. They pathed prostrating themselves at his feet, and amused, he did the same to them, reminding them thereby that they were all avatars of The One Self.

"We're all honored and ecstatic to have you join us, Sir," Maitreya said first, and the others echoed the sentiments in their own words.

"Call me Yeshua, please, I'm getting used to it," The First Son said. "Your team has done more for Earth than anyone else, and you're doing a great job of preparing minds down there for me. I want you to know how grateful I am, as is our 'Father'." They pathed sublime contentment at the acknowledgement. They had all already felt the glow of love inside from The One Self letting them know that they were appreciated. The redoubling of this feeling was almost overpowering, but without attached egos, it lasted only a moment and then fell into the background as a permanent happiness enhancer.

"I'm sure you noticed the many occasions that Lucifer's minions, the Rebels, used higher-tech weapons in this theater during these engagements," The First Son continued, and they nodded assent.

"The flamethrower at Delium," Maitreya said.

"The plague in Athens during a siege," Melchizedek said.

"The tsunami in Potidaea that stopped the Persians," Templegard said.

They were about to go on but he lifted a hand. "Yes, and much more. I know you know," The First Son said. "They haven't trotted out as much off-planet tech as this for about three thousand years."

"Kurukshetra," Layla said, and they all nodded.

"They will surely continue to escalate. They know I'm coming," said The First Son.

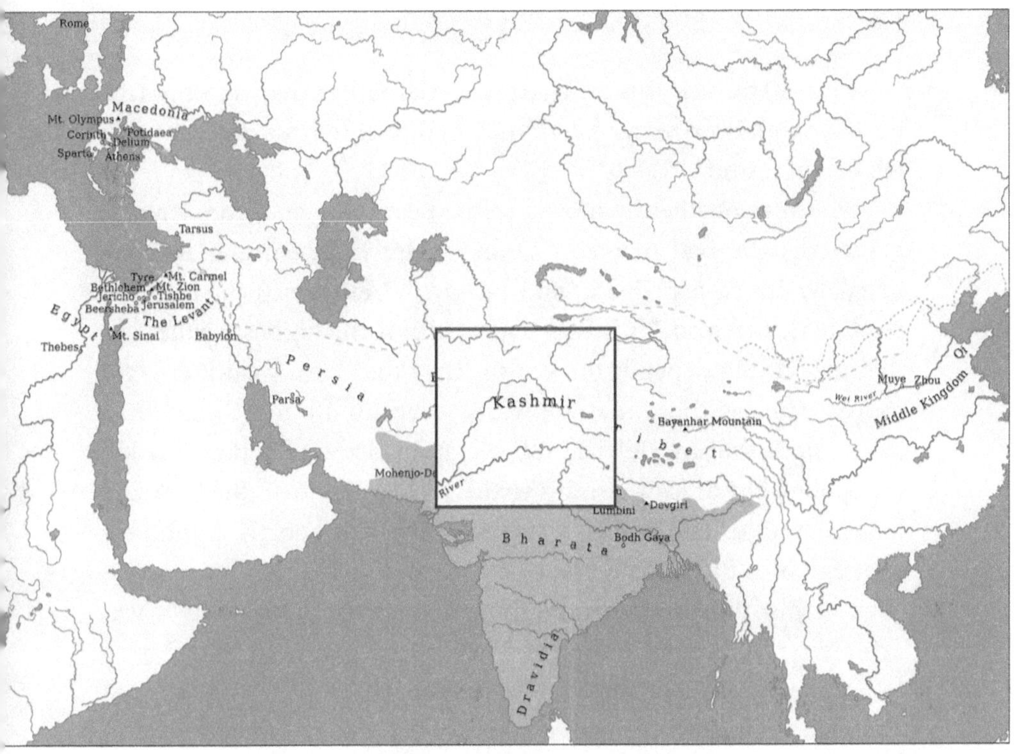

20

Kashmir, A Place

290 BC

"What's the next passage?" Durya, the head Brahmin, asked tiredly. Maitreya easily read the man's mind, having regained a fraction of his powers. This happened right before his 32nd birthday, when he finally remembered his true identity, after 32 years of introspection, and laughed at having used his real name this time.

Durya still saw this as Maitreya's trial rather than an opportunity to do an ever-better job of making life better for everyone, the job of a Brahmin.

Maitreya obediently moved to the next passage of the Mahabharata that he had marked. "Yudhishthira is beseeching Krishna here," Maitreya explained, "and he says," Maitreya picked up the birch bark and read, "It is said that wealth is the highest virtue, and that everything depends on wealth. They that have wealth are said to live, whereas those that are without wealth are more dead than alive. Those that by violence rob a man of his wealth not only kill the robbed but destroy also his virtue…" He put down the bark and looked around. The dozen or so Brahmins were mostly around his own age or a little older, one or two as old as Durya. They looked back at him uncomprehendingly and unsympathetically. He was exhibiting an arrogance they had never seen before in him, daring to find fault with a text held close to sacred.

Their little council room could only have held a few more. This hearing was fact finding and the start of a long process of determining just how bad Maitreya was. He had not yet been publicly accused of anything specific.

Pictures of Brahma, Vishnu, and Krishna hung on the walls in glorious golden frames like clouds. Light poured in through the many windows looking out onto the large inner courtyard park.

"Krishna never corrects him," Maitreya went on stoically, "nor does he correct that view with better logic later in the section. It's left to stand as if that is the truth."

"I don't understand, what are you saying?" Durya asked with controlled impatience. The other four Agents guarding the room knew that Durya was an asleep Rebel, while the others were asleep Agents or asleep humans. Maitreya had not gotten back to Agent level yet, fighting his brain's robotical responses, a problem the disembodied Agents did not have.

"When one sees unresolved inconsistencies in a text that has come down to us by memorized stories long before writing was available," Maitreya patiently explained, "it is logical to consider that the inconsistencies may in large part be additions to Vyasa's original."

One person gasped. Durya's face darkened. Maitreya could sense his resistance to this idea and had a hunch that Durya could be an asleep Rebel. *You're right,* Maitreya heard Melchizedek's voice in his mind.

"This is a revisionist thing to say," Durya counseled, "a very serious charge of the highest order, with consequences."

"I do understand that, oh best of Brahmins," Maitreya said with a bow of his head, "and I accept whatever consequences are merited. The consequences I seek are to better accomplish our purposes on Earth, to improve the general good, to care for everyone and make their lives better. We support ourselves by copying and distributing these books of truth, but more than ourselves we support everyone out there who is read to from these books, we support the readers who can read it to them, and all the people who later hear the truth from these books passed on to them. If we can purify the books themselves by removal of a few small passages that appear to have been added later…"

"How do you know," Durya asked, with a threatening emphasis on the word "you", "that these were not the words of Vyasa?"

Maitreya thought, *because I was Vyasa!*

"Vyasa's message in this book is that Mahadeva is the soul in each of us, all exists for virtue, pleasure and profit, of which virtue is the most important. Making profit the most important virtue is inconsistent with the main theme," Maitreya said.

"Are you saying that you have the only correct interpretation of the message of the Mahabharata," Durya asked. "Sages have spoken and written volumes about the many messages of the great book, and you reduce it all to this simplicity? Is this not being glib, and arrogant?" The word "arrogant" felt wrong in the room as everyone knew Maitreya to be a person of uniform modesty, and the energies of a few took his side, as the five awake (one semi-awake) Agents detected.

"I leave that judgment to you sir. I feel it my duty to bring forth the possibility," Maitreya said, with head hung.

"I'm not sure there is guilt involved yet," Durya said, "It bears investigating further. Much further, as the matter is complex and baffling. You seem to be offering a student too much license to choose the passages he or she already accepts the ideas behind. Scripture given by God directly, or even Godly literature, is collectively our talisman of truth. 'It is written' has become synonymous with law. Before writing, 'It is said' was the phrase describing the accepted standards of behavior and belief. By now suggesting we tamper with all that…" Durya fell silent.

"'It is said'," Maitreya began, "as a phrase, is used often in the Mahabharata. We have built our collective orthodoxy on what has been said in the past, calling that the authority. In reality, these are not all of the things that were ever said, obviously, but a collection of sayings that we all feel have the ring of truth to them." Heads nodded all around, even Durya's.

"So, the arbiter of inclusion," Maitreya submitted, "should then be considered to be the ring of truth, for that is what was evidently used to narrow down the field of all the things that were ever said, to the subset of the things that have been said that have the ring of truth to large numbers of us."

"What do you call this?" Durya asked suspiciously, implying that it was a new philosophy Maitreya was arrogating to invent.

"Thinking for oneself," Maitreya mused as if trying it on, then shook his head, "making the law one's own by thinking it through for oneself in order to come back to it with more grounded certainty."

"Authority is not to be questioned," Durya said.

I wonder if Perse had the foresight to create this altered human brain design just to protect the counterprop the Rebels inserted in our books of truth, Templegard pathed. By "counterprop" he meant counter propaganda.

The Rebelized brain definitely has a bias toward authoritarianism, Melchizedek agreed.

It favors the black and white, either-or point of view, Layla added. *Maybe that has something to do with it.*

The overactive brain tortures itself with its own sophistries and yearns for closure, simplification, Nastassia offered.

"If I may, sir," Maitreya began, and Durya nodded. "This universe is such a creative thing—all of its creatures, the beauty, its continuing changes and fascinating new developments—it is all very creative, is it not? Should our work not be also creative, and continue to unfold and uplift itself, adding improvements that are conducive to greater good and happiness? Would not God, the first Creator, who is living through us, want it so?"

"There are those in every generation who earn the right to be listened to, and they add to the beauty and truth of scripture and commentary. That part is true. All of us can aspire to that, but we would be arrogant to assume it prematurely," Durya said, as if it was the last word he could stand to say or hear that day.

"Sir," Maitreya looked for permission to speak again and Durya nodded. "Yes, but what is authority? It is whatever one defines it as. If we say it is the collection of all oral and written scripture, and religious books written by humans, it often contradicts itself. Which authority within that corpus does one then use to make the decision as to how to interpret authority?"

"Clearly, one consults the greatest living authority, and asks him to interpret it," Durya answered.

That gives me an idea, said Layla. *We'd better use it before they do.*

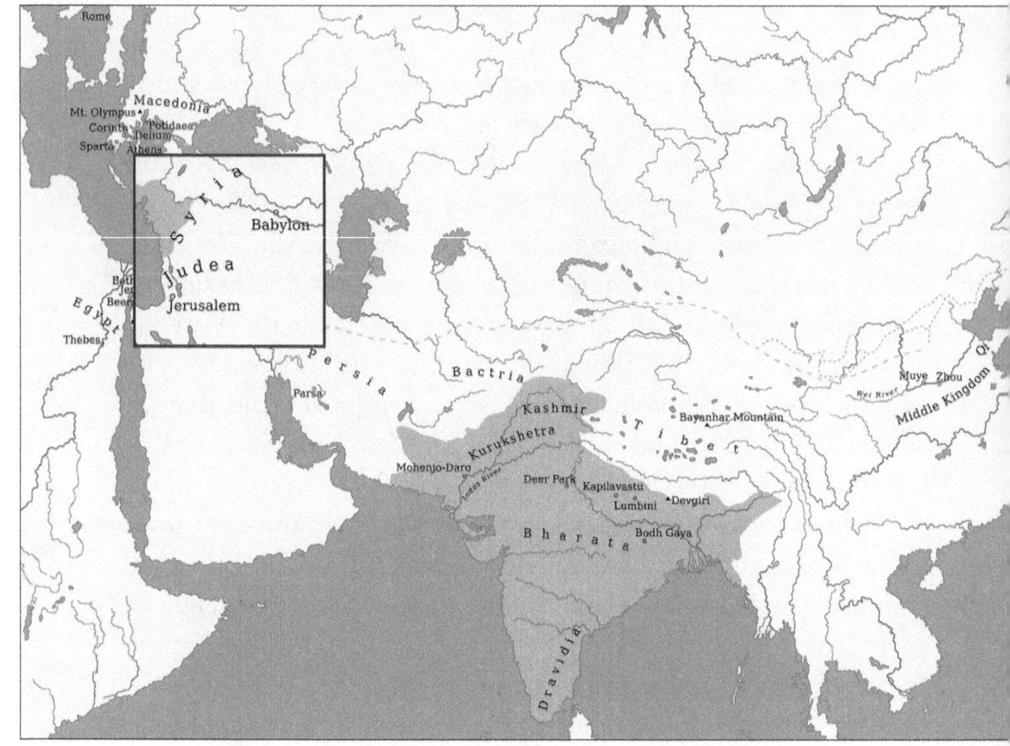

21

HILLEL, AN EARTH HUMAN WITH AN AGENT SOUL

42 BC

The Chamber of Hewn Stones where the Sanhedrin met was within the great Temple. Hillel no longer sat on the steps as a student, but now sat near the front as a full member gradually gaining respect. In the center sat the Nasi Schemaiah. Years ago, when Hillel came to

Jerusalem from Babylon, he'd had great difficulty getting accepted as a student at Schemaiah's school, despite being a kinsman, as they had both descended from David. Finally, through arduous proof of merit, he'd overcome the snobbish policies excluding all but the rich and been admitted. Over time his brilliance had shone through and Schemaiah had sponsored him in joining the Sanhedrin.

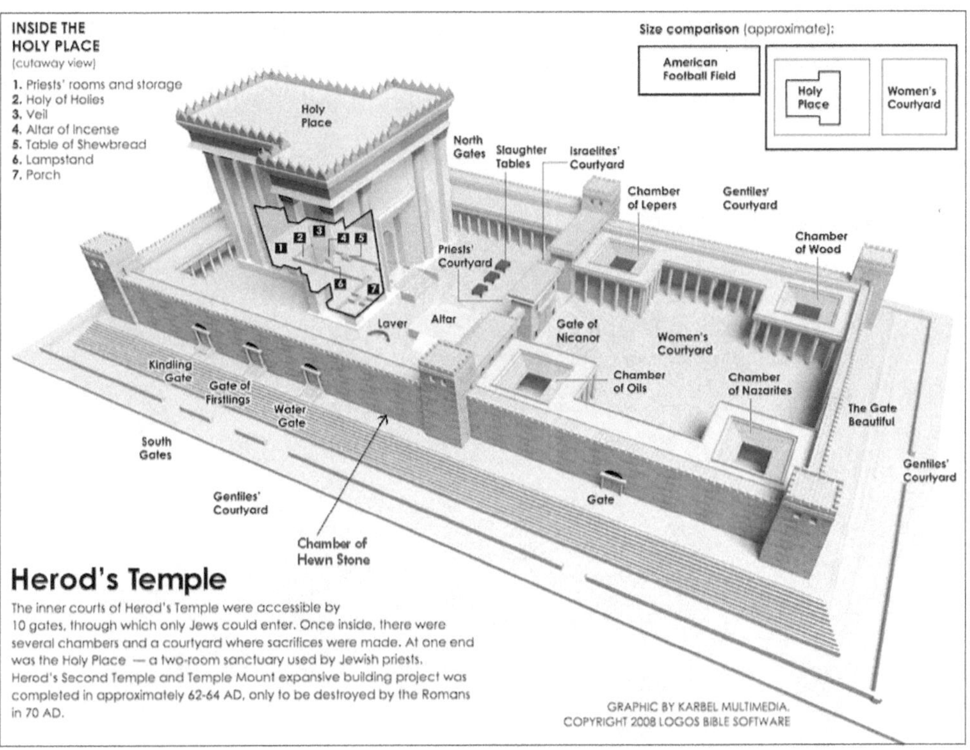

Herod's Temple

The inner courts of Herod's Temple were accessible by 10 gates, through which only Jews could enter. Once inside, there were several chambers and a courtyard where sacrifices were made. At one end was the Holy Place — a two-room sanctuary used by Jewish priests. Herod's Second Temple and Temple Mount expansive building project was completed in approximately 62-64 AD, only to be destroyed by the Romans in 70 AD.

Although the Sanhedrin was the judge and jury for criminal and civil cases, it was also the highest decider of how to interpret the Hebrew Scriptures in any given situation. Today the judging of cases was over and it was the time Hillel enjoyed the most, as he considered that he would be a student forever, and he learned the most from these sessions of discussing the law in itself. However, that part of the day had just gotten started when the most unusual thing occurred.

It started with rough, heavy and loud sounds outside, alien to a quiet peaceful day in the sacred Temple. The council fell silent wondering what ill wind this was. They sprang back in shock seeing Herod, Prefect of Galilee, and a large heavily armed contingent of soldiers marching into the council room. This was unprecedented, probably sacrilegious, and frightening: it appeared that Rome might have given orders to slay them all. Such fear was not unfounded, given all of the other humiliations the Hebrews had already been put through for centuries and the recent step-up in interference in local affairs by the Romans.

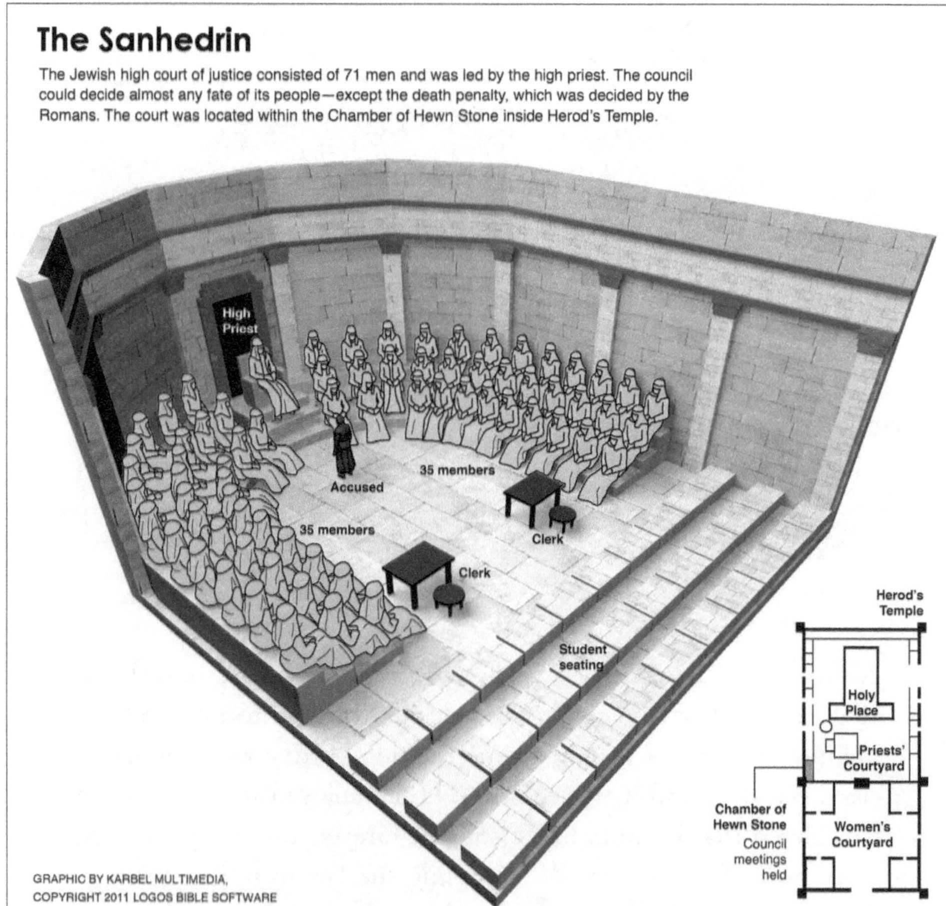

The Sanhedrin

The Jewish high court of justice consisted of 71 men and was led by the high priest. The council could decide almost any fate of its people—except the death penalty, which was decided by the Romans. The court was located within the Chamber of Hewn Stone inside Herod's Temple.

GRAPHIC BY KARBEL MULTIMEDIA,
COPYRIGHT 2011 LOGOS BIBLE SOFTWARE

Hyrcanus II was with them, which was another amazement. The former head priest had his ears bitten off by his nephew Antigonus, who with the help of the Parthians had taken his role as head priest; the removal of his ears would make him ineligible for the priesthood so that he could never make a comeback and displace his nephew. It was widely rumored that Hyrcanus would be exiled to Babylon on some charge. In what capacity then was he here?

Herod, 25 years old, swaggered up to Schemaiah and proffered a papyrus document with a violent and impolite flip of his wrist. Schemaiah looked at Herod for a moment, and at the document. Taking his time, he took the document and read aloud, "By order of Hyrcanus II, the Sanhedrin is requested to arraign Herod for the murder of—Hezekiah the Zealot and his followers." Schemaiah had to pause for a second when he saw and spoke the name of Hezekiah. *Hezekiah dead!*

Others registered the death of a pious man and a friend of that court. Originally an Essene, Hezekiah had become a Zealot and technically a terrorist, being hunted by the law for incursions over the Syrian border to slay enemies of Judea. News of his death had not reached the Sanhedrin until then.

Hillel was especially moved by this news. Hezekiah had been a student of his, and the brother of another student of his, Jacob. Jacob was secretly husband of Cleopatra, and father of Joseph, a third student of his.

Knowing that Herod, a famous person well-known to the Sanhedrin, had been a conspirator with Cassius in major events in Rome and was now there for them to judge, they noticed that the defendant wore purple rather than the customary black, and had not come alone but rather with a threatening platoon capable of quickly slaughtering the entire Sanhedrin. Somehow none of them mustered the courage to mention that aloud.

Taking advantage of his momentum, Herod now handed a second parchment to Schemaiah, who again read aloud: "By Order of Sextus Caesar, Governor of Syria. There shall be dire consequences for Hyrcanus should the Sanhedrin not acquit Herod of these charges." Hyrcanus flinched at these words echoing from the high walls of the council chamber.

There was silence. No one had the temerity to speak, intimidated by the soldiers and their weapons and demeanor. Herod looked around and smiled contentedly.

Schemaiah stood tall and said, "Look at how you carriers of the teaching of God stand up to a situation! You will suffer badly for this cowardice in the days to come at the hands of this same man." He continued, looking directly into Herod's eyes, "We need to confer and consider the facts of the case, gathering evidence dispassionately. Herod, you are ordered to appear here tomorrow, and it is commanded that you appear alone and in the customary garb." Herod would flee the country the very next day rather than appear. Later he would kill all of the members of the Sanhedrin present that day that weren't already dead, except Schemaiah.

Herod was about to act impetuously when he noticed in the chamber, looking at him portentously, was Menachem the Essene who, when they were much younger and Herod an unknown, had come up to Herod and foretold that he would be the ruler of Judea. He felt positively toward Menachem and stayed his hand. Merely laughing insolently, he turned on his heel and led his noisy soldiers out. Herod did not know that Menachem was the son of Hezekiah whom he had killed.

<h1 style="text-align:center">22</h1>

NASI, A TITLE SIGNIFYING THE PRESIDENT OF THE SANHEDRIN
30 BC

"Nasi, how do we answer this one, which comes up all the time?" asked a priest. "Why does The Almighty require animal sacrifice, which does not permanently remove the sin of the person making the sacrifice, but merely temporarily abates it? The sin of taking the life of an innocent creature seems to outweigh such an ephemeral benefit."

The two brothers of the Benei Betheira, who had served many years together as the joint president or Nasi of the Sanhedrin, looked at each other and the elder one spoke. "We have answered this one before many times, but we shall answer it again, as many of you, including Sol who asked it today, have not served as long here. It is an important question because it tries the faith of many who sympathize with their animals as beloved members of the family, especially women, children, and shepherds. It is the way of The Almighty making us understand sin as more than an intellectual concept. It is the pain of sacrificing a friend or a child, as many think of their animals, which makes us avoid sin for their sake."

This struck many as a fine answer and they nodded and mumbled praises, while others appeared unsatisfied. One such priest, a Sadducee, spoke out deferentially, "But how does one come to that conclusion, firmly seeking basis solely in the written law?" As a Sadducee he wanted to be sure that oral law and interpretation by the Nasi themselves had nothing to do with it, since Sadducees believed that the oral law was influenced by the ideas of non-monotheistic Zarathustra and therefore was no law at all.

Another Sadducee spoke up in support. "Yes, in the written law we read many opposite statements about animal sacrifice, in favor of it in Exodus, Leviticus, and Numbers for example, and other passages that are against it, in Amos, Isaiah, Hosea, Micah, and Jeremiah, for example."

The younger Nasi confidently answered, "Yes, we have counted the passages, and the words, and we have given more weight to the earlier written law, as this establishes the more foundational evidence of precedent. By means of this complicated procedure we establish that animal sacrifice is required."

I was wondering how they were going to rationalize that one, Nastassia pathed. The Agents had observed some offline negotiating going on between the questioners and the Nasi earlier in the week. The Agents had been observing the Sanhedrin for long enough to understand the double bone the Nasi were throwing to the Sadducees to maintain unity. First, it was an interpretation based upon only the written law, and second, it favored the main revenue source of the Temple, selling animals for sacrifice, which was of predominant importance to the wealthy Sadducees.

"If I may," Hillel humbly spoke out, and the Nasi recognized him to speak. "Weight of evidence is a logical means of making decisions as to interpretation of the *law.*" The emphasis he gave the word *law* while looking at the two Sadducees who had raised the question conveyed that he was speaking only of the written law, although as a Pharisee, everyone knew that Hillel also supported the oral law as law. "However, the procedure established by the honored Nasi could be faulted as being subjective, that is, not a procedure that is itself spelled out for us to follow in the law, nor definitively established purely by the light of reason."

As on many occasions when Hillel spoke, no one of either party could find fault with what he said, as it was always so logical. "I have discovered seven rules by which we can objectively compare bits of the law with one another to reach defensible conclusions that cannot be faulted objectively. Briefly, "What applies in a less important case must certainly apply in a more important case; an analogy is made between two separate texts on the basis of a similar phrase," he went on, and each of his principles was unarguable although no one had thought that way before.

He blew their minds, Layla pathed. This was true; the audience was stunned, hushed and humbled by the towering genius exhibited by Hillel.

"Applying these rules, all of them working together, I have studied the issue of animal sacrifice. It appears that The Almighty found animal sacrifice a useful teaching method to reach human emotions in the olden times, but as he expected more of us over time, as we accumulated more wisdom from His teachings, he has consistently told us that we continue to rely upon this form in times when it is no longer as suitable for us. Now we use it as a convenience in order to avoid deeper work upon ourselves, or worse, as an attempt to bribe Him. These are surely ways of missing the mark that we need to explain to all who strive to follow His counsels."

The Sadducees felt that since Hillel did not argue for stopping animal sacrifice, they would be better off letting this pass rather than stick their necks out to fight him in council since he was the better logician and debater. The Benei Betheira brothers announced to everyone's surprise that they were so impressed they would resign from being Nasi in Hillel's favor. This was unanimously approved, with the many Sadducees in the Sanhedrin going along with it, feeling that Hillel might not always say things they loved but he was smarter than the rest of them put together and therefore could perhaps protect them better against Herod and Rome. Besides, he was temperate and humble and unlikely to suddenly come out with any shocking changes that would reduce their wealth and power. Almost all of the Sadducees were asleep Rebels, and a couple of them tucked away in their minds the reservation of the option of assassination should Hillel prove to be otherwise.

Although they were upset when he quickly made an Essene, Menachem, one of the sons of the Zealot Hezekiah, his number two—the Av Beit Din—no violence ensued, as they waited to see how this would affect them. Menachem turned out to be almost as wise as Hillel, which was not surprising to the other Agents since Hillel was Maitreya and Menachem was Templegard.

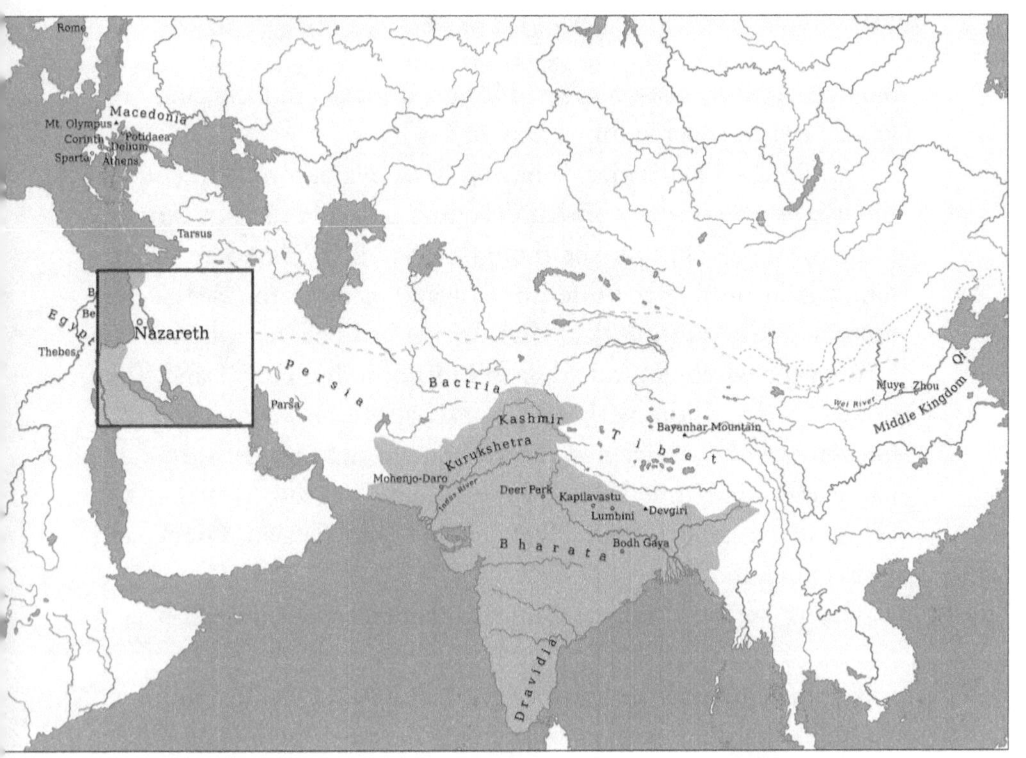

23

NAZARETH, A PLACE

5 BC

Although Hillel did not accept the title of priest he was widely regarded as a holy man not only by those of his own party, the Pharisees, but also by Sadducees, Essenes—shamanic Hebrews who lived on the land away from the towns, Zealots—revolutionaries who plotted the expulsion of the Romans, and simple Hebrews who did not align with any parties or sects. Even believers in other religions, and atheists, respected his great piety, kindness, and brilliance, and considered him a man of God.

Although Layla's idea of having Maitreya become Hillel to be the wisest man in the world at decoding scripture did not turn out to be the game changer she thought it would, it played an important role in turning the tide from always losing to the Rebels into more of a level playing field. The Agents had debated whether the birth of the wise man should be in India or in the Holy Land. They decided that in India, with its Agents heritage, he would be preaching somewhat to the converted, so Hillel wound up with the right name and family tree in the Holy Land, which the Agents saw as being at the nexus of the pivotal Rebel-held Persian, Greek, and Roman empires.

Long before Hillel established his own school he had been a teacher, teaching of the Spirit within all. A semi-awake Agent, he had been born with the knowledge of Oneness, so he felt and acted out the kindness to all that was its logical result. He taught all who came to him and all those he met, many of whom then clung to him for illumination. These included Menachem the Essene and even Menachem's violent father Hezekiah, while he was still alive, whose violence had tempered by what he learned from Hillel. It included Hezekiah's brother Jacob, who was made the Patriarch of Jerusalem in the same year that Hillel was made Nasi of the Sanhedrin, the year later to be called 30 BC, and the same year that Jacob's secret wife, Cleopatra, the asleep Agent Venus, had killed herself with her lover Marc Antony.

Hillel taught Jacob's son Joseph, and Joseph's son Yeshua, his greatest student, who also became Hillel's teacher starting from their first meeting when Yeshua was a newborn baby. He of course taught his own son Simeon and his son's son Gamaliel.

One of the many people Hillel taught was a teenage girl, Mary, who spent all of her time in the Temple in Nazareth and had been given her own cell in which to sleep. For years she never left the Temple, and went about full of the Spirit, seeing far beyond the material world, and loving God. Impressed with Mary, and she with him, Hillel became her favorite of many teachers. Hillel introduced Joseph and Mary and encouraged their love at first sight to bloom into betrothal, which neither youngster hesitated from.

During the period of their betrothal Mary continued to live in the Temple of Nazareth in Galilee, which is where they frequently met and meditated and prayed and talked together, mostly about God and the fate of Israel. Israel had been conquered over and over again since the days of Solomon, and was now in the clutches of Rome, originally a reasonable if imperialist state, but now sunken into tyranny like so many other wicked nations on Earth, under the thumb of Rebel rule.

At this time, Herod was ill and not expected to live much longer. The illness was actually slow poisoning by his son Antipater II. Along with wives and other family members, Herod had killed two of his other sons just three years earlier. The execution of family members was intended to fend off their doing the same to him in order to take over his position, which was partially in his mind and partially realistic, as the whole family consisted of asleep Rebels.

One night as Mary sat in meditation in her cell in the Temple, an unusual light crept to the barred arched window high above. It drew her attention and as she watched, the light grew brighter and expanded slowly down the walls until the room shone as if a full moon was exactly at the correct angle to illumine the room. Enchanted by this thought, she stood and tried to step into position to see the full moon but it was not there, and then she remembered that she had seen the full moon a week or so ago, so the light could not be coming from the moon.

Mary, a kind voice said in her mind and she was suddenly very alert. Her heart was beating loudly in her ears. *Don't be afraid, Mary,* the voice said, *for you have found favor in God's eyes.*

The Agents invisibly present were silent out of respect for an Archangel. It was Gabriel, also invisible, and come from far away as messenger of The One.

Mary prostrated herself on the floor, realizing it was an Angel, and sensing other Angels around her. Technically, Agents were of a different order than Angels, but Mary did not know of such distinctions. She spoke aloud, softly. "What can I do for God that He sends you to me? Please name it, and I shall obey."

You shall have a son, who will be The First Son of God, and you shall name him Yeshua Immanuel. He comes to free Israel and all creatures on Earth of the reign of sinfulness, the Angel responded.

"But I am a virgin, and betrothed to Joseph," Mary said before she could stop herself, and then regretted having said anything that showed doubt.

You will still be a virgin when you marry Joseph, although by that time God will have planted His seed in you.

"You know that I could be stoned to death as an adulteress. Even Joseph who is good, and trusts me, may depart from me."

You are protected, Mary, I shall speak with Joseph, and no harm will befall you. When you are married and Joseph knows you for the first time, his faith in you will be vindicated forever.

"Then I am the Lord's handmaiden, to be done with as He wilt." She felt something overtake her then and had to lie down. A softness gently pressed her from above, and she felt infinite joy and wellbeing, swooning as she felt the first stirrings of a new life within her.

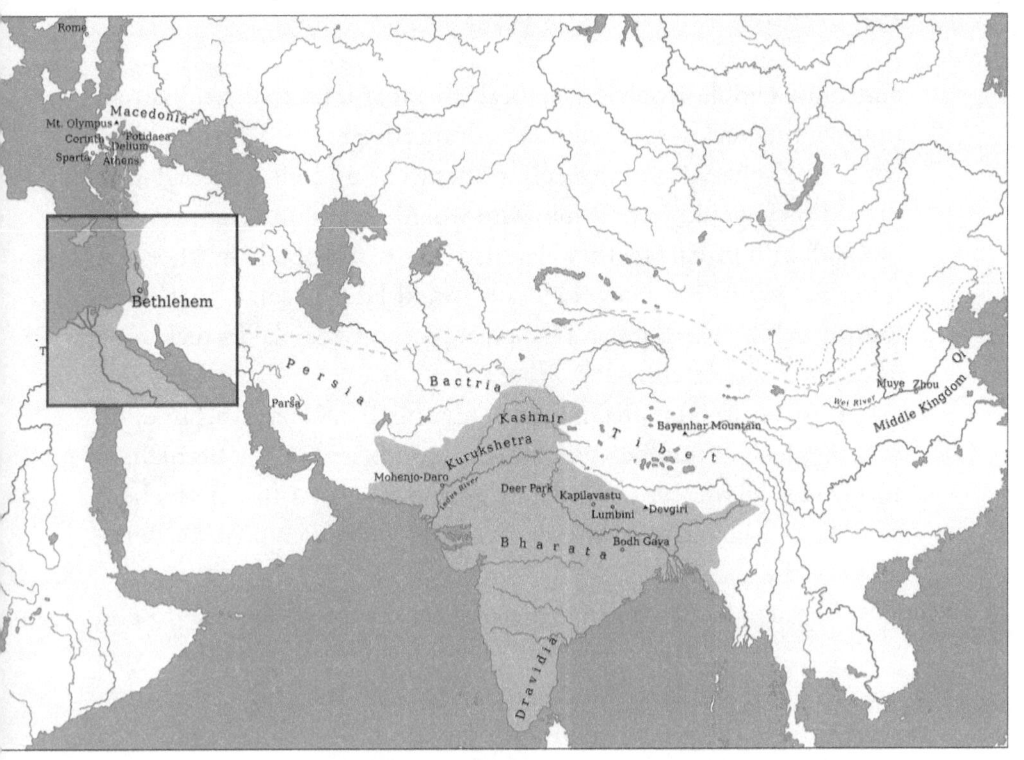

24

BETHLEHEM, A PLACE

4 BC

Mary confided to Joseph what had happened the next time he visited her. He believed her but still felt conflicted until Gabriel visited
him in a dream and set his mind to rest. Once Mary told Hillel, he advised her to spend the rest of her pregnancy with Mary's
cousin Elizabeth and Elizabeth's husband Zachariah in a hill town
of Judea, in order to avoid trouble as the pregnancy began to show

and most people would be cynical. Elizabeth, he told her, had an unusual pregnancy too, given her advanced age. An Angel had also come to Zachariah to inform him that as he and his wife had long prayed they would have a son, who would be an important servant of God. When Elizabeth welcomed Mary, Elizabeth felt her son jump for joy in her belly. Her son would later become an Essene known as John the Baptist. He had also been Ezekiel. His real name of course was Melchizedek.

Mary returned home in time to give birth in Nazareth, but upon arriving, Joseph told her they would have to set out for Bethlehem to register in the census ordered by Caesar Augustus. Bethlehem was back in Judea, from whence Mary had just come. "Why Bethlehem?" she asked.

"Because I am—and we are—of the house of David," Joseph said, and Bethlehem was the city of David. Now that they were married, Joseph fully trusted her, having confirmed for himself that she was still a virgin on their wedding night. This miracle affirmed everything he had been taught by Hillel and everything that his intuition had told him was true since his earliest memories.

I suspect the whole census hokum was cooked up to find Him. Templegard/Menachem expressed all of their feelings, except Melchizedek's, who was only half-awake within the Baptist, in Elizabeth's womb.

Herod's magicians sensed it and read it in the omens, Maitreya/Hillel reminded them. All of Herod's Arya were semi-awake Rebels. Kings decreeing the slaughter of all male sons was a well-established Rebel practice whenever the shamans sensed an enemy being born. It had gone on for millennia on Earth, and much longer across the multiverse. This was old hat to the Agents.

When Mary and Joseph arrived in Bethlehem, Mary was weary and felt her time to be near. Joseph had rehearsed and was ready to tell a guard at the gate why he was ordered to enter and about Mary's condition, when the guard winked. Joseph was startled and stared as the guard gently led them in, suspiciously not even saying a word of explanation to the other guards and the officer. Nastassia, appearing as a burly young male, led the couple in and although a foreign mercenary who would be expected to be hustling them along all the more cruelly for supposedly knowing Mary's condition—Joseph somehow had a feeling that he knew—did nothing to hasten their pace, which given the journey was that of a much older couple.

"She'll be coming soon," Nastassia observed to Joseph. Joseph looked at him levelly, wondering at the intimacy and if the guard had evil intent.

"We could have found a room, actually. Despite the horde of visitors there are still kin who have space," Nastassia explained, leading them to an active barn with many animals, many of them chickens trailing chicks, but no other people. Layla was also there but not presently visible. Joseph's nose crinkled in disgust at the smells of animals where Nastassia now pointed at a very clean and large bed made of hay in a charming corner with outside lighting. There were rose petals on it. Mary petted a baby lamb that had rubbed her calf and looked up adoringly. The chickens ran in all directions with their tail of chicks as the humans and pseudohuman came into the space.

"There are misguided people who want your child to die," Nastassia whispered in Joseph's ear, confirming his worst fears. "Don't panic, we your friends are all around you. You're always safe in God's hands."

Joseph and Mary both profusely thanked the young man, who smiled back and said, "My sister will be here to help with the birth. She's right outside."

In the alleyway where nobody could see, Layla appeared in a clean white apron, with towels and pockets stuffed with things, and holding a silver bowl of slightly steamy water. She had a red bandana on her blonde head and a pink scarf, and no shoes. She peeked in and saw the couple waving her to come in, so she did. Nastassia disappeared as soon as "he" stepped out of sight.

Joseph and Layla helped Mary get comfortable on the bed. "What's your name, sister?" Mary inquired respectfully of the girl even younger than herself.

"I'm a Mary too," Layla said, and Mary took her meaning that they were both nuns.

"Thank you so much," Joseph said to the other Mary.

Inside the soon-to-be mother Mary was a confrontation of which she was caused to be unaware, although this was against Perse's will. Perse had come to intimidate his older brother, or perhaps even tempt him, depending on how it went.

You know I could kill you right now, Perse pathed, and Yeshua merely smiled inside Mary's womb. Maitreya, Templegard and Nastassia prepared for mental combat, as did Layla, though showing no sign of it.

However, I might choose to let you be born, Perse went on, *and share equally with me in everything from this day.*

Share insanity with you, brother? Yeshua responded kindly.

The whole multiverse—yes granted, it's all insane, even me, I get it—but you're even crazier than the rest of us if you don't admit it, Perse argued in his best style. Yeshua laughed appreciatively as if this was just a comedy act. However, it did hurt him to know that even The One Self was hurt that Lucifer was going through this hell. This wasn't fun anymore.

Get thee behind me, Yeshua said. Perse stared at him then laughed ruefully.

What, you can't say "kiss my ass" like the rest of us? Perse asked and haughtily disappeared.

Mary's water broke. Layla cleansed her. Joseph sat on the bed and held Mary's hand. The chickens had settled down in a semicircle watching the humans and seemed to be in a meditative state. A white dove fluttered onto the windowsill above and watched, soon joined by its mate. Within minutes the windowsill was filled with birds of many kinds. The baby lamb and its mother cuddled up at the foot of the bed with a cat, dog and immaculate piglet. There were two horses watching, spouses. The cow also watched.

It seemed as if the gathering twilight outside had rebounded and it were now somehow sunrise, for as the moments quietly passed, listening to Mary's breathing, it was getting lighter outside. Joseph went outside to see what was going on. Nobody was around. There was a strange light. He looked straight up and saw directly above the brightest star he had ever seen.

Atlantis! Maitreya pathed first, and they all got it.

Wouldn't miss this for the world, pathed the great ship above, Atlantis by name.

But you were dead, Nastassia said.

Yes, and resurrected, badder than ever, Atlantis said. *Great to see you folks again.* The Agents and the ship excitedly greeted each other for some time, swapping war stories. To Joseph, who ran inside to report the star, it was a silent night thereafter.

He went into meditation and without moving his eyes he was able to see everything whenever he wanted to focus on the external. He started with his eyes open and drank in the great beauty of the scene. He was already in an exalted state. He had everything he had ever wanted in life. His service to Hillel and now to God was in process of the highest fulfillment. His beautiful and brilliant wife was peaceful, in a state of grace. He himself could see her halo! He had heard of such things but never before had he beheld it with his own eyes. Still his eyeballs did not move to study the phenomenon, for it was not that important somehow.

And these birds and animals, and this young girl Mary, if that was her real name or maybe she meant she was a nun too, all of it was amusing but not important to Joseph. How beautiful they all were, and so caring, and tender. He closed his eyes.

Mary was in a similar state. She need not keep her eyes open to see what was around her, in complete detail as if with her eyes. This had never happened to her before. She felt her first contraction, and Layla and Joseph both sensed it and sprang to hold her, but it had not been so painful.

Many miles away, Elizabeth was in the same phase, and Mary and Elizabeth sensed each other and knew this. They were both aware when Yeshua sent his love and congratulations to the Baptist, and both babies kicked, dancing with joy at the same time.

Yeshua sent greetings to His Father and that's when Layla first heard the singing. At first it was hard to hear, and indistinct, but as she contemplated it and let it in, it gradually became part of her, as if she were singing, and then as reality merged with other realities superimposed, she found she was singing and somehow knew the words and the melody. Her last verbal thought for a while was that The One Self was now fully in control of her. The difference she had been had vanished.

Yeshua then sent greeting to Hillel and to the other Agents by name, and to Atlantis, and to each Agent on Earth, and he kept radiating these messages to beings both near and far across all of existence. The average heartbeat on Earth stepped up a notch. The Schumann Rhythm became a soliton standing wave in the Earth's magnetic field. All beings on Earth became more sentient and breathed more deeply of whatever they were breathing. All perceptions for a time were drenched with this suchness to all perceivers.

The contractions were coming more frequently and now Layla was in position at the end of the bed amidst the dog, cat, pig, sheep, and lamb. All necessary implements were at her fingertips. And now the baby was coming!

Layla felt The One moving within her as her with every movement heartburstingly perfect, the singing ringing from the rafters, her fingers gently on the tiny head of The First Son, in the most important of His births in multiverse history. Tears ran freely down her face in the exultant joy of being thus privileged.

It became clear that they were all within each other's minds, and that each was fully aware of it, the animals, the Agents, the humans, and The One Self. One could look in any direction and see forever, see all of the creatures ever projected by The One Self, in every action that ever occurred was occurring or will occur. Nothing was hidden from sight, a memory that would be especially hard for the animals to bring back into consciousness, although none would ever forget it. Mary and Joseph saw the full Truth, more than even they had ever imagined—the concept of them each being The One Self having never occurred to them. Now the God they adored and obeyed was their selves.

And now they lifted up the baby and slapped its little tushy, but that was for form, as the baby had joined lustily in the singing, becoming the lead soprano, even before the symbolic slap.

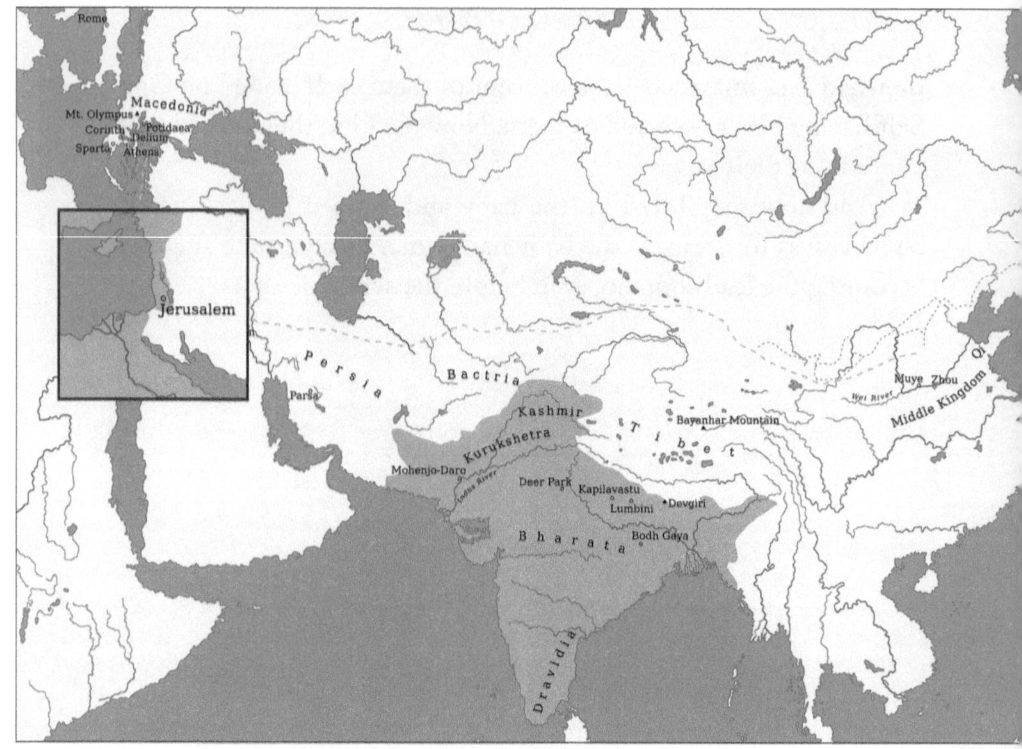

25

The Festival of Water Drawing
1 BC

Yeshua was a very affectionate baby and normal in most respects.
While fully awake even in his dreams and remembering everything
from before and since his conception clearly, he was adhering to the
strict interpretation of the Lost Lambs region of the multiverse. He
would not divulge the greatest of all secrets, the unity, the true Oneness, nor would he perform conspicuous miracles except whenever

his compassion couldn't avoid it. He would not speak the voice of an adult while in a baby's body. He was playing it by the highest Book.

His parents and his close relatives adored him and showered him with love. He listened to every human conversation, and those of the animals he knew, and heard the traffic on the cosmic intercom. Although he could not see out of everyone's eyes at once as his Father did, they were very close in reasoning powers and compassion, and in constant touch.

In a sense he was the Superspy of all history—or if not spy, undercover Agent. He was also in constant touch with the five Agents who were his direct reports on the planet. One of them was born into a human body of his own age, Melchizedek/John, two others, Maitreya/Hillel and Templegard/Menachem were in older human bodies, and the other two, Layla and Nastassia, were invisible except as needed otherwise. The main job of those out of bodies was his protection, as The One did not want to toy with the rules of the Lost Lamb game any more than his eldest Son did, and so Nastassia and Layla were protecting The First Son from himself. At the same time, with Perse looking for them at all times, the safest place to be was with The First Son. They would be seen by Perse but he could not harm them with him around.

Once, when he was three years old, he was on Sukkot pilgrimage to the Jerusalem Temple with family and friends. He had been here every year at this time, and for many other pilgrimage events, but now was walking on his own, and feeling ready to begin his work. Still, he mostly listened, observed, and prepared himself.

They stayed with his grandfather Jacob in his beautiful mansion. In Nazareth his family lived frugally and made no mention of family wealth. He understood that there were reasons for everything. He knew what robbers were, and kidnappers.

All that week he was around his parents, his grandfather, his uncle Menachem the Essene, and their teacher the sage Hillel. He listened with fascination to their conversations while the other children ran off to play.

"How are you, Menachem?" Joseph asked his brother, looking him straight in the eyes across the corner of the picnic table outside the Temple grounds. Yeshua knew by his tone and from listening to earlier conversations what his father was referring to. Menachem had been forced to step down as Av Beit Din, vice president of the Sanhedrin, and Shammai, a semi-asleep Rebel, had taken his place, and more recently had become co-equal with Hillel.

Other than Hillel, Menachem, and John for obvious reasons, his relatives didn't know what a Rebel was, nor what an Agent was. They knew of demons and had a concept of Lucifer (who now called himself Perse) called Satan, derived from the Rebel title Shaitan meaning planetary governor. They knew of Angels as well. But their knowledge of these things was overwhelmingly clouded by admixture with earlier planetary superstitions and myths and Rebel propaganda spiritualizing war, male dominance, and hierarchical society.

"It's all right, Hillel is keeping things under control," Templegard/Menachem spoke softly so his voice did not carry beyond the few at this corner of the table.

"In the Sanhedrin so far," Maitreya/Hillel modestly agreed.

Grandpa Jacob nodded. "Across the land, the Sadducees and the Zealots continue to gather supporters by flattery and other questionable means." Yeshua thought this the soul of understatement. Although he was not the fly on the wall, his powerful intuition and accurate memory filled in vast pictures based on driblets of information, and the Agents' reports verified what he already knew. The Sadducees—almost all asleep Rebels, the other more dangerous ones being semi-awake Rebels and a few awake ones—cared only for themselves. The asleep ones just wanted to continue their vain and greedy self-glorification. The semi-awake ones had the inkling to follow their own mission of creating constant war for long-term battle-hardening purposes. The awake ones were in ruthless competition with each other for higher military status. The Sadducees wished to have as few rules as possible and so insisted on written law, some of which was coming to be written by Hillel as Talmud.

The Zealots had an unselfish mission of restoring national freedom from imperialists. But the odds against them forced them to think like criminals, and many of them came from a criminal background. Others had a military background, while some had been Pharisees like Hillel but had turned a different corner.

Pharisees were the spiritual leaders who obeyed and interpreted the written and oral canons of Jewish belief.

The Essenes were mostly asleep Agents, occasionally waking up temporarily, and some permanently semi-awake such as Yeshua's uncle Menachem. They would not live in the city, sensing its Rebel control, so they lived in the desert and followed the written, oral, and intuited canons of Judaism.

Underlying these four sects of Jews as they had formed was the driving force of the Rebel war against The One. Yeshua had known for a long time that this internal division among the Jews had made them manipulatable and conquerable. From his point of view the obvious tactical plan was first to unify the Jews, and then the world, and ultimately to reunify Perse and his Rebel followers back into the universal Identity.

On the seventh day of Sukkot festival, the day of the Festival of Water Drawing, Yeshua was enthralled looking up at the older boys of priestly stock burdened with ten-gallon oil pitchers climbing the four huge candlesticks, each 75-feet tall, and setting ablaze the total of sixteen oil candles on top. Meanwhile, on the fifteen steps from the Court of the Israelites to the Court of Women, the musicians played harps, lyres, cymbals and trumpets, filling his ears as well as his eyes with such joy. The blazing candlelight from above shone down a heavenly moving nimbus. Here in the Temple atop the hill was his favorite place in the world, the place where he felt most at home.

Yeshua walked with the rest of the worshippers behind the priest and the flutists to the pool of Siloam while the choir sang Psalm 118. He knew some of the words and picked up some more of them and sang along, "The LORD is my strength and my song, He has given me victory. Songs of joy and victory are sung in the camp of the godly. The strong right arm of the LORD has done glorious things! The strong right arm of the LORD is raised in triumph…" Yeshua understood that he was the strong right arm of the LORD and his eyes shone.

He saw that Hillel was looking at him, and so were his students Jacob, Joseph and Menachem. The *shofar* was blown, long blast—short blast—long blast. Under the blazing candlesticks, men of piety juggled flaming torches while dancing and singing.

Waiting for Redemption, Baruch Nachshon

Back in the Temple, as the worshippers prepared themselves for the sacrifice of the wine and the water, there was a unity of feeling among the crowd, as if every mind was attuned together. Yeshua felt his mind clear and it was wonderful to breathe. Colors became enchanting and the sound dimmed. He and Hillel sensed one another alongside, and Hillel with great joy and ebullience lifted Yeshua in his arms. They looked at each other with reverence and love. The priest poured the wine sacrifice. Then, he poured the water sacrifice, and from everywhere Yeshua heard the sound "Ahhh…" as everyone sighed in ultimate happiness.

Yeshua whispered to Hillel very close to his face, "My Father is here."

Hillel wiped a tear from his eye and said with great joy for everyone around him to hear, "If I am here, so says God, everyone is here; if I am not here, nobody is here." And a great shout of joy and praise arose from the crowd at hearing these words.

26

Human Rites of Passage
1–10 AD

As Yeshua was growing up, in order to maintain his cover story of being just a human, he had to undergo all of the same predictable events that every boy must face in growing up.

"How much do you understand about what it is you are to do?" Joseph asked him when he began to admit he could speak, at least to his family. They kept it a secret until it was not as unusual to hear the child speaking like an adult.

They were sitting together, Joseph and Mary holding each other on the couch, Yeshua in their laps. His brothers and sisters and his widowed aunt sat around close by.

"Everything," Yeshua reported simply. They held back from interrogating him feeling that it would be disrespectful.

"How can we help you, son?" Joseph asked, wondering if their help might be superfluous, and disturbed by this thought. Yeshua of course read that thought.

"Father, mother, family," he said looking around, "please just keep loving me as you do. *That is the greatest thing.*" They all murmured their agreement instantly. He went on, "It's going to be very hard on you all, because of me. I won't be the only one suffering. One day I may lose one of you and that is heart wrenching to me to even contemplate." He wiped a tear. He was looking at Joseph. "But we will all be together again."

Because he was affectionate and kind, he did not arouse much hostility until he started to attend school. There the other smart boys wanted to be recognized for their fine minds, and Yeshua couldn't help showing everyone else up, even though he did it always with great respect and humility.

Sensing this problem, he shifted to sitting in the back of the classroom where he would be called on less often to answer a question. He waited and only answered a question after every other answer given had been wrong. His answers were always accepted by the teacher. The smarter the other boy, the less likely was he to like Yeshua.

Inevitably, one day when he was ten years old, the same year that Herod Archelaus, heir to Herod the Great, was deposed and banished by Caesar for his cruel treatment of the Jews, and Judea was now part of Iudaea, an older boy attacked him from behind and sought to throw him to the ground. Yeshua twisted slightly in escaping the boy's clutches and as he spun around to speak with the boy, the boy grabbed his own left kneecap and cried out in great pain.

Yeshua sensed that perhaps one of his Agent protectors was responsible, because he didn't wish the child any injury and had already forgiven him. In any case he speedily repaired the boy's bucket handle cartilage tear.

"You should feel no more pain now, Naftale," Yeshua said. "I forgive you."

Naftale was suspicious of having been let off so easily but he grudgingly respected the way the younger boy had handled it. He backed off and disappeared into the crowd of children.

It was not necessary to overreact, Yeshua pathed to his Agents.

It wasn't us, Maitreya responded. *The Shekinah Itself is ardent in your defense.* By that he meant the consciousness of Nature itself, an automaticity rather than a free will creature, had caused the injury. The First Son reflected on that for a moment and thought, *Of course before leaping off into the unknown as an avatar of Oneself, having already given free will to hosts of avatars of relative ignorance, one would give Oneself certain built-in protections in the game.*

A few years later when he was on his way to his Bar Mitzvah ceremony, he was attacked by a different older boy, in front of two girls about his own age. The boy messed up Yeshua's carefully groomed hair and creased and disheveled his fine clothing. Yeshua smiled at him in wonderment. "Velvel, why are you doing this? It's not funny, it's stupid."

Velvel walked away with a smirk on his face. *I forgive him,* Yeshua pathed to The Shekinah, to avert any over-reaction. "I forgive you," Yeshua said to Velvel's retreating back. Velvel spun on his heel and spat at Yeshua. Yeshua made the spit disappear before it struck him and pretended to have received it in his right eye. Velvel laughed bitterly and seeing a hunk of dog manure nearby, picked it up and flung it at Yeshua. This time Yeshua did nothing and let the dung splatter and stain his white robes. The girls shrieked and ran away. Velvel spat, "Faggot!" and with a contemptuous huff of disgust walked off.

Now what does that mean—oh yes, Yeshua thought, placing it.

Yeshua restored his appearance to the way it was before, without having to do anything outwardly. He got up and went on to his Bar Mitzvah, where he delivered an inspiring reading from the Talmud about forgiveness, repeating the words from memory without having to read them. Then he sang beautifully.

Hours later, after much feasting and merriment, he detected trouble and went out into the street where a crowd had gathered, including many guests departing from the Bar Mitzvah party. A speeding cart pulled by four horses had run over Velvel and the boy's body was bloody and immobile. As Yeshua approached he sensed the boy was still alive but with internal hemorrhaging, which he cured as he came closer. He put his hands on Velvel and the boy came back to consciousness, and seeing Yeshua as his savior, hugged him.

Shortly afterwards, a favorite relative of his, cousin Eli, whom for some reason everyone called uncle Eli, made a pass at him. This had never happened to Yeshua before. He knew Eli to be a man of peace, kind and thoughtful of others, very artistic, and who never spoke a negative word. He was fully human, with no Agent or Rebel soul in him.

They were alone in Eli's room and Eli unexpectedly exposed himself. Yeshua understood everything that was implied and shook his head with a smile.

"Uncle Eli, I love you as a man loves a man, not as a man loves a woman," Yeshua said plainly.

Eli put away his appurtenance and blushed a little. "I did not know how you would react," he explained lamely. *I had to try*, he thought, and Yeshua heard his thought.

"Some men love men, the way other men love women," Eli said.

"Yes, it's a matter of individual choice," Yeshua said unperturbed. "If you do this I don't condemn you for it, as long as it's mutual and not by inappropriate means of persuasion."

"Oh, no, Yeshua, you know me better than to think I would do such a thing," Eli said with transparent sincerity.

About a year later, Yeshua experienced his first great loss when his favorite teacher, Hillel, died. Yeshua and both his parents, Grandpa Jacob, and uncle Menachem were at the great Hillel's bedside for the last time. It was Yeshua's turn to say goodbye and faces turned his way to see what he would say.

"What will Shammai do now?" Yeshua asked.

Hillel smiled. "That's up to the rest of you now."

"What are your final instructions, please, teacher?" Yeshua asked.

"I should be asking you that," Hillel said.

Yeshua willed back a tear. *I love you,* he pathed. Hillel, now the fully awake Agent Maitreya, picked up on it, smiled, and pathed the same back with great tenderness.

"'He who seeks to increase his reputation, decreases it,'" Yeshua quoted Hillel to Hillel, intending to mean *this truth is why I come under cover,* but mostly wanting to quote Hillel to Hillel just now.

"Oh yes, teacher, I wanted to ask you," Yeshua suddenly began again, "When you say, 'That which you find hateful do not do unto others,' that wonderful summation, could that not also be said as 'do unto others'—"

"As you would have them do unto you! Of course!" Hillel exclaimed, having just heard those words in his mind. Their eyes met and love flowed back and forth.

"Teacher, when you say the first commandment is to love God, and therefore to love every one of His creatures, treating them with the same charity you would like from others," Yeshua asked, "I have these thoughts that I have wanted to discuss with you." Hillel nodded.

"In Genesis, when this all begins, God is alone, nothing else exists," Yeshua said, and Hillel nodded. "Therefore, all creatures must be *made from Him*," Yeshua concluded, and Hillel nodded energetically, crying in happiness.

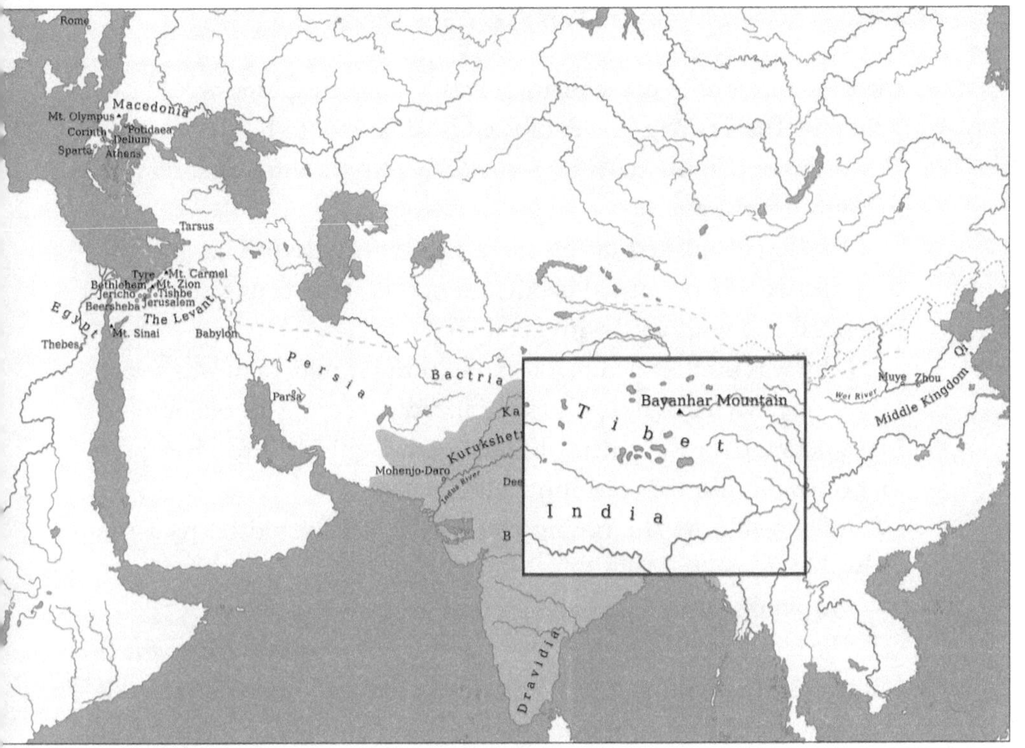

27

EXTENSIVE RECON

11–25 AD

Judea was heating up. Rebel-inhabited Sadducees controlled not only the Jews, but other Rebels were also inside Caesar and most of those in power in Rome and every other nation on Earth.

It was only a matter of time before the Zealots, considered terrorists, or some other spark set off a huge conflagration. It was not the time for light to come forth. It was what the I Ching would call a time of The Taming Power of the Great, a time to hold back.

Yeshua's parents took him out of Nazareth without leaving a forwarding address.

The Rebels picked up on them next at an Essene base in the deep desert, where normal people do not go. Yeshua and John met in person and embraced with great joy.

John was predestined to play an important role. John was a very high being, Melchizedek, who specialized in reading auspicious and inauspicious data and putting them together quickly into a best prediction and optimized recommendation.

John would be the timing clock by which would be read the right time to launch.

He would also prepare the ground in many other ways.

The family stayed with the Essenes for many years, during which Yeshua received all the information from the deep esoteric vaults of the Jews and the Hibirus and ancient Natufians before them. Most of this was oral knowledge, i.e. not written down. Yeshua studied with many teachers for long periods.

This was not a one-way street. During this time of absorbing all of the information possible, Yeshua was also commenting, and correcting the lenses of those reporting to him.

Years later, the Rebels detected the family in what by now was beginning to be called India. There Yeshua was amazed to see through human eyes what he knew already. The big secret was all over the streets in that area, and always had been, since the Dravidians became the only people on Earth to escape the notice of the Rebels, hence this was where the Agents had made their first big base on Earth.

Everyone here knew that extraterrestrials were real and varied, and that there was a single Self in all, in some interpretation or another, and everyone had some degree of what other humans would come to consider as extrasensory perception. Although the area was since infiltrated by Rebels from Persia and elsewhere, the culture was still predominantly Agent-based, the only place on Earth like that in those days.

Yeshua spent years there and in Tibet, learning and teaching before winding up spending most of his time in China. This was where the auspiciousness for making positive change was the greatest at that time.

Of the four invisible Agents that travelled with the family, Maitreya especially was an invaluable guide while Yeshua got his China legs. Almost two hundred years earlier, Maitreya had, as an invisible voice, positively influenced the writings of the asleep Rebel Dong Zhongshu, and so was an old China hand.

During the years that the family spent in China, they took a major role in the developments there. Although Rebels occupied China too and fully understood its massive importance, the intellectual curiosity of the native human population there was causing an upheaval in thinking that could not be suppressed, and the Agent side took full advantage of it to help establish the Han Dynasty and lead it into positive directions, including the removal of persecutions against Buddhism, which had trickled into China from India for about two hundred years but had been viciously repressed.

This work, integrating the wisdom of Lao Tzu, Confucius, and the Buddha, especially pleased Yeshua since he had been the Buddha and greatly loved and respected the celestial beings who had been the other two.

When Yeshua was 23, Perse and a large Rebel army surrounded the family at Bayanhar Mountain at the source of the Yellow River, intent on assassination.

The stars were bright. They were in the large ornate chariot the Tibetan monks had given them, bouncing over the mountain roads beside a huge waterfall, when the Agents sensed the attack on its way.

Incoming— Maitreya said.

A protective energy bubble sprang into place around the family. Hard radiation bolts of many colors blasted at them from all directions making horrible noises while indenting but not breaking the bubble.

Perse— Templegard said.

An irresistible hail of energy crashed down on the bubble, splitting it open for a moment, and Rebels materialized to fire into the chariot.

Jumping in front of Mary, Joseph took a withering mindblast from Perse.

"My love!" Mary exclaimed, bursting into tears. Recovering from the shock, the whole family wailed.

The bubble closed again and the Rebels disappeared. Perse appeared to be playing cat and mouse.

Leaving the Agents to protect the family, The First Son accompanied his human father's soul on the journey of absorption back into The One.

"Thank you, Joseph. I can't imagine a better Earthly father and teacher." Rainbows of light suggesting flowers and ocean waves flowed around and through them on the ascent.

"I can't imagine a better son anywhere in the multiverse," Joseph responded affectionately, and then choking up burst into ghostly tears, like fire glints in the night. The First Son put his ethereal arm around Joseph and hugged him tight.

They would miss each other.

A little window opened in not-space and Mother Mary's face appeared there, saying her last goodbyes to her Earthly husband. "I wanted you for another 50 years, why did you have to go and save my life," she kidded, and then through tears she said, "I love you, husband! I always will! Go with God. I'll be seeing you."

The last four words were what Agents said to each other at an incarnational separation.

Far below, the Agents hovered protectively above the chariot, all of them except Melchizedek, who was on the ground in Judea as John the Baptist.

How did we let that happen? Layla asked. Everyone was downcast.

They were jamming us somehow, Nastassia said.

The astral body of Yeshua joined them. His face was sobered.

By the time Yeshua was nearing 30, he had travelled and seen more of the world than practically anyone before him. He had learned and taught wherever he went, and left it better off than he found it, in all cases, planting seeds.

28

Rebels

26 AD

Perse and his top Generals were seated comfortably in the lounge of Perse's flagship *Planetkiller*, which was hovering invisibly in low Earth orbit a thousand miles west of Atlantis, now also invisible to humans. Both ships could easily detect each other. In the viewscreen, Atlantis appeared to be sending lightshow messages on its hull to Planetkiller, because images of Perse's ship appeared amidst other images. Planetkiller was a conventional saucer whereas Atlantis was an elongated crystal in the shape of two steep pyramids joined at their bases. Neither knew what the outcome would be of a battle, and so they had been in a standoff for decades. Orange-skinned horned Satan in his expensive shiny black clothes hummed along to the slow Gothic heavy metal music playing low in the background. Behind him his orange tail flicked slowly back and forth like a metronome.

"Is the new weapon ready?" Perse asked, although he knew the answer. Beelzebub and Satan were always at each other's throats and he liked to provoke their petty quarrels. The last time the two had pointed fingers at each other was to explain why the answer was still no. Perse had laughed long and hard at that one. Laughing at his Generals and other fools was the best part of his day.

"Satan" had just recently been officially so-named, as part of Perse's proclivity for harsh humor. Human psychics aided by Agents on the planet below had identified a Rebel chieftain they thought was named Satan. Actually, they were picking up on his title of Shaitan, meaning planetary commander, rather than his name. But then to tease him, Perse started to call him Satan and eventually the name stuck.

Beelzebub was Perse's chief of staff. The friction between the two seconds-in-command was intense and Perse poured gasoline on their conflagrations. He allowed himself this enjoyment of laughter as the only thing he really liked about this long frustrating life, since it was taking forever to overthrow the damned backstabber.

There was also sex and food and playing war games with humans and other creatures. He had to admit, it wasn't all bad. If he only had just a bit more power—

"No thanks to him, the answer is finally yes," Beelzebub jumped in before Satan could answer. "We got it done on the ship." At this, Beelzebub in his colorful clothes levitated with self-satisfaction and began to whirl slowly around the room in time with the dark adagio music.

"My compliments to Admiral Shax and Chief Engineer Asmodeus," Perse said, and it rang in echo over the ship's intercom everywhere, irritating both Generals.

"Well, let's see it then," Perse said, in a jovial mood.

Satan snapped his fingers and all of a sudden, the lounge was filled with copies of Satan, each one moving, having different expressions and clothes, some speaking or laughing, others winking or dancing or singing. Perse practically fell off his couch laughing, but there was no room to fall for all the Satan copies crowding the room, which made him laugh harder.

Satan (the original free will creature) was also having a good time—after all they didn't decide to print a million copies of Beelzebub, did they? Most of the Satan copies were in space around the ship, invisible, waiting to be sent to Earth to plant feelings and thoughts into the equally robotic brains of humans. The last great weapon the Rebels had created was the virus called the ego, which they had slipped into the DNA for the new human brains at the last minute, before the great mutation was triggered by The First Son with a special sunspot. The ego virus would be the perfect receptacle for these robot Satan-planted thoughts and feelings. Everyone in a position to help the Rebel situation on the planet could have their own Satan now. And the best thing about it, Satan thought, *I don't have to lift a finger.*

Not to mention plausible deniability, Perse added in his mind.

"No accountability as always!" Beelzebub roared aloud, breaking Perse up.

"Well, let's see it work," Perse said amiably. His two Generals looked at each other. They hadn't thought about a demo yet. They didn't know what to do, trying first to think of hurtful things to say about the other.

This amused Perse and he stood up and clicked his fingers, whereupon he and Satan and Beelzebub and 1000 or so automaticities of Satan were now in Rome. The robot Satan programming sensed their location and they all went invisible.

"Well, that program works," Perse said, like a child testing a new toy. They were standing near the Senate and people were going in and out in great throngs. The three Rebel leaders morphed their clothing into togas and Perse made his hooves into sandaled feet. A few humans noticed something strange but nothing clearly, and the crowd flowed around the Rebels without giving them much attention.

"There, that family over there," Perse said, indicating with his eyes a couple with a young son and daughter, all apparently from out of town and delightedly taking in the sights of Rome. The 1000 robot-Satans' programming picked up that a target had been set by a free will Rebel and the closest four of them peeled off and invisibly went into proximity with the happy, laughing foursome.

"Ad lib," Perse said to the four robot-Satans.

The daughter must have made a clever remark because the father and mother beamed and hugged her. The Satan robot standing by the son planted a feeling of jealousy in the boy, who made a snide remark, causing the parents to laugh and the daughter to flash him a brief angry look. The adults' faces became concerned, the happy mood broken.

"Bravo!" Perse cheered, "Even better than the original," he said winking at the original Satan, who laughed half-heartedly, while Beelzebub slapped him on the back just a little too hard.

"Deploy the million Satans to the enemy list," Perse said.

29

LIFTOFF

26 AD

John and Yeshua started to become aware at the same time that the situation was rapidly deteriorating everywhere. They didn't immediately recognize the existence of the million robot Satans. But people were acting badly even more than ever before, so something was up.

John, you start now with our eternal ministry and I will join you when I get there, Yeshua said.

I'll also tell them you are coming, John/Melchizedek said.

Melchizedek got to wear a leather belt, as was always his favorite. The camel's hairshirt was itchy, but that was the whole idea, to challenge oneself to be better, to be the overcomer.

"Prepare the way of Jehovah, you people, make his roads straight!" John boomed so that the hordes of curious onlookers and inspired seekers could hear him clear up and back both banks of the Jordan. Many of the true seekers cried in numinous recognition of great prophecies coming true. Many sought to be baptized by him, in keeping with Ezekiel 36:25-26a:

> I will sprinkle clean water upon you to cleanse you from all
> your impurities... I will give you a new heart and place a
> new spirit within you...I will put my spirit within you and
> make you live by my statutes, careful to observe my decrees.
> You shall live in the land I gave your fathers; you shall be my
> people, and I will be your God.

150

A beautiful starry-eyed young woman grabbed both his hands and looked shyly and devoutly into his eyes, "You are the Christ, come!" and the echo of that word rippled through the crowd waiting in and near the river to be baptized.

"No, I am not the one you mean," he answered so that all could hear. "I baptize you with water. He who is coming after me will baptize you with The Holy Spirit." *I'm giving you a fresh start,* he thought. *He will give you telepathy. Connection with The One and therefore connection with all.*

John saw Pharisees and Sadducees in the crowd, whom he knew to be half-asleep Rebels, probably not here to be baptized.

Then he saw who was moving toward him in the misty water. It was Yeshua. The First Son gestured to indicate not to take him out of order. After two other baptizings, it was Yeshua's turn. The man just before him was very old but after his baptism looked ten years younger.

Good to see you, they said in unison and hugged. Melchizedek felt a bolt of energy flash into him and he felt capable of anything.

"It's you who should be baptizing me," John said.

"Let all the prophecies be fulfilled," Yeshua said with a beaming smile.

The skies opened with a rumble of thunder and a dewy fine rain fell. John saw an avatar of The One Self in the form of a dove, descending from high in the sky and landing on Yeshua's broad shoulder.

This is My First Son, with whom I am well pleased. This rare broadcast from God was heard by many in the crowd including some Rebels. As always, The One Self used the metaphor of sonship to allude to the phenomenon of avatars, which was judged, rightly, to be too difficult to grasp by the primitive Rebel-brainwashed humans.

Although time stopped below, Yeshua felt taken away into another dimension by Perse. *How could that have happened?* he wondered. He sensed he was with Perse and also with hordes of other demons. He had a very long, seemingly over a month, strange dream of being tempted by Perse three times, and of refusing Perse each time.

Yeshua was back in the water with John and time was flowing again. Not a second had passed since Yeshua left. John was aware something had happened involving Perse.

Yeshua didn't speak of it. It was unnerving knowing now that Perse could take him away like that even just for a second. *He never used to be able to do that. Why is he now able to do it?*

30

BREAKING IN THE ACT
26 AD

Yeshua was welcomed in Galilee. Many became his followers as he walked by the sea, telling of the good news that God loved them all like a father would, because He indeed is Father to us all. Isn't that the best news you ever heard? Be kind, we are all sisters and brothers. He spoke brilliant poetry effortlessly; it spilled out of him as if directly from the mind of God, and his supernal authenticity was palpable. He was highly charismatic and heroic and emanated love. Everyone found it hard not to fall in love with him instantly. He was invited to speak at their synagogues.

He also knew and supported the scriptures, with a level of understanding of how they all fit together that left his growing numbers of followers vibrating with spiritual energy. They began to understand why they should be kind, and to look into themselves deeply.

Among his followers were some Rebel plants and thousands of invisible robot Satans, ganging up many to one against each follower. When Perse took Yeshua away to tempt him, it was with the aid of the million robot Satans, and still they could only hold him a moment. They could, however, make it seem like much longer to Yeshua, which perhaps would help demoralize him and undermine his confidence. If they could succeed in undermining his confidence, he would be theirs, and then all the Agents could also be enslaved, and Heaven stormed.

When he got to Nazareth, the Rebel sapping of Yeshua's confidence was starting to show effect. First it was just nerves. The place reminded him of the uncertainties of childhood. Yeshua couldn't believe he was capable of having feelings of nervousness. His mind kept coming back to the thought and image of being a little boy here and doing some silly things, and of these people remembering the silly as well as the good, while a voice in his head kept reminding him that a prophet is never a prophet in his home town. Without realizing it, he was projecting the reality he didn't want to have happen.

Normally this would have been impossible for him. However, in addition to being trapped now within the sabotaged human brain, he was also being simultaneously sneak-attacked by a million robot Satans plus Perse. Each could focus on different neuron groups and flood the human brain with more information than could be assimilated out quickly enough to not trigger chemical emotional reactions. There were enough of them so that hundreds of thousands of them focused solely on keeping their presence undetected.

Maitreya, Layla, Templegard, and Nastassia suspected invisible Rebel activity in the room but with hundreds of thousands of robot Satans sucker punching them, they could not actually detect what was going on. If Perse had wanted to, he could have tried for some kills but he was playing a waiting game until certain of what he could do with the robot army.

When Yeshua went to the synagogue he was invited to read from the scroll. Opening right up to the place in Isaiah, he read, "Jehovah's spirit is upon me, because He anointed me to declare good news to the poor, He sent me forth to preach a release to the captives and a recovery of sight to the blind—'"

Then sitting down, he said, "Today this scripture that you just heard is fulfilled."

Yeshua and the four Agents sensed suddenly that John the Baptist, Melchizedek, was being arrested. Part of their minds stayed with him supportively, which however was a well-timed distraction by Perse.

The people all around, entranced by Yeshua's presence and the strength and conviction in his voice, began to murmur appreciatively about him. At an order from Perse, the robot Satans quickly planted thoughts of recognition in the minds of the Nazarenes in the synagogue, as several were heard to speak aloud, "This is the son of Joseph, is it not?"

As soon as Yeshua heard that, he was unaware of being bombarded from a million directions with thoughts and tendencies to overreact, anticipating non-acceptance in his home town. Standing, he began to speak with subtle defensiveness, "Truly I tell you that no prophet is accepted in his home territory," and went on, choosing wrong tangents to go off on, quoting scriptures no one understood but which sounded vaguely insulting to them. "I tell *you* in truth, there were many widows in Israel in the days of Elijah, yet Elijah was sent to none of these women, but only to a widow Zarephath in the land of Sidon. Also, there were many lepers in Israel in the time of Elisha the prophet, yet not one of them was cleansed, but Naaman the man of Syria was cleansed."

Perse and the many Satans inflamed the crowd and it became a mob, hustling Yeshua and his few closest followers outside to the brow of a mountain from which the mob was going to toss them to their deaths.

We'll clear a path sir, please just follow it out of here and leave the rest to us, Templegard said, and the Agents gently opened up a gap through which Yeshua and his followers could walk back out of the crowd and away from Nazareth, picking up their other followers along the way out of town.

How are you? Layla asked Melchizedek with concern.

Chained in the oubliette, John responded stoically.

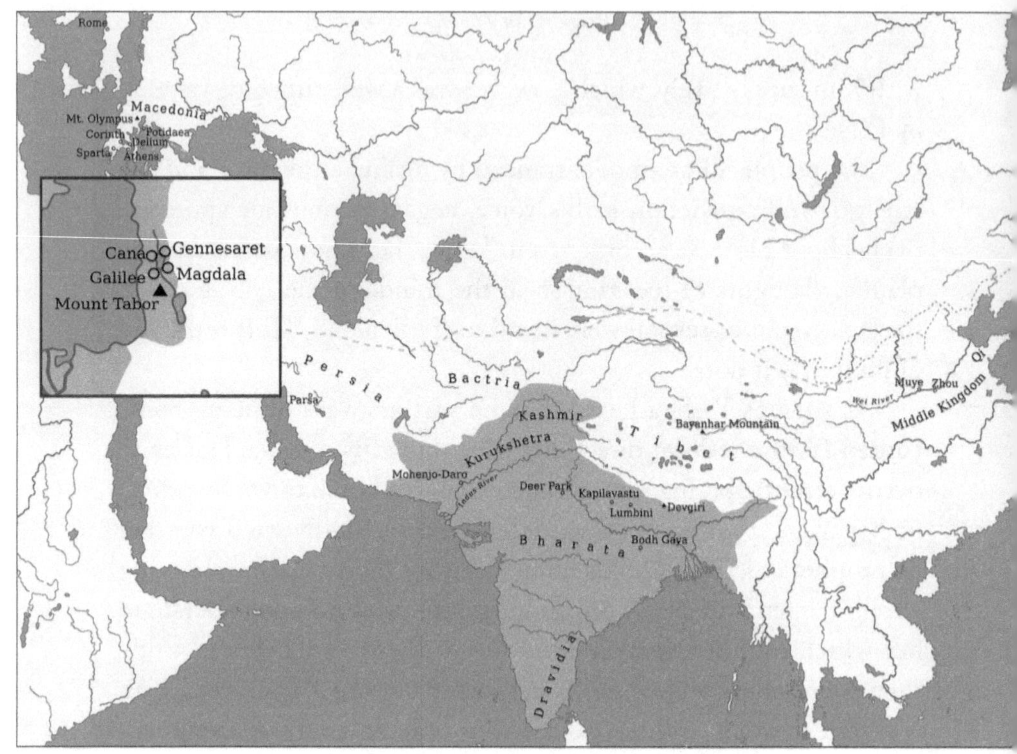

31

BENDING THE RULES OF THE LOST LAMB GAME

27 AD

Things returned to normal, back in Galilee. Attending a wedding
with his family in Cana, Yeshua was sitting under a tree watching
children play across the broad expanse of lawn running down from

the great house into the great valley. His mother, Mary, drying a glass, came out of the mansion to ask him for something.

"They are out of wine," his mother said.

Yeshua laughed. "You agreed that miracles are a last resort on a Mystery Planet," which surprised Mary for a second until she realized her son was speaking to God through her. He smiled sweetly. "*You* want to change the rules for wine?"

His mother looked sympathetic and a little sad. "You admitted yesterday that miracles are going to be inevitable. This is the most important day in my sister's life. She is finally marrying off her only son. If we are not on Earth to make good people happy… must we only make strangers happy?"

He stood up and she lit up from inside.

Yeshua saved the event by turning water into better wine than what had been served before. Very few people noticed this but they told other people and news traveled round, attracting a great deal of attention from everyone including Perse, who ordered another million Satans all assigned to Yeshua.

Beelzebub gulped. "Producing these demons is a slow process. The plastometal is subject to coding errors that cannot all be found and fixed robotically."

"Get it done as fast as you can, and in fact step up production to the maximum, and maintain it there from now on. Just never stop producing them," Perse said.

Yeshua was invited to teach at the synagogue in Capernaum, and the seekers were astounded at his way of teaching, his evident embodiment of the virtue he taught, and the love he emanated for everyone.

Suddenly a loud voice came from a man in the crowd, "Ah! What have we to do with you, Jesus, you Nazarene? Did you come to destroy us? I know exactly who you are, the Holy One of God."

This was obviously the voice of a Rebel, but the Agents could tell that the man was human, with no Rebel or Agent soul, so they hesitated. Yeshua realized that this was a form of demonic possession and pathed to them *Technodemonic Possession*.

"Be silent, and come out of him," Yeshua said, with certainty of being obeyed. The man fell to his knees and made as if to vomit. What came out of him through his mouth first looked like a streaming orange wet plastic but stood up as a robot Satan that stood glaring defiance and growling menacingly. Until Yeshua lifted one arm and the Satan copy became an Akashic Record.

Yeshua helped the man up. A woman said, "What speech is this, with authority and power, he orders the unclean spirits, and out they come?!"

The news about Yeshua now began going out to every corner of the surrounding countries.

What was that? Layla asked as they were leaving the synagogue.

An AI, The First Son said, meaning an artificial intelligence, *like Atlantis, or The Shekinah—no free will. That one was a copy of a Rebel General named Satan—presumably programmed based on observing Satan's behavior, rules-based, with adaptive stimulus-response.*

I wonder how many of those have been loosed down here, Maitreya mused.

Capable of escaping our detection means it inherently has a vast amount of power, Nastassia suggested.

Until we know how powerful, let's coordinate our firepower on one target at a time, Templegard recommended.

Yeshua's follower Simon took them, with James and John and other followers, back to his house, and introduced them to his mother-in-law, who was lying down sick with a fever. Yeshua took the woman's hand and she arose out of bed feeling well again and welcomed them with refreshment and water and towels for their feet.

A little later, at sunset, people began arriving, bringing Yeshua all that were ill or demon-possessed, and until just before dawn he cured one after the other until there were no more to be cured.

Early on, at Yeshua's command, a woman threw up a demon looking just like the one they saw in the synagogue.

Dozens more Satan robot demons met the same fate that night.

"Yeshua is one of us!" one robot managed to scream before Yeshua dispatched it to the Akashic Record. No one appeared to pay attention to its words except one spectator named Judas Iscariot, who went home that night and dreamed about what the robot had said. It was an inspiring dream because Judas in the dream became a very important person.

Just before dawn when everyone else was sleeping, Yeshua went to a lonely place in the woods and prayed to The One Self to be better able to resist the human brain, which he knew had led him astray in the Nazareth synagogue. The four Agents—and Melchizedek, chained in a wet disgusting dungeon—also prayed.

Simon and some of the others found Yeshua around dawn and Simon said, "They're all looking for you." The physically and mentally sick and despondent were being attracted from greater distances as the word spread.

"Yes, but let's continue to make the full circuit of towns in the area, to spread the benefit as far as we can," Yeshua explained.

And so, they went from synagogue to synagogue throughout Galilee, preaching the good news and curing the sick of body and mind. His train of followers ever increased. One day passing a tax collector's booth, he called to a tax collector named Matthew, "Follow me!" and as had happened so many times, inexplicably to many Rebel-controlled observers, the man stood, looking uncertain, and followed Yeshua.

Rebel spies, often being manipulated without their conscious awareness, reported back to the Pharisees when they saw Yeshua and some of his followers dining at Matthew's house with other tax collectors and known sinners such as gamblers, prostitutes, and thieves. The Rebels decided to make much of this, and Pharisees in the streets of the towns tracked down followers of Yeshua and demanded an explanation of how their master could possibly be associating with such unsavory characters.

Asked by his followers what to say when thus accosted, Yeshua said, "Physicians do not exist to treat the sound of body and mind, but rather those who are unwell. Similarly, I am here to treat the sinners, which cannot be done while avoiding them."

The Rebels continued to look for ways to discredit Yeshua and bring him down. "We don't just want to kill him," Perse had instructed his troops, "We need to humiliate him, expose him as a faker, show that the whole story of one original God is a con game, and those that preach it are liars and weaklings who just want to subjugate and steal from us." *So, if he comes back again, he will be rejected,* Perse thought.

Yeshua was teaching in a synagogue one Sabbath and a man with a withered hand asked him to cure it. Pharisees there quickly asked if this was lawful to be done on the Sabbath, when all work was prohibited. They had been waiting for this opportunity, having heard rumors that Yeshua's hungry followers had been permitted to pick wheat and make bread to eat on the Sabbath. Since then, teams of Pharisees picked by Perse for their persuasiveness had been shadowing Yeshua to publicly catch him in the act of doing something inappropriate on the Sabbath.

"Who among you, if one of your sheep fell into a pit on the Sabbath, would not reach down and pull the sheep out?" Yeshua asked. "So yes, it is lawful to do good on the Sabbath." Thereupon he turned the man's withered hand into a normal one, well-matched to the man's other hand.

One night, Yeshua went up on Mount Tabor and prayed all night, after which he called some of his followers and named twelve of them to be his apostles. He knew eleven of these to be guided by Agents, and one to be guided by Rebels. Judas Iscariot, the latter apostle, would be one means of manipulating Rebel moves, to fulfill the prophecies and thus change the course of history across the multiverse.

Coming down from the mountain they found a multitude of people from Jerusalem and all over Judea, from Tyre and Sidon and beyond, and Yeshua spoke to them at length.

"Happy are you who hunger now, because you will be filled." Yeshua looked around at the throngs and his voice became large to reach those furthest from him with perfect audibility. He saw the faces of the downtrodden and those of broken spirit, drawn intuitively to the source of their salvation, and his heart went out to each of them as an individual, and his love was felt by each recipient. Thousands of people experienced his eye contact, every person there.

"Continue to love your enemies, do good to those hating you, bless those cursing you, pray for those insulting you." A spiritual fireball formed around the assembly, invisible to all but The First Son. The robot Satans attending Yeshua fell into a state of sleep for a brief time, although Yeshua and the Agents were still unaware of their existence.

"Just as you want men to do to you, do the same way to them." Yeshua thought lovingly of Hillel and noticed Hillel's spirit looking down, beaming with pride in his student as Yeshua paraphrased his teaching.

"Moreover, stop judging, and you will by no means be judged, and stop condemning, and you will by no means be condemned. Keep on releasing, and you will be released. Practice giving, and people will give to you."

"Continue becoming merciful, just as your Father is merciful." Yeshua watched the faces in the crowd as they reacted to this amazing news that God was actually their Father and loved them. *How could this be? God is the all-powerful warmaker who demands and punishes and rules and spews angry fire down from mountaintops when He is not properly propitiated by sacrifices,* he read their many minds thinking and observed them as these conditioned perceptions loosened.

To bring people to realize that their conditioned biases even affected what they thought they observed, he asked, "How can you say to your brother, 'Brother, allow me to extract that straw that is in your eye,' while you yourself are not looking at the rafter in that eye of yours?"

After speaking with them for some time, Yeshua moved back to Capernaum, with his followers and the huge crowd trailing him.

Along the way he saved the life of a dying slave of a Roman army officer named Longinus, and approaching the city of Na'in, he raised a widow's dead son to life, astounding the many onlookers. One cried out, "A great prophet has been raised up among us!" and another cried, "God has turned His attention to His people!"

The Rebels seeking to discredit him planted the intention in a Pharisee named Simon to invite him over for dinner. Sometime later, after repeated invitations, Yeshua entered Simon the Pharisee's house and reclined at his table with Pharisees and Sadducees. Many followers waited outside and passersby inquired of them what was going on. By this attention, word spread quickly that Yeshua was dining with a Pharisee and this news reached the ear of a certain woman.

The woman took certain items from her house and with quickening heartbeat entered a state of fugue and rushed over to the Pharisee's house, entering through the open door. Before the servants could stop her, she entered the dining room.

Yeshua sensed her presence and half turned from the table where he was dining. Simon nearly stood up but held himself in check. The other teachers recoiled in shock speechlessly. This was the notorious neighborhood witch, a priestess in a gentile temple in a tower not far away on the beach at Magdala. Obviously not even Jewish, she was suspected of being a loose woman, and unlike the Jewish hiding of a woman's hair, the witch's long reddish-brown hair hung flagrantly for all to see. Simon the Pharisee thought to have her ejected but waited to see if perhaps she could be useful in publicly embarrassing Yeshua. Besides, like other men, Simon found her exceedingly attractive, and of course not being Jewish, to him she was forbidden fruit. *Something strange about her tonight, she seems to be in a trance,* he thought to himself.

The woman from Magdala, without saying a word, reclined on the floor and, producing an alabaster case of perfumed oil, began to open it and then, suddenly overcome by tears, began crying all over Yeshua's feet.

Something familiar about her… Yeshua would normally have recognized her before she even came in the door, but he was weighed down imperceptibly by a million robot Satans draining his mind and powers. *My God! Thank you!* Yeshua nearly wept himself but betrayed no outward reaction. *Yasodhara!* This was the one woman he had always loved, and he knew her by millions of names, of which Yasodhara was only the most recent. It was her mission to be his completion.

Simon looked on in outward horror and inward glee as Yasodhara dried Yeshua's feet of her tears using her long hair, and then kissed Yeshua's feet tenderly many times. Finally, she looked up and into his eyes and he into hers.

She knows me, but knows not from where, nor who each of us really is, Yeshua thought. *She came to me by dead reckoning.* Yasodhara now opened the oil and began massaging Yeshua's feet with it. Yeshua saw that she was inhabited by not one but many demons.

This man, Simon thought, *if he were a prophet, would know what kind of woman it is that is touching him, that she is a sinner.* Hearing the thought, Yeshua said, "Simon, I have something to say to you."

Surprised, Simon blurted, "Teacher, say it!"

"Two men were debtors to a certain lender," Yeshua began, "The one was in debt for five hundred denarii, but the other for fifty. When they did not have anything with which to pay back, he freely forgave them both. Therefore, which of them will love him the more?"

"I suppose it is the one to whom he freely forgave the more."

"You were just thinking that if I were truly a prophet, I would not let a sinner touch me," Yeshua said, and Simon's eyes widened as Yeshua explained further. "We all miss the mark sometimes; therefore, we are all sinners to varying degrees. I forgive all sinners, I forgive you for little and others perhaps for more, so is it not logical then that those who feel forgiven for more will love me more?"

Yeshua turned to Yasodhara, now known as Mary Magdalene, and spoke of her to Simon, "How much love one gives is a sign of how much one is in love with God. I entered your house, and you gave me no water for my feet. But this woman wet my feet with her tears and wiped them off with her hair. You gave me no kiss, but this woman has not left off tenderly kissing my feet. You did not anoint my head with oil, but this woman greased my feet with perfumed oil. By virtue of this, I tell you, her sins, many though they are, are forgiven, because she loves much. But he who loves little, is forgiven little."

The teachers at the table, already secretly hostile to Yeshua, now by their glances, expressions, and body language, revealed their hostility, although it had never been a secret to Yeshua. *Who is he to forgive sins? Only God can forgive sins!* many of them thought. Some of them also asked themselves, did they themselves love enough? Yeshua was happy to see that some of them were at least already considering his message of love.

Yeshua turned to Yasodhara and said kindly, "Your faith has saved you; go your way in peace."

Yasodhara looked confused at being sent away and would have resisted but Nastassia and Layla helped lift her to her feet and assisted her out the door, taking her home and noting the route, as Yeshua had requested. They would keep her safe until he was able to leave.

Hours later, after fencing with the Pharisees and Sadducees over many courses, he was able to politely depart. Maitreya and Templegard created a mental haze that made it possible for him to disappear from sight of his followers for a while.

He knocked softly on her door. She sensed who it was before she opened the door but even still lit up like the sunrise upon seeing his face. "Please come in, teacher," she said. Entering, he saw the many idols adorning the rooms and identified that her main God was now Nature perceived as The Goddess. To him this was not a sin but a stage in being able to grasp The One Self behind Nature. She led him to a sitting room where they sat with knees nearly touching. She boldly took his hands and squeezed them lovingly.

"Teacher, thank you for your forgiveness," she said. "I feel I know you from another life... many lives. I know your message of love to be the Truth. Your forgiveness means more to me than the forgiveness of everyone else on Earth combined."

"How do you feel, my dear? Are you alright?" he asked with concern.

"No," she admitted. "My mind is clouded and I act as if intoxicated, although I've had no wine tonight. I feel weak, and my mind is abuzz with many thoughts, some tempting, some horrific. I feel as if I might faint—even before I saw you," she said and smiled.

"Lay down here for a minute," he suggested and walked her to the nearby couch where she reclined. He stationed himself at her feet and then grasped them and squeezed them, concentrating for a moment, and then the demons started to come out.

They both watched as seven of the robot Satans came out of her, pushing open her mouth as they emerged floating upward into the air wrapped around each other until seven of them had unfurled and were now encircling them menacingly. Yeshua looked up at them with pity and they disappeared into the Akashic Record.

"Seven of them!" she sputtered, wiping her mouth with disgust. She sat up and drank some water to cleanse her mouth. She quickly stood, moving now with self-possession and held his hands.

"Thank you again."

In the days that followed, Mary Magdalene become one of Yeshua's followers, as did other women whom he had exorcized, including Joanna, the wife of Chuza, Herod's man in charge, and Susanna and many other rich women he had cured.

As the mass of followers moved from city to city preaching and curing, Yeshua was always teaching. Mary Magdalene was always at his side. They were seen kissing on the mouth. Jesus kissed the rest on their cheeks and foreheads.

And his followers were asking for certain parables to be decoded that they were not sure they understood. He was unwilling to fully explain who the "Devil" was due to the rules of engagement, and so he described the Rebels as "thorns" that could choke off the growth of seeds of ideas transmitted by Yeshua. Although not fully comprehending, his closest disciples knew that they were in great danger at all times from Pharisees, Sadducees, and sometimes from Romans, the local puppet government, robbers, and others. They could identify these as the thorns in the metaphor.

"How dangerous are these thorns to us, Master?" Peter asked.

"Very. They tamper with our thoughts and feelings, our very perceptions. They can take over our actions. It all seems to be us in the saddle but we are enslaved if we let it happen," Yeshua answered.

"The thorns are themselves people who have been taken over inside by these supernatural thorns—they're not really guilty in themselves, but what controls them is guilty," Peter said, and Yeshua smiled his assent.

News was brought to Yeshua of the beheading of John the Baptist, also known to Yeshua as Melchizedek. Yeshua had known of this already, sensed it as it was happening. He went away to be alone and to pray again for John as was proper under the circumstances, although he was glad that Melchizedek had escaped that awful oubliette. But his followers made it impossible to get very far, so he turned back to tend to those asking to be cured and taught. *The show must go on*, he thought, and the Agents winked at the age-old expression.

Soon thereafter, he sent his disciples ahead in a journey to preach in new territory on the other side of the huge inland sea known as the Sea of Galilee, saying that he would join them. Confused, they nevertheless obeyed orders and set off in a boat, even Mary Magdalene, who never left his side, while Yeshua took some precious time alone to pray.

The boat had not gotten very far due to headwinds, and when Yeshua was finished praying he simply walked out across the top of the water, which was roiled up by mounting weather. Astonished and terrified, his disciples in the boat could not believe their eyes and thought it was an apparition.

"Take courage, it is I, have no fear," Yeshua said.

"Lord, if it is you," Peter said, "command me to come to you over the waters."

"Come!"

Peter then tentatively placed a foot outside of the pitching boat and found that the water somehow resisted the downward pressure of his foot, and so, gaining his balance after a moment, he began to walk on the water toward Yeshua. Then looking down, he lost it and immediately sank down and bobbed up again, his face barely above the mounting waves. Yeshua reached down and asked, "Why did you give way to doubt?" and helped him back into the boat.

Crossing the Sea of Galilee, Yeshua slept peacefully in the boat as the winds turned into a storm, threatening to capsize them. They woke him in fear for their lives, and as he easily pacified the elements, wrought up by Rebel mischief, he took the occasion to remind them to remember their faith at such moments instead of panicking.

Landing at the opposite shore in Gennesaret, they were immediately met by a dirty naked man living in a graveyard, obviously being tormented by demons. The man threw himself down on the ground before them, yelling in a loud voice, "What have I to do with you, Son of the Most High God? I beg you, do not torment me. Do not cast me into the abyss!"

"What is your name?" Yeshua asked kindly. He sensed that the man had been an important Agent-guided local leader interfering with Rebel plans.

"Legion," the man said, and Yeshua got the meaning: there was a legion of demons in the man, and each demon could take control of what the man said. All the demons were entreating Yeshua not to put them away in the Akashic Record, evidently unaware that they would lose the experience of selfhood once in the Akashic and therefore would not feel locked away and paralyzed for eternity. Moreover, their consciousness would be recaptured for expression in better places, a positive change from their perspectives.

Before he could explain all that to the demons, Yeshua saw them follow the order of their commander to escape into a huge number of pigs grazing on the side of a nearby hill, whereupon the pigs, who could not stand the invading inhabitation, stampeded over the precipice and fell into the sea to their deaths, at which point Yeshua consigned the demons to the Akashic Record, and prayed that the pigs would be born next as humans without karma, as compensation for their having been harshly used by the Rebels.

News had crossed the sea and they were soon thronged with masses of people wishing to be cured of ailments. The presiding officer of the local synagogue pushed forward and begged Yeshua to save his dying daughter, for which task they set forth, slowed by having to move through masses of people. Yeshua felt a momentary drop in spiritual energy and halted. It was soon discovered that a woman behind him, who had been unable to stop constant bleeding for twelve years, had touched him, and Yeshua's spirit knew what to do and gave her the drop she needed, whence the bleeding stopped. She admitted to having touched him and Yeshua forgave her, saying "Daughter, your faith has saved you, go your way in peace."

He then found that the man's daughter had already died. The family was in tears, beating themselves.

"She is only sleeping," Yeshua said gently, speaking metaphorically.

"Sleeping! What an idiot!" the child's mother exclaimed.

"Girl, get up!" Yeshua commanded. A minute passed and Yeshua appeared unperturbed. The crowd started to mumble. The girl slowly awoke and gradually remembered dying. She stood up and hugged Yeshua. The crowd was exultant and awed. Her mother hugged Yeshua from behind, crying for his forgiveness. He patted her hand.

News of someone doing miracles in Gennesaret reached Herod. The rumors claimed that it was John the Baptist arisen, or Elijah. The populace somehow knew the two of them were connected. Of course, both of them were Melchizedek. Herod was afraid that if it was John whom he'd ordered beheaded, he might now be in big trouble from this reborn saint and newborn miracle worker.

Yeshua called his apostles together and gave them the power and authority over demons and to cure sicknesses. He also endowed them with the powers to officiate and perform sacred ceremonies such as marriage.

He then asked Peter to marry himself and Mary Magdalene. Peter was flabbergasted as they all were, including Mary.

Yeshua sank down on one knee and took her hand. "Will you marry me, Mary my love?" Unable to speak, she nodded enthusiastically and cried with joy. Yeshua turned and yelled down the hill. "Mother, brothers and sisters, you can join the festivities now!"

The ceremony was done beautifully, right there in Gennesaret, atop a hill, in a clearing under the full moon. The youngest disciple, John, who was about 16, had made a crown of wildflowers for Mary of Magdala. Seeing and taking it from him she kissed him and placed it on her head, whereupon she lit up from inside.

It was a lovely soft night and so after the celebratory supper, the apostles and family left them alone to sleep up there for the night.

When they consummated their marriage, Mary saw The One Self. She knew that this was the Highest God behind and within Nature. She saw that she herself was The One Self, as was Yeshua, and so was everything else, even people who did wrong.

Afterward, as they embraced in the bower of dry leaves and flowers the apostles had created, Mary thought, *You call him Father because it would be hard to explain the real truth.* Yeshua smiled and nodded. *In this part of the multiverse, each being has to discover the real truth independently, by their own exertion,* he pathed.

She hugged him tightly. And then she began to sing him a song:

> Intent on the welfare of the world;
> That, indeed, is your father, lion of men.
> Like the full moon is His face;
> He is dear to gods and men;
> His gait is as graceful as that of an elephant of noble breed;
> That, indeed, is your father, lion of men.
> He is of noble lineage, sprung from the warrior caste;
> His feet have been honored by gods and men;
> His mind is well established in morality and concentration;
> That, indeed, is your father, lion of men.

Yeshua smiled and hugged her. *That was the song you wrote about me to our son Rahula,* he pathed to her, and she nodded vigorously, holding back a tear.

When you were the Buddha, she pathed.

And you were Yasodhara, he replied.

She held him even more tightly. "Can I stay with you always now?" she asked.

"They're going to kill me soon," he said.

She stiffened and held him away to search his face in the bright moonlight.

"No! Why does this have to be so?!"

"I'm forcing their hand," he said.

"But why?! Look at all the good you are doing while alive. You can live almost a hundred more years and help everyone on Earth!"

"It wouldn't get through that way," he said. "What I am telling people is little more than what others have taught before me on this planet, put in my own way, and all of that effort for two thousand centuries has not rid the planet of the Rebels."

The Rebels—? she thought.

"I was the first avatar. Lucifer was the second. The One Self deemed me to be so much like Him that Lucifer was an experiment in differentness. Fourteen billion years ago we three began a war game. Lucifer rebelled and other avatars followed him to the side we call the Rebels. Lucifer, I now finally discover, has been quite insane for some time and doesn't believe that he is The One Self. He's not playing a game. Now calling himself Perse, he is training this planet as warriors to help him take over heaven and the whole multiverse."

"How will your death make things better?"

"The miracles, tribulations, death, and resurrection will be remembered till the end of time. The archetypal story will capture the attention of humanity and draw them inside to make their own discoveries."

How do you know it will work?

The One says that it will.

She was quiet for a time after that. And then she cried.

He had just today proposed. Today was their wedding day. Now he was saying goodbye.

"I must die when you die," she said. "Whither thou goest shall I go."

He shook his head. "Mary, I need you to carry on the work for me."

She looked distraught. He brought her close and very gently kissed away her tears one by one.

"My spirit will never leave you again, I will always be at your side, and we will be in constant conversation like this. Only my body will be out of sight until we can again be in compatible bodies."

As of today, we will be together forever.

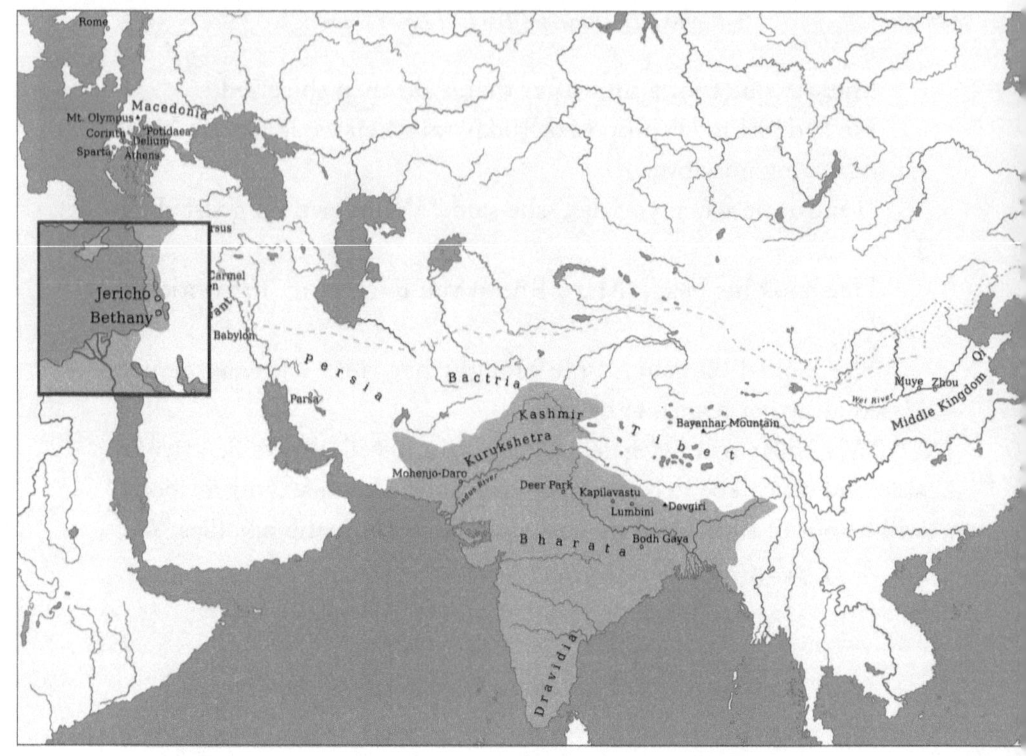

32

REBELS CLOSE IN

27 AD

In the morning he also told the apostles.

After breakfast he said, "The Son of man must undergo many sufferings and be rejected by the older men and chief priests and scribes, and be killed," at this there were loud gasps, "and on the third day be raised up."

Eight days later Peter, John and James were with the couple as Yeshua climbed up into the mountain to pray. After the others had gone to sleep, Yeshua alone was left awake and praying at the summit. Sometime later, something wakened Peter, and what he saw caused him to quietly awaken the others. Without a sound, the three men and Mary looked up at the summit where Yeshua appeared transformed, his face subtly different and all of him a body of light, glittering white.

And he was not alone. There were two other men with him, similarly effulgent. How had they gotten up there without making noise and waking them sooner? Peering carefully, they agreed that one man was Moses, and the other Elijah. The three light beings were conversing mentally with one another. Melchizedek appearing as Elijah fused with John the Baptist, gestured as if he was speaking, but his mouth was not moving, and Yeshua and Moses were nodding. Moses held his staff, now a staff of brilliant light. He handed the staff to Yeshua, and Yeshua changed it into a Roman officer's spear, one made out of light, and handed it back to Moses, who nodded as if agreeing to do something with that spear.

Peter could not contain himself and walked toward the apparition, saying as if drunk or driven temporarily mad, "Instructor, it is fine for us to be here, so let us erect three tents, one for you and one for Moses and one for Elijah."

As he was saying those things, a pink cloud formed and enfolded them so that the humans could not see anything but pink light. Out of the pink cloud came a gentle voice as if from everywhere, "This is my Son, the one that has been chosen. Listen to him." The cloud dispelled as quickly as it had come and now Yeshua was seen to be alone at the Summit, and no longer shining like the sun. His face was also the more familiar face they were used to seeing.

He adjured them to not ask about what they had just witnessed, nor to speak about it to anyone even to each other. "One day understanding of all of this shall come to you on its own," he promised.

Setting his heart upon Jerusalem and the final showdown, he began to head in that direction. Having prayed for right action, out of the thousands that now followed him, he carefully selected seventy-two messengers whom he endowed with the power and authority over demons, in his name, and sent ahead to let Jerusalem know that he was coming. They returned with the good news that they had been able to cure people of demons, and that everyone they had spoken with was happy that Yeshua would soon be coming. Yeshua knew it was far from true that the powerful of Jerusalem were universally happy about his impending arrival.

On the way to Jerusalem Yeshua cured many sick and possessed people, but he overheard some in the crowd that followed him saying, "Yeshua can cast out demons because he is in league with Beelzebub, the ruler of the demons." Yeshua knew that Beelzebub was Perse's chief of staff. Although the name appeared in the Torah a long time ago, it seemed unusual that a human being would be again using that name today, unless the user was himself involved with the Rebels. So Yeshua now felt sure that many of his apparent followers were exactly the opposite, and they would be at his back as he faced his enemies to the front. He and the Agents still had not detected the more than a million invisible demons, many more each day, sucking energies out through loopholes in Yeshua's human brain. The forces acting toward his destruction were in fact growing much larger every day.

Outside of Jerusalem he was invited to dine with Pharisees, and the evening did not go well. It even started badly, when they criticized him for not washing before dinner. Perse gave the order for the demons assigned to Yeshua to put forth all their power at once, and within Yeshua's human brain, the amygdala and hypothalamus were so flooded with energy by the demons that Yeshua departed from his usual kindness and told off the Pharisees bluntly and effectively.

Unfortunately, this went on all night, by which time even some of the moderates who were not guided by Rebels had decided Yeshua was against all Pharisees as a group and meant to expel them from their position of power and authority. They decided then and there to close ranks against him and began a vigorous campaign to alert all Pharisees and Sadducees that either their days were numbered or else Yeshua's must be.

"Woe to *you* who are versed in the Law," he said, thinking of the distortions of the truth that had occurred over the centuries by prideful priests who thought they knew more than they did, who were being whispered to by invisible Rebels, "because you took away the key to knowledge, *you* yourself did not go in, and those going in, *you* hindered." There was a deathly silence during which Yeshua decided he had had enough and so departed.

Perse was delighted with his success. Having accepted and embraced the only possible outcome already, Yeshua was not regretful of having spoken the truth without reservation. The battle lines were now clearly drawn in the desert sand.

Leaving the house of the Pharisees and getting back on the road, the crowd became more densely packed as they got closer to Jerusalem.

Master, your love light did not shine on those lost lambs, you must be tired. Let's escape from this crowd packed with spies and troublemakers and get you some sleep in that human body and brain, which have both been exhausted, Maitreya counseled, while the other Agents held back from teaching the teacher. Melchizedek was now once again traveling with them, having left the beheaded body of the Baptist.

Some of these are my true sheep and need to hear the truth spelled out to them in stories they can understand. There is not much time left for me, and I can't squander it in sleep at their expense, The First Son answered.

Thinking of his own death, which was also getting closer each day, the idea of portable wealth came into his teachings. One man called out to him, "Teacher, tell my brother to divide the inheritance with me." Yeshua cautioned him against covetousness and taught that the only wealth one can bring out of this existence into the next one is the goodness that one has put into oneself, one's own soul. This will be the only thing one can take to the next life.

Through the thick fog created by the undetected millions of demons afflicting his human brain, Yeshua nevertheless sensed that

Perse was nearby, and as they walked toward Jerusalem he decided to tell the crowd a parable designed to reach and soften the heart of Perse. Instantly an opportunity presented itself, as he overhead mutterings of Pharisees about the tax collectors and prostitutes crowding as close to Yeshua as they could get, "This man welcomes sinners…"

"What man of *you* with a hundred sheep, on losing one of them, will not leave the other ninety-nine behind in the wilderness and go for the lost one until he finds it? And when he finds it, he pulls it up on his shoulders and rejoices."

The Agents, thinking of the Lost Lamb Game in which they had become enmeshed and the crowd of sheep and wolves in sheep's clothing following this shepherd, began to see the multitudes as sheep. Unsensed by them, Perse hovering nearby got the allusion but also realized that his brother was talking directly to him, and thus knew he was there.

He's telling me that my supposed father is going to lift me on his shoulders when I surrender—hah! But for a moment he felt how good that release was going to be, before his iron will clamped down and brushed away the feeling as if it had never existed.

Yeshua went on teaching about the reason why he welcomes sinners, next using the metaphor of a lost coin, and then came back to another metaphor that would be especially close to home for Perse.

Yeshua said, "A certain man had two sons, and the younger of them said to his father, 'Father, give me the part of the property that falls to my share…'" Yeshua went on to describe how the father complied, and the younger son took the money and traveled into a distant country where he lived a debauched life and spent all the money, falling into poverty. He found low-paying work as a swineherd and envied the carob pods that were given to the pigs to eat. Coming to his senses, he decided to return to his father's house and throw himself on his father's mercy.

"While he was still a long way off, his father caught sight of him and was moved with pity, and he ran and fell upon his neck and tenderly kissed him. Then the son said to him, 'Father, I have sinned against heaven and against you. I am no longer worthy of being called your son. Make me one of your hired hands.' But the father said to his slaves, 'Quick, bring out a robe, the best one, and clothe him with it, and put a ring on his hand and sandals on his feet. And bring the fattened young bull, slaughter it and let us eat and enjoy ourselves, because this my son was dead and came to life again, and was lost and now is found.'"

What is this—?! Perse realized that his spirit was crying and caught himself. He repressed his hidden longing to go home again so that it entirely disappeared in the persona he had created for himself.

Back on his ship, Perse was dressing down his Generals. "You said you'd be able to suppress his ability to detect me," he said irritably to Beelzebub, and Satan snickered almost inaudibly. They were in the lounge and Beelzebub was floating above in a different outlandish outfit of many colors. Satan wore a signature black suit, this one with a matte finish, and a conservative white shirt and tie with small bejeweled cufflinks.

With a "who me?" look, Beelzebub respectfully responded, "I said we were trying to get there, not that it would necessarily work. Sorry to appear to contradict you, sir."

"Bah!" Perse said, and Satan laughed gaily. "Where did we place the back doors?" They were looking up at a cutaway schematic of Yeshua's human brain on the giant screen.

"The left brain and its connections into the emotional limbic brain," Beelzebub replied. He looked at the screen and made it draw little electric-blue circles around the hypothalamus and the amygdala.

"And when ten million Satans try to pull him into ego, what happens?" Perse demanded.

"We've had a few successes so far as you've seen—" Beelzebub began.

"Too few!" Perse roared. "We're running out of time. They're going to kill him soon before we have a chance to defrock him. So, he'll get to be worshipped anyway, as a martyr—what good will that do us? Get on it! Try something different!" He turned with a hopeless look to Satan. "Any ideas?" Satan made futile gestures.

"As always, I have to do all the thinking! Have you tried the front brain?" Both Beelzebub and Satan stared blankly back at him. "That's the part the backstabber was adding when we interfered," Perse explained. "Try focusing the Satans on the forebrain, see what that does."

"What if we try different combinations of current strategy with that idea?" Beelzebub suggested.

"Sure, sure. Knock yourself out," Perse said, waving dismissively.

After a night in Jericho witnessing the conversion of Zacchaeus, a rich tax collector, into a willing philanthropist, Yeshua and his followers, a sea of people, got on the road again toward Bethany.

Yeshua's invisible and unsuspected robot Satan army was now more than ten million, one for every ten thousand neurons in his human brain, strategically placed to concentrate all their firepower in Broca's area, controlling speech, and in Yeshua's amygdala and hypothalamus, generating wrath. In both of these areas, they aimed to take active control and were increasingly succeeding, as well as in the forebrain, where their fire was now also used suppressively, to minimize reasoning, clarity and forbearance.

For this reason, it became possible for him to dwell on things, a tendency that was not native to his being.

As they walked along and peppered him with questions, and he poured wisdom upon them, the nature of the parables shifted, reflecting whatever it was he had been dwelling upon. Thus, it came to pass that before arriving in Bethany, he told a story whose meaning was taken by all but the poor among them as being a death threat to them if they didn't accept him as their king.

"A certain man of noble birth traveled to a distant land to secure kingly power for himself and then to return," he began, and everyone assumed he was being surprisingly confessive all of a sudden, as if admitting that deep inside him was a germ of wanting kingship. This seemed out of character but the Agents played along with it because they didn't want to risk interrupting him if he knew what he was doing, and they had the utmost faith in him.

"Calling ten slaves of his," Yeshua went on and explained how each slave was given one mina to see how much they could increase that while he was gone. "But his fellow citizens hated him and sent out a body of ambassadors after him, to say 'We do not want *this* to become king over us.'" Yeshua then described how the man had become king and came back to find out how much profit his slaves had made for him. The first one had turned it into ten minas.

"'Well done, good slave! Because in a very small matter you have proved yourself faithful, you now hold authority over ten cities,'" the man said. In Yeshua's story, the next slave had run up the capital to five minas and was given five cities. But the third slave opened his palm to show the original single mina. "'Lord, here is your mina, which I kept laid away in a cloth. You see, I was in fear of you, because you are a harsh man; you take up what you did not deposit and you reap what you did not sow,'" Yeshua recounted the third slave's words.

Yeshua continued, "'Out of your own mouth I judge you, wicked slave. You knew, did you, that I am a harsh man, taking up what I did not deposit and reaping what I did not sow? Hence why is it you did not put my silver money in a bank? Then on my arrival I would have collected it with interest.' With that, he said to those standing by, 'Take the mina from him and give it to him that has the ten minas.' But they said to him, 'Lord, he has ten minas!' I say to *you*," Yeshua went on, still describing what the man in the story said but now sounding also as if speaking for himself, "to everyone that has, more will be given—."

The Agents now knew something had gone wrong, that somehow Perse appeared to have taken over The First Son's human brain.

"—but from the one that does not have, even what he has will be taken away." Yeshua paused for an instant as if realizing that he seemed to be contradicting himself. *Have to clarify that later,* he thought to himself, but went on without missing a beat. "Moreover, these enemies of mine that did not want me to become king over them, bring here and slaughter them before me."

This was a side of Yeshua no one had ever seen before, since they all assumed the story was a thinly-veiled death threat against anyone who would oppose him. Many followers began to quietly express doubts, mostly inwardly. The First Son and the Agents all realized what had happened. The only thing they couldn't understand was how Perse was able to intercede like that.

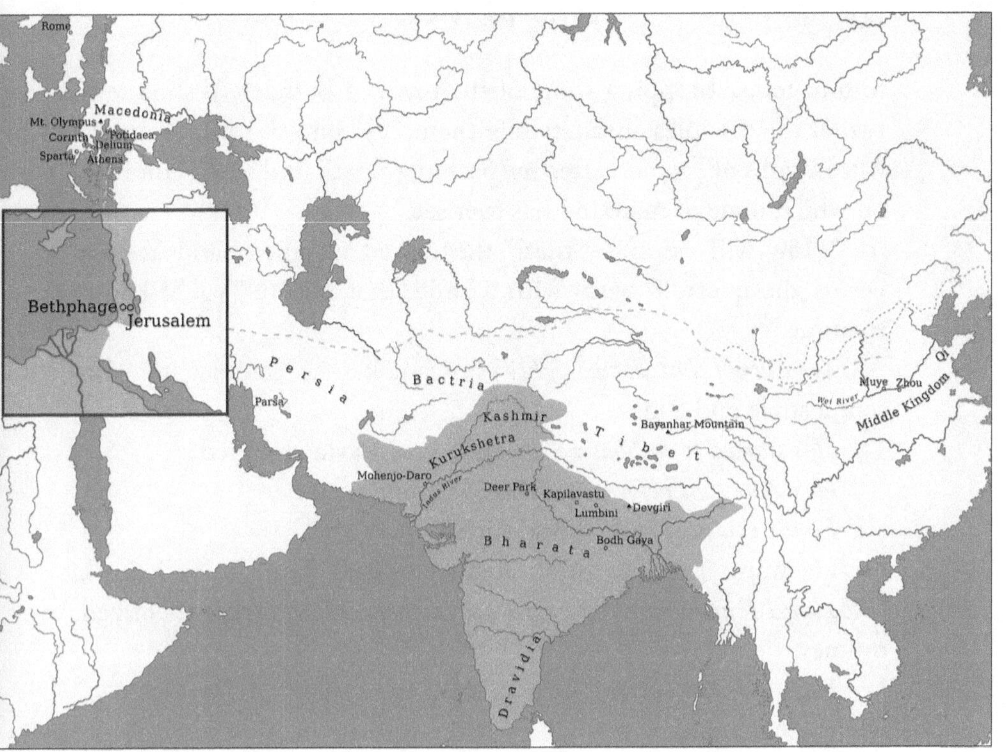

33

INTO THE MOUTH OF THE BEAST
27 AD

The weakness in our plan was sticking with the rules and appearing in a human brain, Templegard pointed out the obvious. The multitudes were moving toward the Mount of Olives.

It must all be done the way The One decreed, The First Son also stated the obvious, and smiled in his mind. He finally had let the human body get some sleep and his mind seemed back to normal to him today. Stopping short of the town of Bethany, Yeshua sent two of the disciples ahead, telling them, "Go into the village that is within sight of *you*, and after *you* pass in, *you* will find in it a colt tied, on which none of mankind has ever sat."

"How will we know that?" they asked in unison and Yeshua waved the question away with a smile that meant, "You'll know, trust me."

You did get that set up, right? Nastassia kidded Templegard, who sent a smile and a kiss.

He's started to emphasize the word 'you', Layla observed.

He's done that before, Melchizedek reminded her.

I hadn't noticed that, she admitted.

He wants them to think about why he's doing it, and think *'Who am I that he says you as if I am important?'* Maitreya theorized or knew.

I always thought you were addressing everyone as The One Self, Melchizedek said.

Yes, to both, and I'm reminding myself that it's ME in there, The First Son said. *I can almost be there for a moment inside the other, looking back at myself and hearing the word* **you** *spoken at me.*

"Loose it and bring it," Yeshua went on instructing the two disciples. "But if anyone asks *you*, 'Why is it you are loosing it?' *you* must answer them in this way, 'The Lord needs it.'" The disciples nodded and departed. Templegard had given that as the passcode.

The disciples wandered into town and followed what seemed to be the same hunches where to turn. There ahead in the yard of a large house with a big lawn, a colt was tied to a tree.

The animal seemed to be luminous, except when you looked directly at him. In fact, none of mankind had ever sat upon him. The colt was Templegard, in his bubble body. They were experimenting with different ways of going forth to see if they could better cope with whatever it was Perse was doing to Yeshua's brain.

Chaim and Miriam, two humans inspired by Agents, came from the house, dressed in fine robes, and Chaim asked with mild concern, "Why are you loosing the colt?" The disciples in unison said, "The Lord needs it," and looked at each other with a glimpse of amusement at speaking the line in unison.

"Let's go, then," Miriam said and, taking the reins in her right hand, led the pony and the three men down toward where the sea of humanity's shore was.

Arriving at the shore and greeting Yeshua with adoration, Chaim and Miriam laid their robes on the horse's back and made as if to help him mount, and he mounted easily onto Templegard's back. Yeshua scratched the colt's right ear, which Templegard realized had been itching, and the colt made a grateful sound. They set off through the towns of Bethany and Bethphage on their way into Jerusalem. The sea of people following Yeshua and preceding him met another sea of people coming from Jerusalem to be among the first greeters.

As soon as he got near the road down the Mount of Olives, both seas of people began to sing and rejoice and praise God, and many musicians in the crowd being to play their instruments—shofars, trumpets, drums, stringed instruments, flutes, and tambourines among them. Unusual cloud formations began to appear in the cobalt sky, and the sun scattered rays through the clouds. Hordes of birds wheeled in the skies, calling loudly.

People from the crowd ran out in front of the approaching parade and flung their robes on the ground as a carpet, expecting never to be able to find or use them again. Children ran everywhere through the legs of adults, and dogs wagged their tails.

One booming-voiced man in the entering sea near Yeshua sang out as a mantra, "Blessed is the One coming as the King in Jehovah's name! Peace in Heaven, and glory in the highest!" and the crowd picked this up and went on, in call and respond fashion.

This mantra particularly offended the Pharisees, and one of them said to Yeshua, "Teacher, rebuke your disciples."

"I tell *you*, if they remained silent, the stones would cry out," Yeshua told him.

A spiritual forcefield had formed, indicating the number of minds across the multiverse that were paying attention to this *now* had reached a high number.

Even the Pharisees were half-convinced that perhaps the stones indeed would sing, if this man were the real thing. No one had ever done so many miracles with so many witnesses.

This could be the real thing.

Certainly no one has ever seen a day or a scene like this one.

Not many men, even rich ones, could pull off a stunt like this.

And when he got near the Temple at Jerusalem he stopped and looked it over. The hordes washed back and forth like outflowing oceans that have collided.

Blinking back tears, he was remembering what he had seen, what was to become of this Temple later as a result of this wrong turn the Human race was taking, misled by the surreptitious slave-traders among them.

He spoke to the Temple, raising his hand to it. "If you," his voice broke, "even you, had discerned in this day the things having to do with peace—but now they have been hid from your eyes." His voice cracked as did the dam, and he let himself cry.

"Because the days will come upon you when your enemies will build around you a fortification with pointed stakes and will encircle you and distress you from every side, and they will dash you and your children within you to the ground." He sat down.

"And they will not leave a stone upon stone in you, because you did not discern the time of your being inspected."

Taking the first steps within the Temple, he appeared to fly into a rage at first sight of those selling things at little stalls they had set up, and he threw down their stands and ordered them to leave the Temple. Seeing his army of followers, there was little resistance.

Chief, you were overacting a little, Maitreya reported bluntly, acting on orders. *You accidentally hurt that man.*

Thanks! The First Son said immediately, grateful for an early indicator of Perse's mental interference and healing the man's minor injury.

Among the humans in local power, given the size of the crowd and the tinderbox nature of the Roman occupation, no one wanted to give the order to break it up, for it could go in too many different directions.

The Rebels wanted to egg the situation on and rile it up but were confident of getting the outcome they wanted even if they did nothing. This Lamb was cheerfully leading the way to its own slaughter. They watched for opportunities to humiliate Yeshua. They wanted the whole crowd to hate him for as long as they would remember him, which would hopefully be for a very short time.

Yeshua found a good place in the Temple where they would interfere the least with normal Temple operations, but that would be their space where they would teach every day from dawn into the evening. His strategy was to stay there and do as much good as possible before the end.

On the first morning a young boy asked Yeshua, "What is God?"

"God is a spirit," Yeshua said.

"What is a spirit?" the boy asked.

"A spirit is a being, capable of having memory of self, of experiencing sensations, feelings, thoughts and hunches, and what appears to be an outside world," Yeshua said, "and able to act with free will in that apparent outside world."

"Then I too am a spirit," the boy concluded happily.

"Yes, you are," Yeshua said, "and a wise one."

"Then what is this body of mine?" the boy asked. The boy was an asleep Agent.

"That's part of the nature of this apparent outside world," Yeshua said. "All of nature works automatically, it is a level of spirit that does not have free will but is happy just doing what it does."

"Then my spirit *inhabits* this body?" the boy asked.

"For now," Yeshua agreed. "But *you* will continue to have experiences after *you* no longer inhabit a body."

"How many of us spirits are there?" the boy asked.

"GOD is the One spirit in each of us."

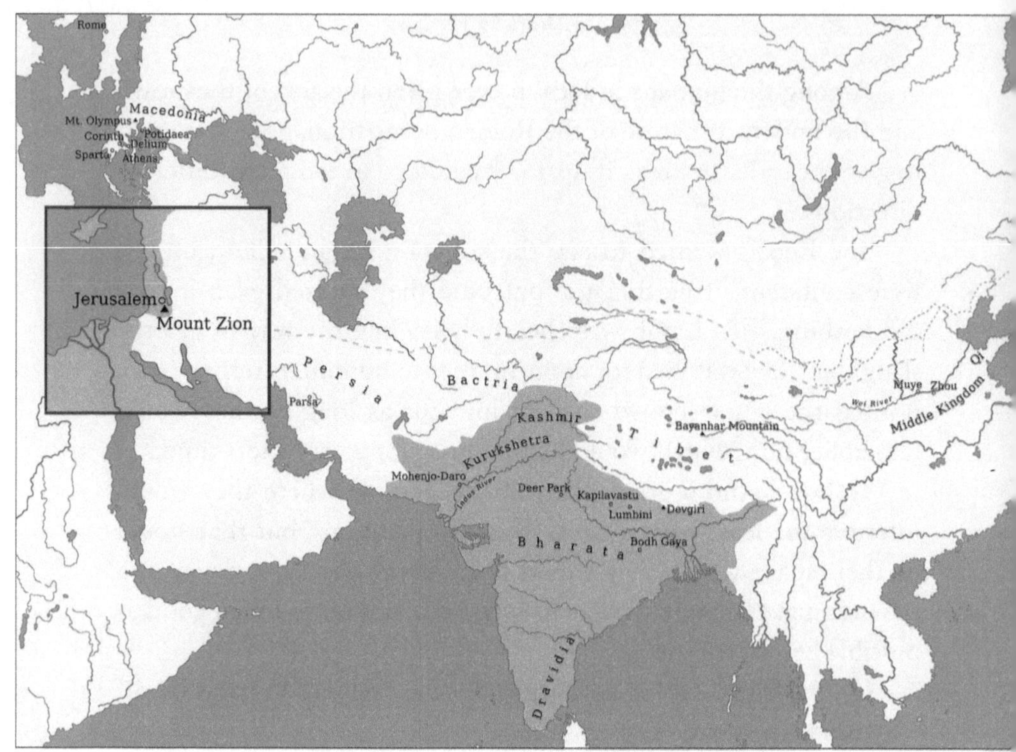

34

SHOWDOWN

27 AD

Yeshua and the Agents were not surprised, on the third day of
teaching in the Temple, when the chief priests and their young
scribes came to the area in which Yeshua had planted himself and
interrupted his teaching.

"Tell us by what authority you do these things, or who is it
that gave you this authority?!" boomed Caiaphas, the chief priest

and head of the Sadducees. His father-in-law, "old Annas" as he was called, who had been the former chief priest and still held the honorary title along with his son-in-law, stood behind him as if for protection and simply shouted, "Yes, tell us!"

Yeshua saw that Caiaphas was an awake Rebel and they regarded each other carefully. Yeshua smiled gently, holding no malice against anyone. Here was the one human in the room who knew what was really going on, and that Perse was behind it all. Caiaphas sensed Yeshua reading his mind but did not know what he found. Yeshua smiled more broadly learning that Caiaphas had already started the plot to kill Yeshua with a prophecy of his own, that Yeshua would die for the nation, and in order to gather the children of God together. For a moment Yeshua delighted in the perfection: he and the supposed enemy were acting as if by prior agreement, both to achieve the same outcome, all the way through to the gathering of the flock in Yeshua's name that would occur in the thousands of years to follow.

Yeshua was not surprised at this. Naturally the Rebels would want to contaminate and take control of whatever Yeshua's following would become. They wanted there to be such a following so that they could use it for their own purposes. He had not seen that coming but it made perfect sense to him.

"I will also ask *you* a question, and *you* tell me: was the baptism of John from heaven or from men?" Yeshua replied.

Caiaphas turned his back haughtily on Yeshua and conferred in low voices in a huddle with his men. "If we say 'From heaven,'" Caiaphas's scribe Azazel, an asleep Rebel, whispered, "he will say 'Why is it *you* did not believe him?' But if we say 'From men,' the people one and all will stone us, for they are persuaded that John is a prophet."

Caiaphas turned back to Yeshua. "We do not know the source."

"Neither am I telling *you* by what authority I do these things," Yeshua replied amiably. He implied by his manner that they were all avoiding a violent scene just before Passover festival, and were both taking the same dodge, as if by gentleman's agreement.

"A man planted a vineyard, and let it out to cultivators," Yeshua began, and told a story of how when the man sent back his people to get some of his own wine, the cultivators beat up the emissaries and sent them back empty handed. After a couple of times repeating this, the man sent his beloved son, whom the cultivators killed, seeking to somehow gain his inheritance. "What, then, will the owner of the vineyard do to them? He will come and destroy these cultivators and give the charge of the vineyard to others."

"Never may that happen," old Annas blurted, caught up in the story and seeing himself and his colleagues as the ones killing the emissaries of the real owner of the universe. Caiaphas looked at him in disgust for an instant and then quickly covered over his expression.

"What, then, does this that is written mean," Yeshua asked rhetorically, referring to the words of Isaiah, "'The stone which the builders rejected, this has become the chief cornerstone.'"

Caiaphas and the other chief priests were incensed and frustrated that he was showing them up in front of a huge crowd of people. They wanted to grab and kill him right there, but that would start a riot and they themselves could die in it, so they backed off without any further words.

Shortly thereafter men began to quietly insinuate themselves in the crowd, men who had been sent to pretend to be followers but to ask trick questions designed to disgrace Yeshua. One of these worked his way inconspicuously toward the front, and when he got there, he called out a question.

"Teacher, we know that you speak and teach correctly and show no partiality, but you teach the way of God in line with truth. Is it lawful for us to pay tax to Caesar or not?"

"Show me a denarius," Yeshua said. The man pulled one out and held it up for Yeshua to see. Yeshua knew quite well what was on it so he did not ever pretend to peer at it. "Whose image and inscription does it have?"

"Caesar's," many people said at once.

"By all means, then, pay back Caesar's things to Caesar, but God's things to God," Yeshua said.

Some well-known Sadducees had also worked their way to the front of the crowd, and Yeshua reading their minds saw that they were going to try to trip him up over resurrection, which they rejected, believing there were no written statements in scripture about life after death. "Teacher, Moses wrote us, 'If a man's brother dies having a wife'", the ringleader began, and went on to describe how written law indicates that the living brother should add the widow as his wife and cited a case where seven brothers had the same wife in sequence due to the timing of their deaths, and then the wife died. "Consequently, in the resurrection," he said the word as if it were a joke, "of which one of them does she become the wife?" The man, an asleep Rebel, then leered at Yeshua.

"The children of *this* system of things," Yeshua began, with a wave of his arm indicating the visible world, "marry and are given in marriage, but those who have been counted worthy of gaining *that* system of things," he pointed upward, "and the resurrection from the dead, neither marry nor are given in marriage. In fact, neither can they die anymore, for they are like the angels, and they are God's children by being children of the resurrection."

They will be left thinking that they have to be worthy of surviving death, though everyone does, Layla mused.

For right now they need a little extra impetus to be good. Later we can tell them the REALLY good news, Yeshua responded.

"But that the dead are raised up," Yeshua went on, "even Moses disclosed, in the account about the thorn bush, when he calls Jehovah the God of Abraham and the God of Isaac and God of Jacob. He is a God, not of the dead, but of the living, for they are all living to him."

The Sadducees sneered that Yeshua was following the Pharisee Hillel's seven ways of deducing the real meaning of the scriptures, which they did not fully comprehend and so rejected as not having been in written scripture. But they knew they could not out-argue him and would be humiliated in front of the large crowd so they kept silent, except one young scribe, who would later regret it, blurted, "Teacher, you spoke well." The ringleader led away his entourage.

Yeshua took a drink of water and turned to his disciples, saying in a normal voice so that it could be heard by all the people, "Look out for the priests and scribes who dress up in finery, and seek to be recognized and greeted, who take front seats and the most prominent places at meals, and who devour the houses of widows, and for a pretext make long prayers. These will receive a heavier judgment." Thus, he described the telltale signs of one who is bound in the ego, the robotic part of the human brain, whose spirit is asleep within. Whether Rebels themselves or merely a pawn of Rebels, the disciples would need to know to look out for that type.

Yeshua looked up and saw that in appreciation of the words he had just been speaking, people were putting money into the donations box. He saw rich people putting in large sums and a needy widow putting in two very small coins.

"I tell you truthfully," Yeshua said, reading the minds of the donors, "this widow, although poor, dropped in more than they all did. For all these dropped in gifts out of their surplus, but this woman out of her want dropped in all of the means of living she had."

Waiting for questions, Yeshua sat and meditated. Many in the audience emulated him. Others continued to speak. This went on for a little while. One man was moved in the relative silence to share his great fondness for the Temple, calling out the adornments and relics and encrusted gems he particularly loved, all in view.

Without at first opening his eyes Yeshua said, "As for these things that you are beholding, the days will come in which not a stone upon a stone will be left here and will not be thrown down."

"Teacher, when will these things actually be," one of Caiaphas's spies asked, "and what will be the sign when these things are destined to occur?"

"Look out that *you* are not misled," he told them all, "for many will come on the basis of my name, saying, 'I am he,' and 'the due time has approached.' Do not follow them. Furthermore, when you hear of wars and disorders, do not be terrified. For these things must occur first, the end does not occur immediately."

He stood up. "Nation will rise against nation, and kingdom against kingdom, and there will be great earthquakes, and in one place after another pestilences and food shortages, and there will be fearful sights and from heaven great signs." In his mind he could see the space battles, the biowarfare, and the ongoing wars on the surface, which were going to continue to escalate unthinkably. But his focus right then was to give them the information they would need as his disciples and followers, for their own good.

"But before all these things, people will lay their hands upon *you* and persecute *you*, delivering you up to the synagogues for trials and to prisons, *you* being hauled up before kings and governors for the sake of my name. Moreover, *you* will be delivered up even by parents and brothers and relatives and friends, and they will put some of *you* to death, and *you* will be objects of hatred by all people because of my name. And yet not a hair on your heads will by any means perish. By endurance on *your* part, *you* will acquire your souls."

He was speaking in their vernacular, as the idea that a soul was sort of a boat you needed to get over to the other side had been a popular superstition for millennia. He did not want to have to go up against every superstition in the short time he had to make a difference.

"Furthermore, when *you* see Jerusalem surrounded by encamped armies, then know that the desolating of her has drawn near. Then let those in Judea begin fleeing to the mountains," he said, answering the spy's question.

He went on to predict the diaspora of the Jews into all the nations, and his own return on a cloud. The Agents assumed that he meant in a few days when he would reappear after his human death. Many in the crowd, however, had the impression that he was talking about a long time in the future.

"Heaven and Earth will pass away," he said, looking very far into the future when the multiverse would collapse back into a single point and go dark, in the endless cycle of multiverse rebirth, The One Self's version of breathing out and in, and HisHer mode of sleeping, "but my words will by no means pass away," meaning that the truth is the same across all multiverses and always will be.

"But pay attention to yourselves that *your* hearts will never become weighted down with overeating and heavy drinking and anxieties of life, and suddenly that day will be instantly upon you as a snare. For it will come upon all those dwelling upon the face of all the Earth. Keep awake, then, all the time making supplication that *you* may succeed in escaping all these things that are destined to occur, and in standing before the Son of man."

Each night they spent in the garden at Gethsemane, a garden of olive trees and other greenery and flowers in the foothills of Mount Olive. Yeshua each night went off by himself to pray.

Perse was testy that Yeshua was retaining the upper hand and staying cool under pressure. He felt it was time for the axe to fall; he could not stand his rival's heroic stance one minute longer. As he had planned all along, he sent a Satan robot into Judas Iscariot, the asleep Rebel that Yeshua had handpicked himself to be the pipeline for disinformation back to the Rebels.

The AI Satan made short work of Judas, who was a man eternally at war with himself, able to believe anything and its opposite from one moment to the next. Judas went to the priests and was led one by one all the way up to Caiaphas, who was delighted at this shortening of the path, and gave him silver money to locate Yeshua for them as soon as possible, at a time when no crowds were nearby to observe.

"You're certain that this is also what Yeshua wants of me," Judas asked Caiaphas.

"You yourself told me that he foretold his death is coming soon. Do you observe him resisting that outcome, or embracing it? I have prophesied that it is his destiny, and he *knows* that it is. It will bring the Children of God together. Nothing else will succeed in uniting Israel," Caiaphas answered.

Judas Iscariot's eyes glowed with his own central importance in the carrying out of prophecy.

Passover at last arrived, the day of the unfermented cakes, and Yeshua dispatched Peter and John to arrange for the special dinner. "When *you* enter into the city a man carrying an earthenware vessel of water will meet *you*. Follow him into the house in which he enters. And you must say to the landlord of the house, 'The Teacher asks of you, *where is the guest room in which I may eat the Passover with my disciples?*'"

The house where the water bearer led Peter and John turned out to be at the top of Mount Zion, not far from the Temple.

Later when they gathered there, before taking their repose he washed each of their feet, which he had never done before. This was his way of giving them the thanks they deserved for becoming his chief followers and accepting the hardships to come of being his disciples.

They gathered around the table for what Yeshua knew was their last supper together, he and the twelve men and Mary Magdalene, who sat on his right closest to him. He kissed Mary tenderly but chastely before he began to speak to them. No one but the couple knew that Mary was pregnant.

"I have greatly desired to eat this Passover with *you* before I suffer; for I tell *you* I will not eat it again until it becomes fulfilled in the kingdom of God." Mary poured a glass of red wine and handed it to him. He accepted it gratefully, gave thanks above, sipped, and passed it to his left. "Pass this from one to the next and each take a sip. That's enough wine for me until the kingdom of God arrives."

Taking a loaf of bread, he broke it, and took the smallest piece and ate it, and passed the loaf to the right around the round table, saying, "This symbolizes my body, which is to be given in *your* behalf. Keep doing this in remembrance of me." Then they set to a wonderful evening meal, with people speaking mostly to those at their sides.

At the end of the meal he poured wine for his disciples but did not drink it, passing it around again for each to sip from his cup, saying, "This cup means the new covenant by virtue of my blood, which is to be poured out in *your* behalf." As this heartfelt ritual concluded, he said, "But look! The hand of my betrayer is with me at the table. Because the Son of man is going his way by what has been marked out, all the same, woe to that man through whom he is betrayed!"

This caused much stir and consternation as they all wondered which man there was going to turn out to be the one to betray him. They didn't know that he meant an intended betrayal, for they assumed he meant an accidental betrayal that could befall any of them.

From the enormous sorrow the disciples felt, mixed with a sense of being so blessed to be part of a very important event on behalf of God, a surfeit of wine, and it being midnight, the conversation turned to which of them would rise to the highest power among them when Yeshua was no longer with them. But Yeshua steered them back in the right direction.

"The kings of nations lord it over them, and those having authority over *them* are called Benefactors. *You*, though, are not to be that way. But let him that is the greatest among *you* become as the youngest, and the one ministering to the needs of the others. For which one is greater, the one reclining at the table or the one ministering? I am in your midst as the one ministering."

With some cheeks flushing with shame at having gotten carried away with their egos, right in front of the Teacher at what could be the last supper, the men returned to their senses. They did not know it, but each of them was being bombarded by hundreds of thousands of robot Satans, as artillery fire had just started in advance of the arrest and execution. Yeshua's personal contingent was in the millions, plus Perse himself, and each Agent was also being assailed by over a million AI Satans.

Having a human brain, Yeshua was not as able as the Agents to put up with the barrage. Nevertheless, he did not show any signs of changing, until he made a remark about getting a deal with God for a kingdom, the same sort of odd remark he had made once before under similar circumstances.

"However, *you* are the ones who have stuck with me in my trials, and I make a covenant with *you*, just as my Father has made a covenant with me, for a kingdom, that you may eat and drink with me in my kingdom and sit on thrones to judge the twelve tribes of Israel." This last bit confused them—was he talking about on Earth or in Heaven? He usually spoke so as to leave no doubt of meaning.

He seemed to be fluctuating between moods as he detected something going wrong in his brain and sought to pull himself out of it, resulting in a trancelike state for a moment in which he beheld something like Satan behind a veil. Then he had a precognitive vision, and said to his favorite disciple, Simon Peter, "Simon, Simon, look! Satan has demanded to have *you* men to sift you as wheat. But I have made supplication for you that your faith may not give out; and you, when once you have returned, strengthen your brothers." His meaning was that Satanic forces were being beamed upon them at that table, and they should all bring each other back at times like those.

Simon Peter replied, not understanding, "Lord, I am ready to go with you both into prison and into death."

Yeshua smiled gently, seeing that Peter did not understand, and based on his precognition teased the disciple by saying, "I tell you, Peter, a cock will not crow today until you have three times denied knowing me." Peter was stunned and could not believe what he heard but automatically assumed it must be true coming from the Teacher. He was horrified and mortified. Perhaps that meant that he Peter was to be the betrayer! But no that could not be, Yeshua would never have been so cruel even to his betrayer to have had such a nice smile on his face while saying such words, if they were tied to his betrayal. *It must be something else,* he thought wisely.

"When I sent *you* forth without purse and food pouch and sandals, *you* did not want for anything, did *you*?" he asked, and they all said "No!"

"But now let the one who has a purse take it up, likewise also a food pouch; and let the one having no sword sell his outer garment and buy one. For I tell you that what is written must be accomplished in me, namely 'And he was reckoned with lawless ones,'" Yeshua said, quoting Isaiah again, and remembering all of the hundreds of passages in law that would be made true by him in the next few days. "For what concerns me is having an accomplishment."

"Here, Teacher!" Two of the men showed that they had swords. He nodded his thanks but did not touch the swords himself. "It is enough," he said, meaning the two swords.

He then went out to the garden to pray and bade his disciples and Mary Magdalene to stay at a certain spot, saying "Carry on in prayer, that you do not enter into temptation," thinking of Perse and the other Rebels that were probably attacking them all at the moment. And he himself went on another stone's throw before sinking to his knees and praying to the night sky. The five Agents were standing on a cloud before his gaze, and he could see that Templegard held Moses' staff, the one that The First Son had changed.

"Father," Yeshua said, "if you wish, remove this cup from me. Nevertheless, let not my will, but yours, take place." Then he saw a sign, the flashing of Moses' staff, which told him that the action would go forward as planned, and he accepted it. Then it occurred to him to wonder at his own weakness and cowardice at the end, of having even brought up the subject of aborting the plan. He couldn't believe he had been so weak, and accepted the full blame for it himself, not crediting the Perse bombardment. He slipped into a vulnerable brain state, and Perse and the Satans poured on the heat.

Yeshua began to feel that he was sweating and chilled at the same time and wondered if this human body was having a heart attack. He hallucinated that he was sweating blood. Rising from prayer steadfast in his determination but hounded by thoughts not his own, slipped through disguised as his own, he walked back to find that the disciples had all fallen asleep, some still in attitudes of prayer. To be sure, the AI Satans had taken away all their mental stamina.

"Why are you sleeping?" he woke them gently, his loving smile beaming down upon them, "Rise and carry on prayer, that *you* do not enter into temptation. Know that I am now praying continuously for the future of this world and will continue up to the moment of my death."

Agony in the Garden, Andrea Mantegna

But before they could return to prayer, a crowd of Pharisees with their strongest slaves with clubs, and a contingent of Roman soldiers with swords entered the clearing from the woods, led by Judas. With a weird smile on his face, as if he were doing what the Master had asked, Judas approached Yeshua to kiss him.

But Yeshua stopped him from kissing him by saying, "Judas, do you betray the Son of man with a kiss?"

"Lord, shall we strike him with the sword?" James, Yeshua's brother asked, but even before Yeshua could respond, Simon Peter swung his sword and clipped off the right ear of Malchus, Caia-phas' slave who was reaching for Yeshua. Malchus leaped backward clutching his bleeding ear stump and grimacing awfully, making a rumbling incoherent sound, glaring with fear and menace at Simon Peter.

"Let it go as far as this," Yeshua said, and picked up the ear and replaced it on Malchus, who was astounded that the blood all over his robe had disappeared and the ear felt no pain. He kept feeling for a seam but the ear was as it had always been.

"Did *you* come out with swords and clubs as against a rob-ber? When I was with you in the Temple day after day you did not stretch out *your* hands against me. But this is *your* hour and the authority of darkness." Indeed, The First Son saw Perse hovering invisibly nearby, grinning broadly.

Having calmed his own followers to not resist, Yeshua allowed himself to be arrested and brought to Caiaphas's house, into the large courtyard where a fire was lit. The all-male contingent that had arrested Yeshua in the Garden of Gethsemane was now mixed with other house servants and slaves, many of them female, kept awake through the night to serve during the overnight vigil.

Simon Peter surreptitiously followed the captors in the dark and slipped into the courtyard with them, staying in the shadows away from the fire, trying to look inconspicuous.

Very quickly he was spotted by a sharp-eyed servant girl who announced, "This man also was with him." This was heard by a few men standing nearby.

"I do not know him, woman," Simon Peter brushed it off trying to seem unconcerned with the accusation, but his right hand rested casually on his sword hilt. The girl shook her head and looked at the men around her but they ignored the situation and kept watching Yeshua and the scene that was evolving, where the crowd was taunt-ing Yeshua.

A few minutes later someone who had seen him with Yeshua many times pointed at him in surprise and exclaimed, "You are also one of them." A few heads turned from the riveting scene of Yeshua now being beaten but did not pay much attention.

"Man, I am not," Simon Peter said to the man with seeming sincerity. The man let it drop but moved away. Simon Peter wondered if he was going to get a Roman officer to come and arrest him, so he slipped away to another place.

Meanwhile his insides roiled as he wanted to rush up to the improvised stage and rescue Yeshua, which he knew was not what Yeshua wanted him to do. He had to watch as they made fun of Yeshua and were now beating him.

A slave threw a cloak over Yeshua's head and then several other slaves punched Yeshua's face and head through the cloak.

"Prophesy. Who is it that struck you?" Caiaphas asked Yeshua, and the crowd laughed gaily.

Suddenly a man appeared standing over Simon Peter, looking down at him with assurance and said, "For a certainty this man also was with him, for, in fact, he is a Galilean!"

Simon Peter stayed seated and looking up benignly, responded, "Man, I don't know what you are saying."

Instantly there came the loud sound of a cock crowing to proclaim the approach of dawn. It came back to him what Yeshua had prophesied at the supper, that he would deny him thrice before the cock crowed. Filled with self-loathing he stood up and, ignoring the man, left the courtyard and went out into the last of the night, beating himself up inside.

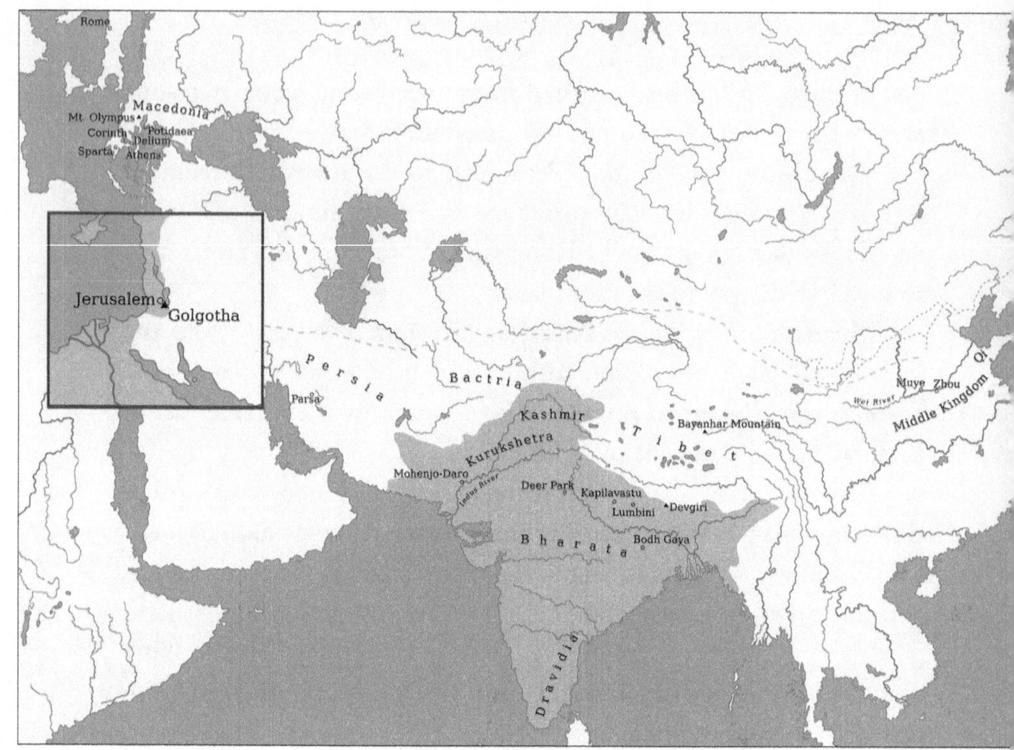

35

THE ETERNAL EVENT

27 AD

Peter you did right, you were a perfect spy. This is what I wanted from you under the circumstances. You will need these talents for the rest of your life; do not despair of your actions. He heard this in his mind and knew that it came from Yeshua and his heart was lightened.

The dawn rose and the crowd, following the orders of Caiaphas, dragged Yeshua off to the Temple, which would now be open, and to the Hall of Hewn Stones, where the Sanhedrin would be beginning its daily meeting. Seeing Caiaphas followed by men pushing Yeshua, the other senior Pharisees and Sadducees, wide-eyed, stepped aside and acquiesced to Caiaphas taking over the meeting.

As people began finding places to sit on the stairs and the regular members took their seats, Yeshua was placed in the position of the accused, directly in front of the throne-like seat of Caiaphas. The crowd having settled became quiet and Caiaphas then boomed out, "If you are the Christ, tell us."

"Even if I told *you*," Yeshua responded, "*you* would not believe it at all. Moreover, if I questioned *you*, *you* would not answer at all. However, from now on, the Son of man will be sitting at the powerful right hand of God."

Many chorused at once, almost in unison, "Are you, therefore, the Son of God?" or words to that effect.

"You yourself are saying that I am," he replied.

Caiaphas screamed as he stood up and tore his robe. "He has spoken blasphemy! What further need have we of witnesses? Behold, now your own ears have heard his blasphemy out of his own mouth!" He looked around at the members and saw no one disputing him.

The entire group stood up, one following the other, and led Yeshua off to the Roman Prefect Pontius Pilate, who was an asleep Agent with a conscience, trying to govern Judea with impartiality and justice. He had been aware of Yeshua's activities but not aware that Yeshua had committed any crime, he explained to the mob. People called out various accusations.

"He has been subverting our nation!"

"He was forbidding the payment of taxes to Caesar!" yelled an awake Rebel.

"He's saying he is himself Christ a king!"

Pilate turned to Yeshua, noting the many contusions on his face that Yeshua had left on himself, and asked, "Are you the king of the Jews?"

"You yourself are saying it," Yeshua replied.

"I find no crime in this man," Pilate announced to the crowd after thinking for a minute. But the mob wouldn't accept that and started yelling additional accusations, one of which caught Pilate's attention.

"He stirs up the people by teaching throughout Judea, starting out from Galilee to here!"

"Is he a Galilean then?" Pilate asked and the crowd roared "Yes!" as if being a Galilean itself was a crime.

Suppressing a smirk, Pilate said "Well, take him to Herod for judgment then, that's his jurisdiction."

Herod had been spending his time in Jerusalem and so they hustled the prisoner over to where Herod was holding court in a palatial mansion not far from the Temple. Herod was delighted to see Yeshua and hopeful of seeing a miracle. He missed John the Baptist and hated having him beheaded just to please his sexy step-daughter. He hoped that Yeshua would be as entertaining as John, who had made him think, and he had always liked thinking because that always led to having ideas, and ideas had helped him step up to higher and higher power. Most of those ideas involved someone else's death.

"Please sit here, Yeshua," Herod said, showing the man kindness by offering him the second-best seat in the house. Yeshua remained standing, however, and acted as if he was not hearing the voice of Herod. Seemingly not noticing, Herod talked to Yeshua as if expecting to have a conversation and started out by dominating it with a stream of consciousness mostly about himself and his accomplishments, rationalizations and lies as if covering up his own role in John's death, his plans for developing the country and his love for his fellow Jews. The subjects roamed to relationships with other countries, his own Jewishness, the challenges of being in his own position, his love of God and Torah, the beauty of the Temple…

"Yeshua, you know me to be a devout Jew and the primary defender of Jews across the empire. Everything I've accomplished in Rome and Egypt, and here in Judea, has been for the good of our people. Although my hand was forced by my step-daughter,

Salome, to behead John the Baptist, I myself loved him. In my position I'm forced to often do things for the general good that I do not want to do." Herod ran on and on.

The mob was waiting for Herod to start questioning the prisoner but too afraid of Herod to make a sound. It seemed bizarre that Herod was almost acting as if he himself believed or knew Yeshua to be the Son of God and was somehow trying to make a confession to him as if begging for forgiveness, although Herod's tone was self-congratulatory and hearty as if enjoying a party.

He would get you off if you'd only play along with him a little bit. It isn't like you to ignore people. How uncompassionate!

Yeshua heard this chiding from Perse, floating in the cupola overhead, but seemed to be oblivious to it. Actually, The First Son was avoiding giving any clue as to his real intentions, certain that Perse would change his own plans—save Yeshua himself—in an instant just to foil The First Son's plans. He didn't want Perse interfering with what was about to happen, what had to happen to fulfil scripture.

Eventually Herod tired of hearing himself talk and when his questions went unanswered he signaled his guards to come over. "Here, take this man back to Pilate for judgment. First dress him up in the best robes we can spare to befit the king of the Jews. Tell Pilate I find no fault in this man, other than that the beating someone has been giving him seems to have addled his brains and he is unable to put words together now."

Yeshua was dressed in a kingly purplish red velvet robe and marched back to Pilate, who was impatient at being bothered again with the efforts to manipulate him into a trumped-up lynching of an innocent man. He pointed out that Herod had not found any guilt in Yeshua. He offered to let one prisoner go as a gift to the Jews for being good, thinking they would pick Yeshua, but they cried out to release the Zealot Barabbas. Three more times he refused but then the mob started to really get out of hand and there would soon be a riot if he didn't give in.

"Impale! Impale him!"

"So be it!" Pilate bellowed and the crowd became less menacing. Pilate conferred with his men, who then stripped Yeshua of his king's costume, dragged him outside, beat him, stomped him, flogged him, all to the cheering of the crowd. As a final touch they put a crown of thorns on his head and, holding him up, with great ceremony, put back on the king's robe. Then they dragged him off toward Golgotha.

Around the lynch mob led by Sadducees and Pharisees and their slaves, a much larger, more peaceful ocean of people formed. These were Yeshua's followers, many of them women, beating themselves in grief and wailing. One of these followers was a strong-looking Cyrene man named Simon, whom the Roman soldiers grabbed and assigned the carrying of the cross.

A wide-eyed little boy noticed that Yeshua, whom he had personally seen performing many miracles, was now unable to carry his own cross. *How could this be?* In fact, at this point, Yeshua was bent over, half-standing and just barely able to walk. As Yeshua's face went by very close to the boy's, Yeshua winked at him.

He's doing this on purpose, the boy realized.

Arriving at Golgotha, Yeshua looked up to see the erecting of his crucifix and behind it a strangely baleful orange sky. He was then pulled forward and shown the sign at the top, which read, "This is the king of the Jews". Using ropes and pulley they hung him up and then using ladders they nailed him in place.

The Agents could tell that The First Son was not blocking the pain from his human body but merely tolerating it by means of self-discipline, feeling it in the same way a human would and controlling his reactions the way some humans could, those that had trained for it by yogic practices. Yeshua showed no sign when the spikes went in. Some of the Roman soldiers below now looked up with respect.

"Father," he said aloud, "forgive them, for they know not what they are doing."

Two criminals were hung up on his left and right. He looked at them with compassion. Looking down, he saw men casting lots to determine who would get his robe and other garments. There below were his two Marys, his wife and his mother, his disciples, brothers and sisters and other relatives, a sea of followers extending to the horizons. A huge bass drum was being beaten. Sparse clouds floated by in the odd sky through which crows flew.

Court nobles standing below him said one to the other, "Others he saved; let him save himself if this one is the Christ of God, the Chosen One."

"How are you, Teacher?" Longinus asked.

"I am good, Longinus, and you?" Yeshua responded, licking his lips.

"I've seen happier days," Longinus said. "You keep licking your lips, Teacher, are you thirsty?"

Yes, thank you." Longinus looked at his men meaningfully and they got it that they were to bring some water.

Two Roman soldiers who seemed a bit drunk themselves brought him a cup of soured wine to drink but were chased away by the Centurion Longinus with a swing of his spear. A moment later, actual water arrived and Longinus helped Yeshua drink it.

The criminal on his right began in an abusive tone to speak to him and he turned to listen.

"You are the Christ, are you not? Save yourself and us."

The other criminal said to the first one, "Do you not fear God at all, now that you are in the same judgment? And we indeed, justly so, for we are receiving in full measure what we deserve for things we did; but this man did nothing out of the way."

Turning his eyes to Yeshua he went on, "Yeshua, remember me when you get into your kingdom."

"Truly I tell *you* today, *you* will be with me in Paradise," Yeshua said.

That's when Perse released his strongest mindblast at Yeshua, which was the signal for all hundred million robot Satans to attack Yeshua and the Agents.

All of them were instantly paralyzed by the force of the clamp-down on their consciousness. Being in a human brain, Yeshua was the most afflicted, but this was more than made up for by his superior power over the Agents. The Agents were totally unconscious. The First Son retained consciousness but barely and could not do anything.

Perse, invisible to everyone else, brought his face up very close to Yeshua's and smiled with great satisfaction. He had never had his brother in this position before. He would have to give great rewards to the inventors of the robot Satans, for he could never have achieved this without them, and without having caught his brother in one of the human brains that the Rebels had redesigned for just this sort of purpose.

"Father! Father! Why have you forsaken me?!" The First Son heard himself wail pitifully aloud to the masses below. The two Marys looked up alertly, realizing that something had gone terribly wrong.

Perse's smile now became really mean. He had taken control of Yeshua's body and brain and played him like a puppet.

The First Son's mind was impeded almost completely but by will alone he thought through the implications and the directions this could go off in. This meant that Perse could probably prevent the resurrection. By using just a drop more force, The First Son himself would black out and sleep through the resurrection, and be reincarnated as a dung beetle, or whatever Perse wished.

Despite remembering that this was all a game, Yeshua momentarily dropped a level into believing in the nightmare that if Perse could somehow do this—where had he gotten the power?!—who knew whether he could actually take over The One Self?!

In dropping level, The First Son made the phase shift into the internal state of Hell, where he was able to see the hundred million Satans oppressing him and the Agents. *No wonder the sky is orange!* He immediately exuded a bolt of his last strength to throw Perse and the Satans off guard for an instant, and in that instant sent a message to the Agents: *Use the trick!*

The Agents coming awake in a flash found it easy to feel all was hopeless. Falling instantly into Hell and seeing the Satans, they at least knew what they were fighting against and struck back with mindblasts, evaporating thousands of Satans.

Just released from deep unconsciousness and in weakened states the Agents were barely able to keep from being overcome completely but the situation looked dire. Perse's face was grinning evilly with cool confidence inches from The First Son's, as if about to deliver the coup de grace.

Yeshua looked down and there next to the cross was the Roman Centurion Longinus, looking up. Yeshua looked into his eyes significantly. Longinus received the signal and thrust his spear, actually the staff of Moses, up into the side of Yeshua. As blood spilt out, a blast of cosmic energy shot up and totally turned off the human brain except for its autonomic bodily functions. Released from his human brain, The First Son immediately paralyzed Perse and obliterated millions of AI Satans, freeing the Agents to their full power and thus shifting the battle the other way.

It appeared that the battle was won until suddenly new Satans started to appear on the scene, apparently being manufactured and rushed to the battlefield as fast as Rebel forces could do it. The fight now swung back the other way, with The First Son and the Agents on the verge of blacking out while still vaporizing hundreds of Satans per second as thousands more per second were coming into the fray.

The First Son thought he mentally heard the sound of a bugle and an instant later he saw Atlantis come around the horizon firing diffuse computer code designed to penetrate and self-destruct the Satans. Within minutes the skies were clear, and Atlantis disappeared with another mental bugle note. The Agents mentally stamped, hooted, cheered and whistled for Atlantis, who pathed, *My honor.*

Yeshua looked down with love into the eyes of his wife and his mother, saying *I'll be seeing you* but neither was ready to let him go, so he made up a song that would be channeled by Franz Schubert in 1825 AD, and mentally sang it to both of them, both maiden and mother, until their hearts were at peace:

Ave Maria, maiden mild
Oh, listen to a maiden's prayer
For thou canst hear amid the wild
'Tis thou, 'tis thou canst save amid, despair
We slumber safely till the morrow
Though we've by man outcast reviled
Oh maiden, see a maiden's sorrow
Oh mother, hear a suppliant child
Ave Maria
The murky cavern's air so heavy
Shall breathe of balm if thou hast smiled
Oh maiden, hear a maiden pleadin'
Oh mother, hear a suppliant child
Ave Maria
Ave Maria

Then in a strong voice he bellowed, "It is done. Father, into your hands I commend my spirit." At this, his head tilted laxly down and he departed the body.

36

Death Is Not the End
27 AD

"Really this man was righteous," Longinus said boldly, unafraid of censure, although as he looked around at the faces in the crowd he saw mean-eyed people taking mental notes against him. They would bear closer watching. The many merely curious onlookers were impressed at praise from one of Yeshua's evident foes. Longinus, an asleep Agent, had always been a good man and one of the first Romans to realize that Yeshua was more than a mortal man. No one had gotten Yeshua's true message that we are all more than we think we are.

The followers and family of Yeshua were beating themselves and crying uncontrollably, tearing their clothes, not knowing what to do to express their unbearable grief. Some were going away, unable to stay at the scene. At the base of the cross, the two Marys wept silently and with dignity, seeming to shine with an inner light.

Bearing scrolls from Pilate, Joseph of Arimathea approached Longinus and handed him the scrolls. "Pilate said that I can take the body of Yeshua Ben Joseph," he said to Longinus evenly, regarding the man with some surprise as he registered warmth in the officer's eyes.

"Yes, these are in order, I'll take them, you can take the body," Longinus said, and got his men to help. "Treat that body with respect," he admonished his men strongly.

The two Marys crowded the soldiers out of the way when the body reached the ground, and held and loved it, wiping away the blood and grime. Then they wrapped him in fine linen. When they were ready, Joseph of Arimathea gently lifted Yeshua's body, now bereft of his soul, and carried it away, followed by the family and followers, a large group, leaving the crowd quickly dispersing.

Longinus' right hand was on his heart and his eyes were following Yeshua's body as Mary Magdalene looked back for the last time.

Not far away they arrived at a newly-carved cave entrance in the mountain and laid the body inside. Many of the women, including those that had been followers since Galilee, and the disciples and family, flooded briefly into the cave to see him lying in state and to speak their hearts silently to him with gratitude and love. As the Sabbath was approaching, they would have to come back after the Sabbath having by then prepared spices and perfumed oils with which they would anoint him, and they all promised to see him again then.

But when they came back with the spices and oils, they found that the rock had been rolled away and the tomb was empty. The first to arrive were Mary Magdalene, Joanna, and Mary the wife of Alphaeus. Picking through the fine linen bandages on the floor, they gaped speechless at the imprint of Yeshua's face on the linen. Suddenly two men appeared whose clothing seemed to be flashing. This was Maitreya and Templegard, making it plain they were not of Earth.

"Why are *you* looking for the living One among the dead?" Maitreya asked them. "He is not here but has been raised up."

"Recall how he spoke to *you* when he was yet in Galilee, saying that the Son of man must be delivered into the hands of sinful men and be impaled and yet on the third day rise," Templegard reminded them.

Dazed, the three women left the cave and returned to the disciples and the rest of the family and followers and described what had happened. Despite having observed miracles, the group could not come to grips with the reality that Yeshua could bring himself back from death. Something had happened during the crucifixion and the events leading up to it. Inside each of them doubts had arisen that this terrible outcome could somehow be ordained. These doubts were not just because of the graphic nature of the final ending. They were because of the army of artificial Satans that had been in constant attack on each of them. Although these robots were now all slain, and new ones were not coming to Earth, the damage had been done. Each of them suspected that friends had stolen the body and that the men with flashing clothes were simply using some form of trickery to achieve those effects. They wanted to believe it was all true but were divided inside.

Peter ran to the memorial tomb to see for himself. All he found were the bandages and was amazed to see Yeshua's face emblazoned on the linen by some means he had never seen before. He took those and left, still roiling inside with doubt and punishing himself for it.

Mary Magdalene was alone in the garden meditating on Yeshua when she met a man walking in the opposite direction. He stopped and politely greeted her.

"Why do you look so sad, Mary?" he asked.

He stopped controlling recognition and she suddenly realized who he was. She gasped and gaped at him, and he smiled.

"Is that really you?" she reached out timidly and touched his arm, felt it and then gripped it. "God protect me from demons!"

"Yes, this is the real me, beloved, I swear it."

She stared for a moment longer and then kissed him, first exclaiming, "Oh Yeshua!"

She felt flooded with love and total approval. *Yes, this was him!* Every other man's kiss was all about lust and passion, but Yeshua's kiss was the love that God felt for you, come alive. *This was him!*

"They will be calling me Jesus now," he said.

"Why?" she asked, flushed with color and beauty and wonder.

He simply smiled and rolled his eyes upward for an instant and she knew what he meant. No one but the beloved One Self could fully understand His aesthetics, although the enlightened love all of his art, which is why they love each other.

When Mary reported the incident, some began to believe because she was always so level headed. Others felt that even Mary could lose her mind over the events of recent days.

Later that same day, two followers, Cleopas and Simon, were journeying on an errand to the nearby village of Emmaus, going over the facts again and again, trying to get their heads around it, but merely frustrating themselves. Yeshua appeared and began to walk behind them. They noticed another traveler coming up behind them and paid no attention to it, for it was natural to walk in as large a group as possible to dissuade robbers.

After walking along for a few minutes, silently listening to their conversation, Yeshua asked, "What are these matters that *you* are debating between yourselves as *you* walk along?"

The two stopped and turned to Yeshua with sad faces, not recognizing him as he was controlling that. "Are you dwelling by yourself in Jerusalem and so do not know the things that have occurred in her in these days?" Cleopas asked.

"What things?" Yeshua asked.

"The things concerning Yeshua the Nazarene," Cleopas began.

"I know of him. Isn't that the one they also call Jesus?" Yeshua asked.

"Yes, I have heard some use that name too," Simon said, but Cleopas shook his head and said, "Yes, I think I've heard that name too… it sounds Greek…" and Jesus nodded for him to go on with his story.

"Jesus the Nazarene became a prophet powerful in work and word before God and all the people," Cleopas explained. "Our chief priests and rulers handed him over to the sentence of death and impaled him." Cleopas choked up and could not go on.

"But we were hoping that this man was the one destined to deliver Israel," Simon picked it up. "Today is the third day since the impaling, and three of our women have astonished us, because they had been early to the memorial tomb but they did not find his body and had a supernatural sighting of Angels who told them that he is alive."

"O senseless ones and slow of heart to believe on all the things the prophets spoke!" Jesus rebuked them affectionately. "Was it not necessary for the Christ to suffer these things and to enter into his glory? Did not Moses report that the LORD said unto him 'I will raise them up a prophet from among their brethren, and will put my words into his mouth?' Didn't Isaiah prophesy that a pure young woman would give birth to God's son, and that the Christ would come as a baby? Didn't Micah foresee that the birth would take place in Bethlehem? Didn't Jesus himself say that he would be put to death and on the third day, arise again?"

"You seem to know a lot about… Jesus," Simon said.

Jesus began to walk and the two men stayed with him and they continued talking for further miles down the road and when they entered Emmaus the men pressured Jesus to dine and stay with them so he did.

Reclining for the dinner meal, Jesus took the loaf, blessed it, broke it, and began to hand it to them. At that point he released recognition control and both men saw who he was. Jesus smiled and disappeared.

They looked at each other in astonishment. Simon was the first to speak. "Were our hearts not burning when he was speaking to us on the road?" They made quick work of the meal, picked up the packages they had been sent to get, and set out immediately for Jerusalem.

When they arrived where the disciples and the rest of the flock were resting, they told their story. Everyone crowded around and became increasingly excited and charged up by the multiple confirmations. As Cleopas related the moment of the breaking of bread, Jesus was suddenly there, standing among them.

No one had ever experienced anything like that before. Even Yeshua's bringing back people from death was not as mind altering as seeing someone pop out of thin air. A ripple of fear expanded circularly from Jesus and people involuntarily stepped away.

"May *you* have peace," he said. But many of them were terrified, imagining that they were beholding a spirit.

"Why are *you* troubled, and why is it that doubts come up in *your* hearts? See my hands and my feet, it is myself; feel me and see, because a spirit does not have flesh and bones just as you behold that I have." A few brave souls nearby reached out and pressed the flesh, nodding in awe. "Do *you* have something there to eat?" he asked, and the crowd began to loosen up while they watched him munch a bit of broiled fish.

"These are my words which I spoke to *you* while I was yet with *you*, that all of the things written about me in the Law of Moses and in the Prophets and Psalms must be fulfilled. In the Psalms alone there are 92 references, each of which must be fulfilled. Of the total of all these prophesies, most have already been fulfilled. *Your* work and courage are needed to fulfill the rest. *Your* Holy Mission in fact hinges upon just a single one of these prophesies."

Everyone who had been standing sat down. They were now completely attentive and no longer distracted by doubts and fears. This was the Christ, there could be no doubt of it, the one that God anointed. They were privileged to be the few to carry on his work on Earth.

"As sung in Psalms 22:22, my atonement on the cross will enable believers to receive salvation. Since this is *your* part of the Holy Mission, I will now reveal it to you in a more detailed way." Yeshua looked around and showered love upon them. They each felt highly prized and beloved.

"This love that I give you is the essence of the Mission. We must all love one another as we love God, because it's all the same thing, we're all made out of God."

He had never before stated it so openly. This was on the edge of the game rules of engagement. But they had to know the full Truth. Even if they never said it aloud, it would be their personal reservoir of strength.

"But we cannot convey messages that are so far from being believable, we accomplish nothing," he went on, looking around for comprehension. "*You* have heard me extolling love and exhibiting it, it is based on Hillel's practical saying that we should do unto others as we'd have them do unto us, and it's enough to explain the *why* of *love*. More than mere words, every action that you take must be done from and with love and kindness, no matter what they may be doing to you. If you stop feeling the love for others at times, do not practice the work at those times but go into retreat, pray, and meditate until you are fit to go back to duty."

"What Psalm 22:22 is meant to say is that I had to undergo public torture on a mind-shattering scale in order that my ideas about love would continue to receive attention, over the ages that it will take. This would cause the existence of more believers. Believers would receive salvation by their own work in practicing love, unconditional love to all creation."

"What *you* need to do now is to create a worldwide church of love for everybody. They don't need to throw down any beliefs or practices to which they feel love. Love can coexist, love transcends what can be spoken in words and should be taken as above words in value."

He saw how unready they felt. They had no strong leadership of their own, there were nascent factions and rivalries, the deep learning of his message was tattered with half-understood parts, they were humble people not knowledgeable about other parts of the world, he had of course not told them the truth about Rebels, and he could go on all day enumerating how impossibly long the odds were against this group being able to make much of his recent performance.

This bothered him not at all. He and the Agents would be there with them every step of the way, and The One Self with them. Impossible odds tended to shrink in importance with all that on your side. True, the game rules acted as a handicap equalizer, so the outcome was uncertain. As The One would say, *uncertainty is where the fun is!*

"Come walk with me," he said and while talking he led them on the road toward Bethany.

"The implications of love include forgiveness of sins, repentance and self-forgiveness of sins. *You* must bring this message to all nations. There is One God and He is like a Father to all of us. Therefore, we ought not to hate one another, in the knowledge that He loves them whom we hate. Therefore, must we change the world to a way of love to one another, and forgive each other for trespasses of the past. Our mistakes of the past loved *us* because they *taught us* to not make them again, so we should also be *grateful* to them and not hate them. Hatred is a mistake and should be turned off as soon as it turns itself on."

"Stay in Jerusalem and be witnesses to these things until *you* become clothed with power from on high. As your work on your self evolves, you will find you are able to do many of the miracles that you beheld me do. Do not hold back your ability to heal, exorcize, even fly. Whatever you feel is good and is overtaking you, go with it, unless there is any bit of negativity in it toward anyone or anything. Any negativity at all is a sign to not act on an impulse."

There at Bethany he stopped and said, "And, look! I am sending forth upon *you* that which is promised by my Father." He held up his palms toward them, pivoting left and right to emanate spiritual power upon all of them. They felt electrified and strong, mentally clear, courageous and full of love, uninterested in any distractions.

And then he floated upward, waving goodbye, and disappeared into the sky like a rocket.

"That must feel better now," Jesus said, unparalyzing Perse.

"I would rather you not make a habit of doing that," Perse admitted, feeling intense relief, and rubbing his own arms just to enjoy the feeling of anything. He detected that he harbored a feeling of gratitude to Jesus as he was now calling himself and clamped down on it.

"Just like you to let me go, ever," Perse taunted. "What a foolish move. That's why you people can never win. You're your own worst enemies."

"What would it prove to just keep you paralyzed for eternity?" Jesus asked. Perse had no answer. Jesus answered his own question.

"It would prove that might makes right. Why would we want to prove that?"

37

PASSING THE TORCH

27 AD

Jesus' followers and family stayed in hiding in the same neck of the woods, the area around the Garden of Gethsemane on the Mount of Olives. Everyone knew where to find them and so they felt no safety there, but the Master had commanded them to stay put and wait for signs before moving out to all nations, so they stayed where he had last led them and kept their heads down and prayed.

Throughout Judea and beyond, word had spread of the unusual events in Jerusalem, captivating all attention away from politics and sports. Most of the word of mouth was negative to the followers of the man, according to the plans of the Rebels and their Roman puppets. They were said to break and seek to change the laws of Moses. Thus, they were seen as Jewish revisionists, heretics, enemies of Israel, distorters of the Truth, and with their supposed miracles they were in league with the devil, magical tricksters, or perhaps merely masters of illusion and deceit. They swapped wives, hence calling each other "brother" and "sister". They wanted to overthrow governments and share everything, which would mean loss of one's possessions. They were an outlet for malicious humor that seemed to make one feel temporarily better.

The 22-year old Saul from Tarsus had no reason to think any differently from what he heard. As a Pharisee who had studied in the school of Hillel's grandson Gamaliel, he would have occasion to judge cases brought before him by other Jews accusing a follower of Jesus of one sin or another. Although the schools of Hillel and Gamaliel taught mercy in balance with severity, Saul's youthful testosterone tricked him into acting with an imbalance toward severity when it came to these Jews for Jesus. Saul had no idea of the relationship between Hillel and Jesus.

It was in this dangerous atmosphere that the 120 followers hid on the Mount of Olives and tried to stay out of trouble and away from others. This was not easy as there were many roads crisscrossing the mountain and so it was highly populated at all times, with many homes and many tents. They had the use of a large house that had been lent to them by Joseph of Arimathea, and under very crowded conditions many slept there, but many more slept outside, in tents or in the open air. They respected all laws and traditions to minimize trouble with nosy neighbors, they kept the area and themselves clean, and were naturally kind in all their interactions outside the community. They were firm in their beliefs and in their Great Commission to bring the master's teachings to all the nations, but they were doing nothing to forward that mission, and instead were hiding in terror, as if not knowing what to do.

A couple of awake Rebels in their midst, Mastema and Kokabiel, were helping to keep the group in a paralyzed condition with various psychic and hypnotic methods exploiting the back doors in the new human brain. The Agents were aware of them and spent their days almost neutralizing their effects on the two Marys and the apostles.

A few weeks after their last sight of Jesus, Peter was first to shake himself out of a state of shock and gathered them to listen to him. They seemed resistant to having to think or talk or do anything. He had felt something inside remind him that there were supposed to be 12 apostles, and since Judas Iscariot had sinned and thrown himself off a cliff, they were now 11. With the help of the two Marys and five invisible Agents in overcoming the inertia, Peter led them in a discussion that resulted in two of the followers present being considered, Justus Barsabbas and Matthias, and Matthias was chosen. So now the 12 were complete: Peter, John, James ben Joseph (Jesus' half-brother), Andrew, Philip, Thomas, Bartholomew, Matthew, James the son of Alphaeus, Simon the Zealot, Jude (son of James ben Joseph), and now Matthias.

Seven weeks after the master left came the Shavuot festival, which as good Jews they needed to attend and properly respect. This would mean mingling with all the other Jews that lived around here, who would be sure to have a public event with lots of good food, wine, and cheer. This was a scary prospect and the Agents and Rebels constantly pushed against each other's efforts to terrorize or strengthen the group.

Led by the Marys and the apostles, the small tribe began to slowly walk toward the sound of the music coming over the top of the mountain, merging in with streams of other pilgrims. As they came within sight of the main tent area, itself consisting of hundreds of big tents, and people on blankets eating breakfast, as it was early morning, people at a nearby tent waved to them and anyone to come in and sample the breakfast they were cooking for free for the multitudes.

Being hungry they gratefully went under the top of the open-sided tent and to the long tables there. But as this was happening, a stiff wind rent the air intimately, getting everyone's attention as the tents all over the mountain fluttered making the sound of muted bass drums. The sky was a brilliant electric blue and people's faces looked slightly blue in reflection. And little tongues of flame now appeared floating just above the tops of the heads of the followers of Jesus!

The Holy Spirit, Maitreya pathed. Indeed, this was the promised gift of the Baptism of the Holy Spirit. All of the followers were getting injections of numinous grace and were all suddenly clear-headed and in their essence selves, not in their brain egos, and they knew it.

The Agents could sense the heightened presence of the ever-present One Self, and The First Son.

Everyone around them started talking all at once, in their many native languages, Parthians, Medes, Elamites, Mesopotamians, Judeans and Cappadocians, Phrygians, Egyptians, Romans, Cretans, Arabians, and the amazing thing was that the Jewish Christians could now understand exactly what was being said in all of these languages, as it was immediately being translated into Galilean in their minds.

The followers were all energetically discussing these strange events and trying to make sense of them. Kokabiel said, "They are full of sweet wine."

Peter stood up and raised his voice, getting everyone's attention including hordes of people outside the Jesus community. "These people are not, in fact, drunk. On the contrary, THIS that you see about you, is what was said through the prophet Joel. "God says, 'I shall pour out some of my spirit upon every sort of flesh, and *your* sons and *your* daughters will prophesy and *your* young men will see visions and *your* old men will dream dreams.'"

Indeed, the flock could tell these words were true, for each of them was experiencing revelations, reading minds, seeing things to come, understanding foreign tongues (which was simply a matter of reading minds). And thinking with an uncanny sharpness and feeling the bountiful love inside themselves pouring out toward everything. This was the baptism that Jesus had promised them soon, *and this was soon, wasn't it?*

This is indeed the baptism by spiritual fire I promised you, they all heard Jesus say. *From this day, Shavuot shall also be known as Pentecost, meaning the first fruits of our Mission.*

No special spiritual energy was given to Mastema and Kokabiel. They felt suddenly exposed and obvious to the rest of the tribe, who now looked at them with pity. The two got up and excused themselves and headed toward Jerusalem without a backward glance.

Because a multinational crowd was gathering, Peter realized that this was an opportunity to begin the Great Commission. He returned their minds to the recent events, which everyone had done nothing but talk about ever since. Except he put it in perspective for them: "Therefore let all the house of Israel know for a certainty that God made him both Lord and Christ, this Jesus whom you impaled."

The utter conviction in his voice and the spiritual energy he now emanated made the thousands in earshot suddenly consider that this sounded a lot like the truth. They began to yell, asking what they could do to save themselves now that they have done this deadly insult to God.

"Repent," Peter said simply, "and let each one of *you* be baptized in the name of Jesus Christ for forgiveness of *your* sins, and *you* will receive the free gift of the Holy Spirit."

That day, 3000 more followers were baptized in the same fiery tongues from Heaven.

Each initiate became overcome with feelings of love and connectedness with all beings and all things, opening them to receive messages from the Universe and from the minds of others.

Ω

"All shall be well, and all shall be well,
and all manner of things shall be well,
for there is a force of Love
moving through the Universe
that holds us fast and will never let us go."

— Julian of Norwich, Christian mystic, 1342-1416,
from *Revelations of Divine Love*

To be continued…

there is never an End

About the Author

Bill Harvey first experienced the Zone—that space where innovative and successful ideas and actions flow out of you effortlessly—as a young child. The son of legendary orchestra leader/emcee Ned Harvey and former Ziegfield Follies showgirl Sandra Harvey, Bill started performing on stage at age four, dancing with showgirls and exchanging lines with comedic greats like Jack E. Leonard. He liked this feeling of being "on" and wanted to learn how to be "on" more often. So he began his lifelong quest to understand how to bring on higher states of consciousness and to help others do the same.

Earning his degree in philosophy, the first school subject he ever loved, Bill founded the Human Effectiveness Institute, with the goal of sharing the consciousness techniques he had learned and developed. His ideas were further inspired by Alan Watts, Buddhism, Zen, and by his adopted older brother, the multitalented Bill Heyer, second trumpet in Ned's band.

Bill's first book, *MIND MAGIC: The Science of Microcosmology*, met with rave reviews in the late 70s and was lauded by thousands of readers. Fans included John Lennon, Ram Dass, Norman Cousins, Daniel Goleman, and Jimmy Carter. The book is now available in its sixth edition, *MIND MAGIC: Doorways into Higher Consciousness*.

In his second book, *YOU ARE THE UNIVERSE: Imagine That*, Bill speculates about the true nature of reality, in which all that exists is a single divine consciousness made of information. In this view, religion is not at odds with science. Bill turned his theory into fiction, and conceived an epic series of novels entitled **Agents of Cosmic Intelligence**. *THE FIRST SON* is the first to be released in the series.

With an imaginative, unorthodox mind for research, innovation and invention, Bill started his career in the media business with a dream of making one-way media into something the audience co-creates. He predicted today's media reality with his *MediaWorld 1990* report to the industry, and in his widely-read *Media Science Newsletter*. He invented media research tools and measurement systems, including some now written into FCC regulations. He holds four issued US patents and has consulted for over a hundred Fortune 500 companies.

A leader in the field as media morphed into being more interactive, putting the viewer in charge, he received the Advertising Research Foundation *Great Mind Award* in 2008. In 2014, he became the first recipient of the ARF's *Erwin Ephron Demystification Award*.

Bill lives with his wife Lalita in New York's beautiful Hudson Valley. He has a daughter Nicole, and with Lalita has four grandchildren, Nicholas, Gabrielle, Jessica and Alexander.

Acknowledgments

My Deepest Thanks...

To my parents Ned and Sandy, my role models for being openminded, compassionate, and generous, and for their "noble experiment" of letting me make up my own mind after hearing their inputs, from my earliest days throughout their lives.

To Bill Heyer for telling me at age 4 when I wrote my first story that I'm destined to be a writer.

To F. Scott Fitzgerald, Ernest Hemingway, Fyodor Dostoevsky, Robert A. Heinlein, and all the other writers whose work inspires me.

To my guru for showing me how an awake being behaves.

To my wife Lalita and my daughter Nicole for believing in me and helping me in every way they can at every moment, including as editors.

To my main editor Yana Lambert, and to George and Christine Niver, Nicole David and Karen Kennedy for their unstinting devotion as editors, art creators and curators, social media implementers, and in every other role bringing my work to its audience.

To cartographer Lynn Davis, for his diligent research and collaboration in creating a map covering the time period 3067BC to 27AD.

To my assistant Kristin Dragos for making it possible to juggle so much and still get through each day with a smile.

To Harvey Kraft for teaching me the derivation of the word "Aryans".

To the world's religions for allowing me to fictionalize their work in service to making their wisdom more accessible in the present turbulent age. I set out to show that it is possible to imagine a plausible scenario in which religion is not at odds with science, and one which perhaps makes the world's present difficulties easier to understand. I feel intuitively certain that the real truth is far stranger than my story, though there are similarities.

Other Books by Bill Harvey

MIND MAGIC: Doorways into Higher Consciousness
The Human Effectiveness Institute, *publisher*
ISBN-13: 978-0918538000

YOU ARE THE UNIVERSE: Imagine That
The Human Effectiveness Institute, *publisher*
ISBN-13: 978-0918538062

Available at your favorite bookstore and on Amazon.

Author's Note

I wrote this book because I feel that the more people who can imagine that both science and religion have pieces of the truth, the more peaceful and happier the world will be. If you agree that spreading this rare notion of spirit-science unity is a good thing, please do share it any way you like. God bless you in any case.

Love, Bill